Shanghai, Kyoto, Mexico City

RHAPSODY IN A CIRCLE

GUERNICA WORLD EDITIONS 91

RHAPSODY IN A CIRCLE

MARLON L. FICK

GUERNICA
World
EDITIONS

TORONTO—CHICAGO—BUFFALO—LANCASTER (U.K.)

2025

Guernica Editions Founder: Antonio D'Alfonso

Michael Mirolla, general editor
Scott Walker, editor
Cover and interior design: Errol F. Richardson
Cover Art: Francisca Esteve

Guernica Editions Inc.
1241 Marble Rock Rd., Gananoque (ON), Canada K7G 2V4
2250 Military Road, Tonawanda, N.Y. 14150-6000 U.S.A.
www.guernicaeditions.com

Distributors:
Independent Publishers Group (IPG)
600 North Pulaski Road, Chicago IL 60624
University of Toronto Press Distribution (UTP)
5201 Dufferin Street, Toronto (ON), Canada M3H 5T8

First edition.
Printed in Canada.

Legal Deposit—First Quarter
Library of Congress Catalog Card Number: 2024942565
Library and Archives Canada Cataloguing in Publication
Title: Rhapsody in a circle / Marlon L. Flick.
Names: Fick, Marlon L., 1960- author.
Series: Guernica world editions (Series) ; 91.
Description: Series statement: Guernica world editions ; 91
Identifiers: Canadiana (print) 20240434501 | Canadiana (ebook) 2024043451X | ISBN 9781771839631
(softcover) | ISBN 9781771839648 (EPUB)
Subjects: LCGFT: Novels.
Classification: LCC PS3606.I35 R43 2025 | DDC 813/.6—dc23

for
my mother, Joyce,
who convinced me to tell this story as if it were fictional,
saying that "otherwise no one will believe it"
and for
my wife, Paquita

... and thus disclosed the innocent Stevie, seated very good and quiet at a deal table, drawing circles, circles, circles; innumerable circles, concentric, eccentric, a coruscating whirl of circles that by their tangled multitude of repeated curves, uniformity of form, and confusion of intersecting lines suggested a rendering of cosmic chaos, the symbolism of a mad art attempting the inconceivable.

—*from* Joseph Conrad's *The Secret Agent*

Characters

Bolivar Collins (Aka Francisco Barranca, Aka Robert Segovia)

In Mexico

Teodesia Segovia Collins (wife of Bolivar Collins)
Karli Collins (daughter of Bolivar Collins and Teodesia)
Paco Segovia (son of Bolivar and Teodesia)
Father Sebastián (a young Mexican priest)
Wayne Williams (Aka Robin Ward; American financier with Wall Street Industrial Bank)
Eduardo Aguilar (head of Zeta Drug Cartel)
Martha Aguilar (wife of Eduardo Aguilar)
José Luis López (employee of Eduardo Aguilar)
Carmelita (Carmen) Vaghina (Aka Isa Aramara Barranca; employee of Eduardo Aguilar)

In Nicaragua

Captain Tomás (also Colonel Tomás, Aka Professor Martinez Saracho; Nicaragua Deputy Director of National Security)
Professor Espejo (associate of Professor Martinez Saracho)

In Pakistan

Sahib (a Servant)
Nadia Siddiqui (graduate teaching assistant & unknown employer)
Farooq (Head of the Commission, Pakistan Department of Education)
The Chancellor (head of the women's university)
VC (Vice Chancellor of the women's university)
Hasam (Director of International Affairs)
The Retired General, Kahn (board member, women's university)
Mohammed Al Dost (prominent Imam in Islamabad)
Samina (graduate student)
Humaira Kahn No. 1 (graduate student)
Humaira Kahn No. 2 (graduate student)

Hina Shahid (graduate student)
Serein Asad (graduate student)
Sidra Kahn (graduate student)
Zaib Sughra (graduate student)
Rafia (graduate Student)
Simba Shah (student)
Tabina Bari (student)
Mustaf Asad (sex slave merchant and drug merchant in Islamabad)
Hasan Jalil (an Afghani refugee boy, age 8)
Ayesha Jalil (formerly Hasan Jalil)
Mohammed Jinah (merchant, Chaklala Market)
Nasir (friend of Mohammed Jinah)
Altaf (friend of Mohammed Jinah)
Ahmed (brother of Mohammed Jinah)
The Captain (chief of Francisco Barranca's bodyguards)
The Inquisitor
The Knifer
The Knifer's Assistant (employee of Mustaf Asad)
A Geology Professor
Anoosh (owner of a book store in Sadr Market, Rawalpindi)
Tahmina Zara (Professor of Spanish, Islamabad International University)
Uncle Jinah (uncle of Mohammed Jinah, Abbotabad)
Fatima Abbas (employer unknown, citizenship unknown)
Masood (boyfriend of Fatima Abbas)
Professor Q or Professor Qadir (candidate for professor at the women's university)
Michael Kilduff (United Nations pilot)
Tatiana Puchnecheva (with the United Nations Human Rights Watch)
Mahmood (rug merchant)

Not-So-Fictional Personages

Prince Charles and Camilla, Duchess of Cornwall
Hillary Clinton (United States Senator)
Benazir Bhutto (presidential candidate, Pakistan)
Daniel Ortega (President of Nicaragua)
Fidel Castro (President of Cuba)
General Parvez Musharraf (President of Pakistan)

Chapter 1

Rawalpindi, January 2007

Dawn's call to prayer woke a curious flock of scavenger kites that rose and circled a smoldering heap of rubbish beside Sadr Market. A high window gradually turned from dark to grey, like the hue of an old black and white photograph, and thin limbs of a Jerusalem Thorn tree leaned heavily against the filmy glass.

With his head still muzzy, Francisco Barranca could not remember his dream. Upon waking, he could not recall his recent past, nor could his attenuated body remember what it should have felt—now it was battered and splotched in purple and blue with open, malicious and infected sores. Memory is something like a bird that flies inside a bird, and Barranca's memory bird had broken wings. He wanted to move, to sit up in the frowsty bed, but this proved arduous. His fevers had returned, too—fevers that climbed perilously high a week earlier in Mumbai. This was not Mumbai. Not Queen Victoria's Gateway. And the only gateway was a single inscrutable door that was shut and locked from the outside. The hapless events of the past few days had altered everything, and now he was back in beleaguered Pakistan where a nearby mosque broadcast blaringly the call to prayer from the minaret through a bullhorn in a tortured, electronically distorted foreign language, though he knew the words very well. They were not calling the bloody infidel to prayer; they were, however, rousing the imperious guards from sleep.

Am I who I say I am? kept running through his mind. *I am only a teacher … I do not know anything about …* Upon waking, Barranca had learned to rehearse, to get into his character. His feigned identity as Barranca had become so much a part of him that he could lose himself behind the veils. If he had not mastered this ability, whoever he was would have ceased to exist. He did not speak his thoughts out loud. One of them might hear.

A candle still burned. Its flicker caught a small bronze statue of Parvati, consort of Shiva, and cast her shadow against the wall.

The shadow danced gracefully—her arms and hips came to life in a world of shadows. She was more real to Barranca than what awaited him. He embraced her shadow with his eyes and swayed back and forth with his memories … *oh my Teodesia* … A broken necklace of tears rolled off his cheek when he tried to remember her face. He had taken a photograph from his wallet dozens of times, but it was not Teodesia, it was a fictional wife with a made-up name, "Isa Aramara," and the photo was Carmelita, really. Whatever her name was, she—Carmelita—was also beautiful. Their names swam around in him. *Teodesia*, his wife. *Carmelita*, an acquaintance, and, like him, a prisoner, but on the other side of the world. *Isa Aramara*, just random words, one of the veils, like reality, a shade, not a solid, but a shade that traverses dust.

Barranca had grown tired of the incessant questions—*Where is she, your wife? Why is she dark like us? Why isn't she here in Pakistan? Do you have children?* Some responded to the picture with shock: "You married a blackie?" The question disgusted him, but he had pretended not to notice their racism, or their assumption that to be a white man you must be a racist: "You're white! Americans can't marry blackies! Americans are all racists!" Teodesia was also dark, darker than many of them, and more beautiful than most, but they were commenting on Carmelita, who was actually from Brazil and whose name was not Isa. "Did you know," Barranca once said, "that the first known racial slur occurs in the Sanskrit language, probably from Old Persian, the word *barnish*, from which we derive the English word *varnish*, although the word then referred simultaneously to your color and your caste?"

It was January of the year Barranca would turn forty-seven. The hair around his temples had turned grey, but the rest was the same pile of disheveled reddish blond as before. His face had turned permanently dim and serious, with the gaze of a ghost. Forty-six is not "old," but this life, the wars and what went with them, had turned him into a very old man who frets about the humiliations of aging. He had been away from home, forced to be away from home, for five years. Those pains that the mind inflict on the body tried to seep through his physical wounds. His right ear was stoppered with dry blood, but his left ear heard the call to prayer, in Arabic, "Divine Arabic," not in Urdu. Now he associated the call with violence—*God is great. There is no God but God.* It was a tautology, a circular statement in which the supplicant was trapped as surely as he was a prisoner in a house surrounded by guards and high walls.

One of the guards is Shi'ite. Tonight is the night of Ashura and one of the guards will be away, leaving just the other to guard me. Barranca's mind began searching frantically. He trembled from weakness. If they beat him again today, he may not have enough strength left, but he couldn't afford the thought. His eyes searched the pale green room and the high grey window's photograph of Jerusalem Thorns for anything he could use as a tool, a weapon. They would hear the glass shatter—broken glass would not help.

Lackadaisical and witless, the guards did not consider this broken down man to be very dangerous. He could have, for example, used his little statue of Parvati, but it was slim and no taller than the length of a hand. Striking out with Parvati would only incur their anger, and chances were great that a guard could squeeze the trigger finger on his sawed-off 12-gauge faster than Barranca could raise his arm. They had left him with a small bag of possessions: Parvati, some clothes and books, his cigarettes and matches. What could he do? Light a match and set them on fire? They removed his razor and his mirror—better to not see himself or what he'd become. They left a pencil stub which he could sharpen on the coarse, gritty wall, but it wasn't long enough to stick in a man's throat. No pen. And it is not true, the saying that "the pen is mightier than the sword," or it depended upon whose pen was doing the slaying. Maybe, he thought, he could recite bad poetry to them and they would suddenly find themselves in hell. None of these feeble options for striking out would work, so he continued to dwell on a possible course of action. Then that very day, the day preceding the night of Ashura, an opportunity presented itself. When the guards let him wander around the yard inside the compound, he spied a heap of trash, and in it, a lead pipe, which he quickly hid under his achkan, and later, under his mattress.

He had heard one of the guards talking outside the door. He was telling the other guard their orders. The conversation was in Urdu.

ہم اسے یہاں صدر میں پھانسی نہیں دے سکتے ۔ کل ہم اسے مارگلہ کی پہاڑیوں پر لے جائیں گے ۔ یہ محترمہ کی خواہش ہے ۔ پہلے ہم یہ جاننے کی کوشش کرتے ہیں کہ اس نے کمیشن کو کیا کہا ہے ۔ محترمہ کی پوزیشن اس پر منحصر ہے، لہذا ہماری ملازمتیں اس پر منحصر ہیں ۔

"We cannot execute him here in Sadr. Tomorrow we are to take him to the Margalla hills. That is the Ma'am's wish. First we try again to find out what he has told the Commission. The Ma'am's position depends on it, so our jobs depend on it—understand?"

Barranca could not see the other man nod through the closed door. Nor could the guards see him listening or know that he understood.

He was thirsty, but they had taken away the clean water along with food. Eventually thirst won over fear of dirty water and he drank from the toilet's open tank, the lid having been removed for its potential use as a weapon.

The realities of his situation circulated in his mind with the poet, Homer, whose central character found himself in faraway, unhospitable lands among suspicious hosts. If the truth were known to all, this man, Francisco Barranca, was not a spy, not really, although whether one was or wasn't did not really matter in Pakistan where real and not real bore little relevance. This place had been one of Odysseus's stops. In Homer's *Odyssey*, Odysseus encounters all types: good, bad, ugly, friendly, unfriendly, beautiful, trustworthy, untrustworthy. It was a story about hospitality. When Odysseus's boat drifted onto the subcontinent's shores a few thousand years earlier, Odysseus discovered the same habits, the same incessant questions asked of a stranger without the slightest notion of reciprocity. He had to tell his story as many times as asked until the natives could make up their minds whether to invite him to dinner or kill him. Their hospitality had grown famous over the next several thousand years as visitors from all over the world mistook their intense interest in strangers for kindness, their subtle interrogations for "friendly" questions.

Mostly Odysseus told the truth; Barranca did not. He wanted to but couldn't. And when one is living a fictional, unreal life, one begins to pace in circles like a caged tiger. The natives laid out dishes of Biryani, figs, dates, rice with saffron, tea … They were part of a greater plan to uncover his caliginous purpose; this much was already assumed from the beginning. There were, however, those who were good to him and whose curiosity was spontaneous, not asking the pre-scripted questions one asks to ascertain whether or not someone is a spy.

The sun was up now. He sensed that in a brief hour of desultory sleep here and there Teodesia's face had appeared to him, or he could see her long legs striding back to the house from the market in their home in Jlalpan in central Mexico, and he could hear her call out his real name, "Bolivar!" He believed he might still be able to dream her wondrous face, but he also feared that he could no longer remember the faces of their children, utterly without guile, as he breathed in the chilling vapor of loneliness.

The memory loss was not only from typhoid fever, or the beatings, or food and sleep deprivation and dehydration. One of the Taliban's bombs had taken the greatest part of his memory. His mind simply threw up a wall. He was aware, the very next day, that he could not picture his son or daughter, or even his long-gone mother and father. Somehow events like these erase one's personal life and leave only general knowledge. Paradoxically, he could remember books. His memory of written words was etched onto a sequestered tablet in a deep recess hidden inside his brain, there forever, as intractable as the presence in the absence of a wound. Words from books could come to him as easily as singing comes to a bird. And he could discuss any book endlessly with the book simply lying on his desk in front of the classroom, citing even its page numbers without having to stop and look, a feat that impressed some people and frightened others. But the rest of him was washed away, as if his memory had leached out of him right after the explosion. Now his personal memory was shards of shrapnel and broken glass. It had become the human viscera that the authorities washed into the canal with fire hoses. He was holding a small arm in one hand and another small arm, both from different small bodies, as he gazed through the smoke. One of the arms he tried to reattach to a little girl who was on fire. He laid the arms on the ground and tried to snuff out the fire with his bare hands. But it was no use because she was already dead. Logic was telling him that neither of the arms belonged to her, so he continued to look for their owners. That's when he became aware of a faint muffle of warped sound, sirens or screams, or the mournful cries of whales deep in the ocean, and the wet iron smell of blood and saffron and sulfur and cloves from the vendor's spiced meat kabobs.

Thirsty, he drank the dirty water from the toilet tank. Canal water that was drawn from the fetid, unfiltered river of Rawalpindi.

After morning prayers, the door opened and the two men grabbed him and dragged him into an adjoining room where they kept plastic on the floor. They sat him down in a chair and taped his wrists behind him. They taped his chest to the back of the chair and his legs to the seat of the chair. *I am no man*—it was a line from Homer, Odysseus had proudly claimed his name was "no man" to the Cyclops. The line was running through Barranca's mind like a sutra or a holy chant to ward away evil.

The inquisitor came in. He was a clean-shaven man in his twenties sporting a thin brown Oxford tie against a clean white shirt, and he was sedulous in his task. The guards stepped back as he began.

"Now, my friend ..."

"I am not your friend," Barranca said.

"Forgive me. It is a custom here. Hospitality. You are our guest. Now, my friend, we have some questions."

"They are the same questions."

"But today you will have new or better answers. You say your name is Francisco Barranca. You are from the United States? What exactly is your business here?"

"You hired me to evaluate the curricula and advise. In addition, you wish me to teach, so that is what I do. For this you receive millions from the Commission and you skim. I found out and that is why I'm sitting in this chair, and when they catch you, you will be the one in the chair or hanging from a rope ... or is it with your head in a basket?"

"Yes, this is what you have reported. I believe the consequences of your lie will come back to you. Still, what I would like to know is who you have implicated in your fairy tale? You see, you may have hurt the innocent in your zeal. So you will tell me the names you put in that report."

"I'm sure you don't need me for that."

"No names? Ah, you wish us to beat them out of you."

"I will be dead soon. What does it matter?"

"Let us put aside this … what do you call it … 'foreplay'—a word from decadent American English. We have a tip that you are here to assassinate someone, someone very important to Pakistan, and this little game that you play with the Commission is merely a diversion."

Francisco Barranca knew the real jailer, the one giving the orders, not the young man in front of him. It was neither the school's Chancellor—the "Ma'am" he'd overheard them say—nor the Higher Education Commission. As long as he breathed, the school he worked for—where he kept his real identity covered—collected great sums of money. For them, he was more valuable alive. But who was the double inside the school or the Commission? There was a leak somewhere. A lot more than a few million dollars a year was enough motive to end these past few years of play-acting. The real jailer was Wayne Williams. Williams, the "Financier," Williams, the shadow—or whatever he was. On the other side of the world, Williams was rolling the dice for hundreds of lives. Or he was circumnavigating the globe in the deepest and most dangerous currents of the underworld. Only when death finally came to Barranca, would he journey to such depths with Odysseus to speak to the seer, Tiresias, and tasting the blood of ghosts, know the truth. But Barranca was already in Hell—it was a place he had come to believe was very real. There is a hell and no heaven. Let the beating begin again.

Maybe they have Teodesia. Maybe her being alive was a false message. Maybe they have already killed her. I've said too much. Who is this inquisitor, really?

"If you do not cooperate, what should we do? Should we give you to the Taliban or to the ISI?"

"Your question assumes you are neither. Interesting."

Motioning to the guards, the inquisitor ordered, "Cut him loose and bring him some tea and *rhoti*."

"Sir!"

One of the guards cut Barranca free and moved a table to within reach while the other guard went for the tea and flat bread. The inquisitor continued …

"You are not from the United States. You are an Anglo, yet a Mexican national with a degree from Princeton, yes?"

"Whatever you say."

"I confess I believe you are perfect for the job, but what sort of job is it, really?"

"My job is teaching your idiot children to think themselves out of the parochial bubble you made for them. And what for? Because Musharraf is worried that the Paki rupee is weaker than the Indian rupee."

"Is that what you think? Everything is about money to you Westerners. You all think you are so important. To me, you are no one. You are a plague in my country that must be purged with fire. You are a scavenger."

"I confess as much. Why not simply let me go home?"

"Go? Go free? Commit hideous crimes and just walk away? No, my friend. You will pay. You will pay for the deaths of many children. You will pay for polluting their minds. You will pay for raping Nadia!"

"Nadia?" Barranca was only surprised because he had not heard her name in so long.

"Oh, you are surprised that I know about that? Oh, I know about all of your victims. And you would have gone on raping young girls if I had not stopped you. And do you know that we will castrate you for this before we kill you?"

"You know full well that I rejected Nadia. I refused all of her advances. You know this. What is the point of trying to convince me of your elaborate ruse if you mean to kill me anyway?"

"No, my friend, here in Pakistan, we value the truth. Truth is part of our devotion to Allah. And we are not without evidence. We have your violation on tape."

He paused …

"You are married, yes?"

"Yes."

"Her name is Isa? You are married even though you are a homo?"

Barranca's face twisted into a laugh which opened a scab covering his split lip. It was too absurd. The fantasy. *Maybe Plato was right to banish poets as liars from the Republic—at least the bad poets should be banished. I, Barranca, "raped" Nadia and dozens of others, and now I'm a homosexual, only Barranca is not my name and my job in Pakistan is that of a simple courier, a small cog in a large machine of banks and armies and cartels.*

Every day the inquisitor asked the same questions, each time throwing in a new question or two, and in so doing he had revealed more to Barranca than vice versa. Now, by mid-morning, Teodesia's face had come fully into view, welling up from deep inside his broken body. He could see her calling his name. That was what kept him alive for four years. That was his purpose—to keep Teodesia and the children safe. Follow orders and they lived. The inquisitor interrupted his thoughts.

"Tell me again about these old wounds. They are war wounds?"

Barranca only had to tell the truth. Nothing about the old leg and chest wounds contradicted his cover.

"From Nicaragua. I served in the Nicaraguan army. That was more than twenty years ago."

"And after the war, you went to Harvard."

"Princeton."

"Right, Princeton."

There was a man named Francisco Barranca at Princeton in the 1990s, and he had immigrated there from Nicaragua, but the true account had placed him on the side of the Contras, not the Sandinistas. Barranca wondered if the inquisitor knew this.

"What were you doing at that bookstore all those Sundays?"

"Is this a trick question? I get books. You have the reports. You know how many cigarettes I smoke in a day, how many spoons of sugar I have in my morning coffee—all very relevant to your national security. Your sycophant Nadia reported every word of every class and followed me like a pestering little dog. You know I eat lentils and *rohti* for lunch and drink tea-white on the verandah by the bottlebrush tree where sometimes a green parrot sits on a branch and squawks. In the afternoon I grade papers or write my reports for Dr. Farooq. At five o'clock in the afternoon, my bodyguards arrive to take me to one of the so-called safe houses, shuffling me around from Pindi to Islamabad to Peshawar. Sometimes, in the middle of the night, one of your gunmen knocks on the door and whisks me off to yet another safe house, without so much as a why or a wherefore—no 'imminent threat,' just 'Let's go.' On Fridays, I leave with the guards for visits to the other universities to evaluate their curricula and weed out their frauds. But they keep their fake professors because they're highborn or some general's kid, so the truth is meaningless. Even your questions are part of a mirage."

The interrogation was over. It was the last one and Barranca knew it. His only edge was that they didn't seem to know he understood Urdu or that he had heard the kill order. In the afternoon, one of the guards brought him food, the second time in a day, after a week without food or clean water. A last supper was the extent of their sense of mercy. It consisted of *rhoti*, some rice with cloves, and tea-white. He ate alone wondering if Teodesia and Karlita, his daughter, were alive. He wondered if they thought he had abandoned them. He wondered if his son was still angry with the world and everything in it. He forgot much of the past, but he remembered the Black Suburban and wondered if anyone in their little pueblo, Jlalpan, had seen him being kidnapped. In the morning they would take him to the Margalla Hills and make it look like a Taliban killing. The bullhorns blew the call for evening prayers. The Shi'ite guard would be leaving now to observe the Night of Ashura. Barranca slipped the bar under his achkan and carefully grasped the handrail down the curved steps to the main room. The lone guard was facing east, genuflecting on his rug, his shotgun laying parallel beside him. He was lost in ritual motions and prayers. Barranca thought of a moment in Shakespeare's *Hamlet* when Hamlet hesitates to slay the usurper King, his uncle, fearing that his soul might fly to heaven. But Barranca did not believe in heaven. He didn't hesitate. He struck the man on the head with the iron pipe with such a force that the blow made a sound like an egg when it drops on the floor. Then he took the keys to the compound. Now he retrieved his small pack. He did not know if the guard was dead or unconscious, but he hobbled past him on his bad leg without looking, unlocked the metal door to the compound unaware of exactly where he was, and stepped out into the street. It was Sadr Market, the night of Ashura. He walked a few steps into the street. He was just in time to witness a most terrifying scene of holiness and blood.

Chapter 2

Sinaloa, July 2002

Eduardo Aguilar was fat and quiet, like a Buddha except in all other aspects, since no serenity or harmony dwelled beneath the surface of his calm. He sat in a big leather chair with a small glass of gold tequila in one hand and a Ducado cigarette burning in the other. When he did speak, he was boorishly devoid of any decorum. Bolivar Collins could see a row of Starlings perching outside on a phone line. They looked like musical notes—all of them the same notes on only one line. The American was talking, a man named Wayne Williams.

"Mr. Collins, I represent a financial company, maybe you have heard of us … 'Wall Street Industrial Bank.' Sr. Aguilar oversees our office here in Sinaloa."

Bolivar Collins did not know he was in Sinaloa. His home was in the state of Querétaro, a long way from Sinaloa. Aguilar's men had covered his head with a black sack. He did not know Williams or Aguilar, either. He did not know why he had been brought here.

"We've watched you," Williams said. "Your career—very impressive—you have a set of skills that could be useful to us. It's what? A symptom of your autism—though mild I'm told—that makes you something like a savant? You can see patterns where others can't, right?"

"I don't know what you're talking about. I'd like to go home. Thank you all the same."

"Yet, unlike other autistics, you've learned how to analyze and interpret social cues? I find you quite interesting, Mr. Collins."

"I am of no use to you. I'd like to go home."

"If I may … I'd like to lay it out for you, just the same. You see, I know all about your activities in Nicaragua. Do you know that fighting for the other team is 'treason'? I can have you extradited like that." He snapped his fingers to punctuate "that". "Or you can come to work for us. Stand trial for treason or … oh, Mr. Collins, please, as you consider your options, remember that Mr. Aguilar would regret any harm that might be done to your family."

Bolivar Collins felt nauseous. He had repressed the horrors of the past, memories that existed now as if in old books we closed and placed on the shelf beyond reach. These years now were peaceful. Jlalpan was small. Teodesia was a fine companion, wife, and mother of his children. She had welcomed their return to what had been her girlhood home, especially after the trauma she knew in Nicaragua. Neither of them ever spoke of those days or of the world's cruelty. Typically, days began early. He drank a cup of coffee with Teodesia at six o'clock, had some buttered toast and yogurt. When he was fully awake he would say "Good Morning, darling." And Teodesia would say, "*Buenas días, mi amor.*" And Collins would go to his office to write until lunch. Teodesia would call for him around one o'clock and their lunches were a leisurely two hours, longer when the kids were not in school. On occasions, Collins skipped work and took Teodesia and their two children to Tequisquiapan or the city of Querétaro, seldom as far as Mexico City, except on one occasion to show Karli and Paco the museums. After lunch, Collins wrote a little more, ending somewhere in the middle of a thought, somewhere where he could easily pick up the following day. Meanwhile, Teodesia had her garden and the fruit trees, her magazines, gossip with her *amigas*. Apart from school, Karli had a dozen projects ranging from writing books, like her father, to piano lessons, to chemistry experiments, the likes of which had never been reproduced, but she had very long and involved explanations for every new combination, invention, work of art, astronomical discovery, etc. Teodesia called her their "Baby da Vincita." Paco, on the other hand, was inward and brooding and contumacious. He spent his free time in the tree house his father helped him build. Up there, Paco reigned supreme, conceiving all manner of plots and schemes to destroy his rapacious enemies, who were usually the kids from school who called him a "dirty gringo." And because Paco was more private, his mother and father found it increasingly difficult to understand him and know him. Still, even with the occasional quarrels with Paco—between Paco and Teodesia, mainly—their lives were as smooth as twilight greeting the night, a way of life that could not have been farther from the worlds of these men, Aguilar and Williams.

"With your ability with languages," Williams said, "your understanding of cultures, you will be an asset. It would be a shame to waste your talents."

"Excuse me, Mr. ..."

"Williams. Wayne Williams."

"Excuse me, Mr. Williams, all this seems like a lot of drama for ... what did you call it? ... a job offer. Perhaps you could describe the job you would have me do. I ask this because I think I recognize your associate from the news. Mr. Aguilar, isn't it?"

Eduardo Aguilar sat very quietly with his tequila and his cigarettes. He listened but remained expressionless. He was a man of power and reach. His pictures in the paper, his business in banking and casinos, even his trafficking, were simple matters of well-known fact. A dozen bodies hung from the international bridge spanning Nuevo Leon, Mexico, and Laredo, Texas on his orders. Why should he care if Collins "recognized" him? The only man who ever impressed Eduardo Aguilar was himself. Perhaps, as a child, his father had impressed him, once upon a time. His father was a hard man and a heavy drinker. Sometimes, halfway through a bottle he would begin to weep and squeeze his little boy, muttering some story little "Eddie" (or, "Eduardito") had already heard about the evils of the intoxication of women, very bad women, and their snake-like deceptive qualities. But since the age of thirteen, Sr. Eduardo had stopped being impressed by anyone. He rose through the ranks of the cartel, first a courier and a packer, later a soldier, then a bodyguard—all the while gaining the trust of high-ranking cartel men whom he later killed.

Now Sr. Eduardo Aguilar lived in luxury in Sinaloa. He had guards. He had other guards to guard his guards. He had a home with more rooms than God Himself—"In my Father's home, there are many rooms. I will go to prepare one for you! said Jesucristo," Aguilar loved to say, followed by chuckles, throat clearing, and a wheezing cough. Maybe he had fewer servants than God, but he did have servants, and the best tequilas, a grand piano that he did not play, a large library filled with leather bound books which he did not read, and expensive paintings by very famous painters whom he'd never heard of—one of them a "Rembrandt." And although he was approaching his seventies, he also had women, a dozen or so, who lived there, albeit against their will. All of them were beautiful, and all of them had the simple job of looking and acting beautiful to impress whomever Aguilar wanted impressed. He had heard of Muslims, men who were rumored to keep many wives, and despite his allegiance to the One and Only Holy Apostolic Roman Church, he could not help but admire them, whoever they were. He had also been told of the Shogun War Lords of Japan who kept many geishas for amusement. And he had heard of the lazy Sultans and their libidinous harems, but he did not know the difference between a Shogun and a Sultan. It did not matter. These Muslims wanted to do business with him, and their keeping of many wives was sufficient logic, or affinity, to expand his business, which is why Williams had come down from New York.

Mr. Williams of New York had already proven to be a reliable silent partner, and even though Aguilar trusted no one, not even Williams, in just one year their deals had netted Aguilar over 340 million dollars and had increased the strength of his growing army incrementally, making Aguilar stronger than the Federales and the Mexican Army combined. Now Aguilar was ready to explore new markets in the Middle East, and Williams was the man. By now, he was convinced that Williams was not a DEA agent, but Williams was vague about his other affiliations and clients. After a year of business, Aguilar let Williams have limited Power of Attorney on Aguilar's behalf in both Mexico and the United States.

Aguilar was uneducated and foolish, but not about his business. He could read people easier than a newspaper. If a man even looked the wrong way in a negotiation, Aguilar would kill him. About Williams, Aguilar knew that he kept things hidden. He knew that his motives did not always have to do with money—the money was simply a means to various ends. Aguilar knew in a day, upon meeting him, that he was not simply a banker because Williams knew things that bankers did not know or care about: the various kinds of flower teas in China, the way the Day of the Dead reminded him of ancestor worship in Africa, and the kill radius of an RPG. All Aguilar had to do was let him talk and Williams would size himself up all by himself—Aguilar noted that Williams could also speak like some of the senators he owned. He could speak and say nothing, and this amused Aguilar. He could tell from his build that he was ex-military, but the sort who still kept a gun close. While Williams talked percentages and pay schedules, Aguilar noted his serious blue-eyed gaze and military posture. *He must be a very successful man like myself,* he thought, *possibly more successful.* On one occasion the two men were having a glass of tequila beside the pool, and when Williams answered the telephone, he suddenly switched to some utterly demonic tongue that Aguilar did not recognize. "What is that? Chinese or Arab?"

"Oh, no Señor, that language was Pashto."

"I never heard of it," Aguilar said. Aguilar told one of his guards to get his globe from the library and then he made Williams show him where people speak "Pashto."

"It is," Williams said, "one of the languages of these areas ... Here in Pakistan and Afghanistan. Urdu and Punjabi are also spoken in this area."

On another occasion the two men had been drinking rather a lot, celebrating a grand success in business. Williams, slurring a little, asked Aguilar if he could fight one of the guards—for fun. Aguilar thought about this as well as any man could in a fog of alcohol. "Are you sure you want to do that? You might get hurt."

Williams insisted. "I really feel like having a go at that one, you know, keep myself in shape."

Aguilar thought ... *Let him have Sebastián.* "Sebastián! Come here!" he yelled.

Sebastián Marco came quickly.

"Don Aguilar, sir?"

"Let Mr. Williams have a go at you, will you?"

"Certainly, Don Aguilar."

The two men squared off on a patch of green between the pool and a row of palm trees, and before Don Aguilar could take another sip of his tequila or tap the ash of his cigarette and commence to watch, Sebastián was laid out on the well-manicured lawn, temporarily unconscious.

The women who were sunning themselves by the pool saw this and were impressed. Even a buzzard was impressed—it left its perch on a saguaro cactus and circled once high over the unconscious man, Sebastián Marco. The feral animal that lives inside of us smells blood and becomes aroused. Sometime, hours after midnight, one of them, Carmelita Vaghina, risked her life going on tip-toes surreptitiously down a long hall to Williams's room to be with him.

Chapter 3

Rawalpindi, January 2007

ON THE NIGHT OF Ashura, a long procession of faithful Shi'ite men was stirring the dust on a street and marching in Francisco Barranca's direction, making a great noise with the clashing of swords and screams of devotion. The moon was full and flashed across the silver blades that they swung in the air and flailed themselves with. All of them had cut through their clothes and deep into their backs, self-flagellating with the swords. Francisco had seen a similar spectacle years earlier in Mexico City, the faithful crawling up the avenue of Guadalupe on pilgrimage to the Basilica, edging their way on bloody knees. Such behavior, he thought, was disgusting. He stepped into the shadow of an alley and watched. The men bore deep cuts and their blood dripped into the street. They must have numbered five or six hundred. By the next day, the rotting blood would cover the streets of Sadr Market and the air would fill up with black flies and draw the scavenger kites into circles overhead.

Now Francisco had his bearings. He was not far from old man Mahmood's rug shop. He didn't trust Mahmood still after five years, but he had no other choice. He had to get off the street before someone spotted him. The rug shop had been one of the first clandestine stops Francisco made under orders from Williams and Aguilar. There he passed along a ciphered code, which in turn arranged a shipment from the poppy fields of Afghanistan to the port of Karachi where it would be loaded on a ship bound for Rotterdam, and there transferred to a ship bound for Miami. The same route in reverse was used to bring new weapons from the United States to the Taliban. Williams had men everywhere, working on the inside. Francisco began to understand that Williams was even more powerful than Aguilar. Aguilar had dozens of trucks rolling across the US-Mexico border, but Williams had carte blanche in several countries, though his name appeared nowhere on any invoice or customs' form. In return for these shipments, the jihadists received both money and all manner of military toys. And they received their goods cheaply due to competition in the marketplace. US sellers had to compete with suppliers in Dubai, Beijing, Tehran, and Moscow … It was a complex operation and no one, with the exception of Williams himself, knew every link in the chain.

Many of the older jihadists enjoyed the same trade routes from back when they called themselves the Mujahidin. Even then, some of their weapons came from traders behind enemy lines. It was so commonplace that the word *Kalashnikov* was part of a small child's burgeoning vocabulary.

The first time Francisco slipped away, eluding his Pakistani employer, The Higher Education Commission, to meet the old man Mahmood, the bearded old fellow invited him to sit down and have a cup of tea, so Francisco knew that he was not among the strictest observers of Islamic laws, laws that forbid communing with infidels. So, Francisco sipped on his tea while the old man gently probed him with questions. Three young men were present, sitting in a semicircle and eating lentils with lamb, sopping up the sauce with *rhoti*. Francisco noticed that one of the young men was remarkably handsome, almost felicific, with very long eyelashes. None of these young men took much interest in the old man Mahmood or the American until Francisco (the American) unwittingly violated a taboo by asking if the young men would be joining them for tea. The pretty one stared back at Francisco with frightening coldness. "They do not speak English," the old man said, "or Urdu, for that matter." The dulcet one was the most vociferous. He chastised his fellows for not dressing "thusly" in the proper manner of the Prophet, motioning at his own properly donned baggy white pants that were tied of with strings at his ankles just over his sandals—his fellows feigned listening, like squat limpets clinging to his words while they crouched over their lentils. Nothing, no matter how trivial, would escape the eye of Allah, and for their degree of observance, they could expect rewards from Allah reciprocally. Conversely, any deviance from His path will incur his wrath a thousandfold, unless these deficiencies were rectified—penance for an unclean thought; penance unless you enter the toilet with your right foot and exit the toilet with your left foot; if you see a dog or a puppy, you must punt it as far as possible for a heavenly field goal; send an enemy of Allah to Hell; never say you have killed your enemy, but rather proclaim that he or she is now in Hell. "Today, 85 Shi'as are in Hell—all praise to Allah," one of them said. Allah must be credited for all things, no matter how small, and no matter if it be for good or evil. "Typhoid and cholera have spread through the stinking refugee camps where the cowards live and now more than three hundred are in Hell—praise be to Allah," one said. "Praise Allah," the other two said in chorus.

Francisco was not sure what penalty awaited them if they were to have accepted his offer to join them for tea.

Finally, the time came to address the business at hand. Mahmood leaned over and asked Francisco quietly for the information he needed.

"The Mayflower," Francisco said.

"Fine. Fine. That concludes our business."

"No, I'm afraid not. I must have this put on a note and wrapped in a tapestry and mailed to this address. Otherwise, I will be in trouble."

"I see. It is not a problem. Give me the address."

Francisco handed it to him. The old man Mahmood put on a pair of spectacles and looked at an address to a place in Mexico City that neither he nor Francisco knew.

"Fine. Fine. Pick out a tapestry. The children make them because their fingers are small and very nimble. They do excellent work, yes?"

Francisco pointed to one of the tapestries on the wall, one that was filled with tiny red and yellow finches.

"Fine," Mahmood said, "it will be going out tomorrow by DHL. Very fast. Five days. Ok?"

Chapter 4

Sinaloa, July 2002

EVERY ROOM OF EDUARDO Aguilar's estate had hidden cameras except for Aguilar's bedroom. Behind a console, José Luis López sat and monitored the activity. He was a short, plump man with fat lips, a smirk, and a quickly receding hairline. His mouth bore an unnatural divot that pooled with spittle and leaked down his puffy cheek. The room where he spent every afternoon and night was filled with monitors. The sounds and sights of forty-one of forty-two rooms were his world—the 42nd being that of Aguilar's. Here he was a little god who could see into the lives of those who had wandered into his domain. He could raise and lower the volume from his control panel, which resembled a cockpit. He watched with lurid excitement and short quick breaths as Carmelita Vaghina entered Williams's room. He watched them pet each other and listened to their moans, and he put his hand inside his pants as if he were fumbling around for change while their two bodies slammed together in the strange pleasure that looks like pain or aggression to small children. To López, though he was unaware, it tripped a wire in his head that turned on a light in that same part of his inner child brain—aggression. He knew if he reported Carmelita Vaghina to his boss that he would have the cheap tramp executed, probably her pretty head lopped off and her body chopped up and strewn around the desert in Sinaloa. *No*, he thought, *I have a better idea*. She could do things for him, instead. Dirty things. Secret things. She would have to do it. From that night on, Carmelita—the sweet, intoxicating *Brasileña*—belonged to José Luis, whenever she was not summoned by Aguilar.

Chapter 5

Rawalpindi, August 2003

THE NIGHT FRANCISCO BARRANCA arrived in Pakistan, he couldn't sleep—it being the middle of the day in Mexico. In a few hours it would be the morning of the first day, a Sunday, so he waited for the sun. When it began to turn the eastern horizon to luminous grey, Francisco took his cane and went for a walk. His bodyguards were still asleep on mats on the front terrace. Francisco did not know that he wasn't supposed to go anywhere without a bodyguard, and he crept quietly, out of politeness rather than stealth, and managed to not wake them.

This neighborhood was called Chaklala, in the city of Rawalpindi. From here he walked to Sadr Market using only a memorized map in his head. He wore sneakers and blue jeans, a white shirt—this attire, along with his disheveled pile of reddish blond hair would make him instantly the subject of attention as it marked him as either European or American, and it had only been a year since Daniel Pearl was taken and executed by the Taliban. The thought did cross his mind. "Kafir"—the Urdu word from Arabic for "infidel"—slipped from the mouths of women and children, anyone who had already risen to begin their labors. In Old Sadr Market, he found the bookstore. The first thing he noticed was a tall stack of Korans beside another tall stack of Adolf Hitler's autobiography, *Mein Kampf*, as if one were a primer on how to best interpret the other. *North wall, last bookcase on the right, behind the row of books on the next to highest shelf… The first name of the author will begin with A.* And there it was in his hand, Alfred Lord Tennyson's great epic poem to a departed friend, *In Memoriam.* "Begin reading it backwards from the end to complete the message by assembling the typographical errors until you reach the word stop," Williams had said. The message was "The Mayflower Stop."

By this time, it was close to nine o'clock. He gave the storekeeper fifteen rupees for the book and left. The message would only mean something to a rug merchant a block away, a man named Mahmood, so that is where he was to proceed. Beyond this, Francisco did not know the meaning of the message. To Mahmood it would translate to an actual boat, a Libyan freighter docked at the Port of Karachi, and to a place and date where a transaction was to occur, one involving 400 kilos of heroin encased inside vats of wax honey in 50-gallon drums waiting to be loaded deep inside the bowels of the massive ship.

September the 7th in the year 2003 was, as was written, a Sunday. The messages were to be picked up and deciphered only on Sundays that fell on either a prime number or on the first of a month—in this case, seven. By ten o'clock the temperature had already risen to 103 degrees Fahrenheit. By afternoon it would reach 118. Francisco still had to meet the rug merchant, Mahmood, and walk back to Chaklala. After they met, Francisco was only part of the way back to his quarters when an old Nissan clattered up beside him. Inside, the driver motioned for him to get in.

"Excuse me, but who are you?" Francisco asked.

"I your driver. Get in. Not safe you here."

"I'm fine," replied Francisco, "I like walking."

The driver kept the Nissan rolling beside him, just over two miles per hour, and he pleaded and insisted piteously until Francisco relented and got in the backseat. Then the car turned onto the Pindi causeway and headed to Chaklala. The driver liked to talk.

"Here are many attacks," he said, as they crossed the main bridge in Pindi. "They hide trees along river … launch missiles. Already five attacks on President."

Francisco knew they were passing General Musharraf's compound, having memorized the map.

"Many attacks," the driver said. "Do not cross bridge by walk on foot. You they shoot from either side. How you say … You not Kansas, anymore. This … Pakistan. Oh, stay out that neighborhood." The driver pointed north. "Don't shop that market." Again pointing somewhere. "Next time take you your guards—that why they paid. That market there … safer for shop." He pointed to Chaklala Market. "Fewer bombs there."

In the following days Francisco realized what a rare thing it was to receive even the smallest piece of practical advice.

That day, the Vice Chancellor of the women's college arrived at the house in Chaklala to brief Francisco on his duties. She was a short, plump little woman in Indian dress with actual gold threads embroidered into the cloth, tantamount to frippery in a country so poor, he thought. Her dress was "salwar kameez," and so lavish it brought to mind a warning he'd read in *The Gospel of Sri Ramakrishna*: "stay away from women and gold"—especially women, for they are the ones who entice men to seek out gold. She had received her PhD from Stanford in the 1960s. When she spoke she was a bit diffident and a little obtuse. She made statements without first framing them, but Francisco quickly became used to such ambiguities, finding them to be abundant throughout the land. It was a little like trying to catch a fly ball in pitch dark. *If ambiguities could grow on trees and were edible, he thought, they would save their people from so much starvation.*

The VC handed him his schedule. There would be an early morning meeting on Monday to introduce him to administrators and other members of the faculty, and then at eight o'clock in the morning, he would be teaching his first class, a graduate seminar on American Literature. The following day he would meet his students in Literary Critical Theory. Monday and Wednesday, American Literature. Tuesday and Thursday, Critical Theory. Thursday afternoons, he will leave to visit other universities in order to assess their faculty and curricula, and then return to Rawalpindi on Saturday night. His reports for the Commission of Higher Education, or Dr. Farooq, were due each Monday. Then the VC left. She did not introduce him to the guards. She only said that they were the guards and he was to do as they said, or as they indicated, since they did not speak English. She turned to them and told them in Urdu, "This is the Professor," and they both snapped to attention. One of the guards was older, about sixty-five, and the VC addressed him as "Captain," so presumably he was retired military.

There was another boarder who stepped outside onto the terrace just as the VC had left. He said his name, but Francisco forgot it after just a few weeks. Everything about the man was fake. Clearly he was a spy, but for whom? His business was not as he professed, geology.

"We are doing a survey there in the Margalla Hills," he said, pointing. "We are looking for additional fault lines to help us plan for earthquakes."

"Oh," Francisco said. "What sort of rock forms the foothills? Sedimentary? Metamorphic?"

"Sedimentary."

Wrong, thought Francisco. *The hills are volcanic igneous, probably with pockets of metamorphic rock. This man is not a geologist. So what is his purpose?*

"I see," Francisco said.

Francisco went up a curved staircase made of white marble and did a little more unpacking. The window in his room was open. Next door someone was playing music on a stereo. It was an Indian raga. He sat down by the window to listen, trying to discern its key signature. *It was certainly dominated by a minor key, but which? East or West, we live with the same sun and moon, the same rotations—there are 24 key signatures once we minus the equivalent keys, and these correspond to the lunar cycles, the twelve full bright moons drawing us into the brightest lights of the major keys, and the twelve dark or new moons, which our hearts echo with melancholy. The waxing and waning were essentially the way we express, in music, augmenting and diminishing. The solar rotations were there, as well, most obviously visible when the cycles were laid out in the sequential black and white keys on a piano—eighty-eight of them, which when multiplied and rounded, mirrored the 360-degree rotation of the earth around the sun. The scales of the west were embedded in the raga, too; they were simply sliding through a few more tones, perhaps as much as 1/32nd tones. It was difficult to tell.* Francisco loved music because it could never lie—not good music. Bad music lied, but good music of whatever kind or culture never lied. He thought it was one of humanity's better endeavors, but as for that, few people ever bothered to listen to music very carefully. He wondered if his daughter, Karli, was practicing and what she would be practicing, or if his having gone missing had completely disrupted everything about their lives.

At three o'clock in the afternoon, a new driver, another guard, and a strikingly beautiful but very small woman arrived. She could not have been older than twenty-five. She was so tiny that Francisco wondered if she might be an actual dwarf, but her proportions seemed normal—that is, her head, her hands, seemed to be in concert with the rest of her. The geologist, dilatory in his movements, was just finishing a late lunch and now he was rubbing his stomach, letting out a gusty belch, followed by an unidentified stench.

"I am Nadia. I will take you to buy the things you need."

The geologist greeted her casually and returned to his room.

"How do you do. Pleased to meet you," Francisco replied.

Francisco knew enough not to offer his hand to her, but she violated Islamic tradition and stuck hers out to shake his, which she did firmly.

Nadia spoke very quickly and moved from side to side nervously, beginning all of her sentences with an overly solicitous "sir," though with no clear tone of respect. The effect was irksome. She was so small and bouncy that she reminded Francisco more of a Christmas toy than a real person. But there was something about her that was surreptitious.

Nadia ordered the house servant to bring them some tea-white, or *chai*. Now her own sense of power became evident. A diamond on the side of her lovely nose glistened brightly in defiance of *Sharia* law—as some interpreted it. Her clothes were stylish and colorful, but chosen to not step over the legal line of Muslim acceptability—as defined in this region, the subcontinent, the penumbra between the Far East and Middle East.

"Sir, I am your graduate teaching assistant."

"That's very nice. However, it would be wonderful if you would not call me 'sir.' Call me Francisco, or, if you must, 'Professor'."

"Sir, we must all say 'sir.' It's our tradition."

She continued to move as she spoke, plopping down on a wicker chair and reaching into her handbag for his schedule, the same one the VC had just outlined for him verbally. The servant, whose name was Sahib, brought out two cups of tea. Francisco looked over the pages while Nadia kept talking.

"Your first trips for the Commission will be to Punjab University, then International Islamic University, then Karachi University. I suspect you'll be busy."

"What is my enrollment?"

"Close to one hundred, but don't worry, I'll help you. I'll mark your papers."

"No, I think I'll do that."

"Oh, and here is your telephone. You must have it with you at all times."

"Why? Must I? I don't use telephones."

Nadia did not answer him; she continued almost machine-like.

"Your driver will come for you at 6:30."

"But I don't use phones. The ringing disturbs me. Especially cell phones."

"Your servant … His name is Sahib. He will make you anything that he knows how to cook, but he doesn't speak English. You can call me and hand him the phone. Here is a menu. Just point."

Francisco had to pretend that he did not understand Urdu, so he was conscious of his facial movements and his eyes whenever Nadia used Urdu to bark an order at Sahib.

"You will hand over your reports for the Commission to me. I will take care of this."

Francisco had stopped listening and was focusing on the course outlines, and suddenly interrupted Nadia.

"You do realize that Critical Theory did not really begin until the 1920s and this class outline ends with T.S. Eliot's *Uses and Abuses of Poetry*, about the time that Critical Theory actually begins? What about the Russians? The Germans? The French? The Americans?"

"Sir, you can tell us what we need to know."

"It appears that the study of English came to a halt when the British packed up and left. We'll have to revise this."

Nadia's demeanor changed its tyrannical aura to the bewildered look one normally sees on the face of a college freshman.

"The Russians?" she asked, nervously.

"Roman Jakobson, for one."

"The Romans, you mean?" Such ignorance might have been cute coming from a child.

"In studies of aphasia, Jakobson discovered how the brain's structures are reflected in syntax, and by doing so he inadvertently founded the basis for modern critical theory. Tomorrow, I will give you a list of theorists. See if it is possible to track down any of their works."

"Yes, sir."

"Professor or Mister."

"Yes, sir. Mister."

Francisco was awash in a torrent of first impressions of Nadia, and likewise, so was she. She considered herself the most erudite at the women's college; confronted with unknown names or ideas caused her to panic. Anything beyond her purview or domination cannot possibly exist. These Romans or Russians, if they did exist, had nothing to do with a course on Literary Theory. Was it possible that something beyond her control could exist? Also, Francisco presented an authentic air of self-control, one that came naturally. But worse than this, he showed no sign of fascination for her, no curiosity despite her well-wrought flamboyance and her wiles. This troubled Nadia. She bit her lip in confusion and squinted at the distance.

The afternoon was beginning to recede into evening, and the scavenger kites had disappeared from the sky to roost in the trees along the river between Sadr and Chaklala.

"I am instructed to take you to eat and then shop. What kind of food do you like?

"What are my choices?"

"Pakistani food."

"Fine."

Francisco's training in Sinaloa was language intensive. He was taught to understand Urdu, but never to speak it. He was trained not to acknowledge any comprehension. He was shown pictures of people such as Mahmood. He was made to memorize the maps of five cities and a dozen villages. But Williams himself did not care a wit about the abecedarian cultural ways of other peoples, thus Francisco was not presented with any cultural information; and although Barranca's education was ample, he was not well-versed in the ways of this benighted backwash of the world. His life in Africa, Europe, and Latin America did not prepare him for the uncertainties of Pakistan.

That night he ate Biryani, picking cloves out of the rice. At dinner Nadia asked him forty or so more questions but never actually let him answer any of them. He began to think of her as not only a small person, small as in nearly a dwarf, but also as a bantam child, about age three, asking "why" and not waiting for an answer. The more she talked, the more Francisco's mind drifted back in memory to the company of Teodesia. He searched high walls in his mind for a way to reach her, even if it were for a moment, or the freedom just to write her a secret note to tell her he loved her and he loved their children, and he loved their life together. Teodesia was still very youthful, still beautiful, and she was graceful—not like this exotic little creature blathering uncontrollably and quite apparently ignorant of almost everything.

Normally, Francisco welcomed the society of women. He loved women, and not simply as a man who wants a woman. He loved their company more than the company of men, generally. He liked almost everything about them—their way of thinking about the world was different, their preoccupations and the things they considered to be "problems." And each differed from the other as one star to another in the night sky. Nadia's dark complexion was almost the same as Teodesia's. But the resemblance ended there.

Teodesia had a playful spirit. She was genuinely interested in other people. Nadia merely feigned a pretend interest for some dark purpose. Teodesia could have beaten him in a foot race were they to have turned back the years to before Francisco's war injuries when he could sprint fast enough to make the university's track team. For curiosity once, he measured out one hundred yards and timed Teodesia in a hundred-yard dash at 10.9 seconds. Nadia could not keep up with Francisco even though he used a cane. Her walk resembled a kid pedaling a bicycle as fast as she could. Her stride measured no more than a foot. Teodesia was calm and composed. Nadia was nervous and easily distracted. Still, Nadia was sensuous, like the sirens in Homer's Odyssey singing out messages of wantonness with their eyes.

Nadia interrupted the answers to one of her questions to ask Francisco if she could see a photograph of his wife. So Francisco took a photo out of his wallet and handed it to her. It was, however, a photograph of Carmelita Vaghina.

"Her name is Isa Aramara," he said.

He barely knew Carmelita. They had just begun to get to know each other in Sinaloa. Now her function was to be a face in a picture, a false representation of a woman who didn't exist, the supposed wife of Francisco Barranca. Even photographs of his parents and grandparents had false names.

There was a detectable jealousy in the way Nadia looked at Isa Aramara's picture. And she blurted …

"You married a blackie … like me!?"

Carmelita Vaghina had spent most of her time outside, in or by the swimming pool, so she had a cinnamon, rubicund tan.

Chapter 6

Sinaloa, August 2003

IT WAS 117 DEGREES in the shade in Sinaloa. After a year, the prisoner/spy-in-training, Francisco, was allowed to go into the city, Culiacán, with José Luis López. Williams wanted only to see if Francisco would run. When not monitoring the estate's security systems, López handled pick-ups of laundered money at one of the casinos in town. The largest of these establishments was co-owned by Aguilar and the state's governor. The two of them also owned the only airport around, in Juárez, in the state of Chihuahua, so it was not a secret to anyone why taxation on airfare in and out of Juárez, even for domestic travel, drove up the cost of tickets. It was cheaper to fly from Tokyo to Paris then from México City to Juárez. For Aguilar and the officials, these costs were justified—to fly large shipments of drugs across several borders cost untold quantities of added costs to pay off DEA agents and customs officers, and line the pockets of a long list of Americans. The industry's web was so vast that Aguilar's accountants and their computers could only estimate the costs on spreadsheets. Aguilar employed twenty-nine accountants in an office building on Reforma Avenue in México City. He employed a number of lawyers, too. He did not employ anyone in the field of Human Resources because he did not consider his employees to be human; they were commodities like everyone else. It was a lesson he'd learned in college, a prestigious university in Monterrey called "The Tec"—a university that specialized not in education but in how to make money.

López had not removed his tie even in 117 degrees of heat. The sun struck the cinderblock buildings and blistered its latex layers of white paint. The sun and the city were too bright to see through the glare on the windshield. Black vultures were circling over something just on the edge of the city. Francisco felt dizzy. His head was full of Urdu, months and months of Urdu, and now a collection of fictional "facts" that were to serve as a cover story. Asalamalaikum, Carmelita Vaghina is your wife; here is her photo, but her name is Isa Aramara. She was born in Sao Paolo, but really she was born in Rio; you were married in Puerto Vallarta in 2001. You do not have children. She works as a nurse in Culiacán. You are a professor from Tec de Monterrey, a professor of literature. You are a book person and we cannot train it out of you, so we have figured out how to let you remain a book person. You attended Princeton. You did not attend NYU. Princeton. If they check, and they will, you were born in Mexico of an American mother and a Mexican father in 1960 in San Miguel de Allende. Your father, Jorge Barranca, was a geologist who worked for Pemex and your mother, an American named Marsha Branham, was a housewife. Her parents, your grandparents, were Julia Barnes and Clyde Mason. You didn't know them. Your father's parents were Ana Laura Mendez Licea and Victor Barranca Salanova. You grew up in San Miguel de Allende. After graduating from the Tec, you received your graduate degrees from Princeton. Here are all the papers, all translated, all with the appropriate apostilles and supporting documents. With your joint citizenship, you now have a US passport and a Mexican passport. Your visa for Pakistan is issued to your US passport because Pakistan does not have diplomatic relations with Mexico. Your other interests include American sports, especially baseball and football, so make a habit of reading everything I give you to read. And, no, I don't really care if you are or aren't actually interested in it.

Francisco looked at one of the copies of *Sports Illustrated* on the coffee table.

"Who are the Ravens?"

"You're joking."

"Titans?"

"Football team. Tennessee."

"Tennessee has a professional football team? Since when?"

Williams ignored him and continued. *Your favorite TV show is called* Baywatch. *And, yes they have heard of* Baywatch *in Pakistan even if you haven't. They love it for two reasons. One, they are just as salacious as anyone else, possibly more so, Muslim or not, and two, the show confirms their belief that all American women are whores. More about that later. Now back to Urdu. I'm going to play a dialogue for you while you pretend to not understand a word. When it is over, I want you to summarize it.*

López and Francisco walked inside the dark, air-conditioned casino and into the noise of bells and slot machines and the rattle of a spinning wheel of roulette. A woman in a bikini approached them with cocktail trays. She was sporting a live cockatoo on her shoulder, but López waved them away. Francisco followed him to an office. As soon as the man in the office saw López, he got up and went to a safe, opened it, and passed its contents to López's briefcase.

For several more days the last strokes of paint were applied to Francisco Barranca. *Here is your invitation letter from the Education Commission in Pakistan. You will be flying from México City to Paris, from Paris to Islamabad. Use your Mexican passport to leave Mexico, but then switch to your US passport. Slip the Mexican passport back into your jacket in the airplane bathroom and sew it shut with this needle and thread. In Paris, they will run a facial recognition test, but you'll pass, so don't start sweating and fuck up before you get there. If you fuck up, all your patriotism for Cuba and Nicaragua will only lead to the same consequences—another family, all of them dead. Understand?*

These sessions went on until Williams was convinced that Francisco had fully absorbed his part. Williams wanted Barranca to begin to doubt the existence of Bolivar Collins, or that his real self would simply seem like a dream. When Williams handed him a new wallet, Francisco stared at a photograph of Carmelita, his "wife," whose name appeared as Isa Aramara Barranca, and the actual face of his wife, Teodesia, was supposed to float up into the clouds. "She will be safe as long as you do your job," Williams said. Teodesia's face was now Carmen's, and Carmen's name was Isa Aramara.

"Why bother making up this wife? Why not just make me single?"

"Because married men are less suspicious."

Francisco whispered his name to himself to verify his existence: *Bolivar. Bolivar Collins.*

Williams had long since stopped calling him by his real name—by the second day of his abduction, a year earlier.

"Francisco, what team do you think will win the World Cup? France? Brazil? Francisco, would you like a tequila? Francisco, give me the names of your maternal grandparents …"

Who in the hell is Francisco? I am Bolivar. I was born in St. Louis, Missouri. I want to go home to Teodesia. What is happening to me? To my family? But it never stopped. It just went deeper into unreality until the unreal began to feel normal.

"They may torture you. If they torture you, nothing you say will make any difference. If they find out who you really are, it has no effect on us. The Americans may execute you for treason, but that is only if you manage somehow to escape. You don't know enough about us to even constitute a nuisance. Understand?"

One day Williams entered the room with a box of books.

"Today we'll be talking about your cover job. The first item is a notebook of your correspondence with your new employer for the past six months."

Williams dumped the box of books on the table.

"I assume you are familiar with some of these. I want you to look through them and start talking about them."

Mostly they were American classics that anyone would know—books by Twain, Hawthorne, Melville, Whitman, Dickinson ... There was a large anthology of Literary Criticism, edited by Hazard Adams, *Critical Theory Since Plato.*

"Maybe I can save us both a little time," Francisco said. "Why don't you simply choose one and open it to any page."

"You're joking."

"Try me. I don't always get it right."

Williams opened Whitman's *Leaves of Grass* arbitrarily.

"Page 509."

"Which edition?"

"1889. Modern Library's Deathbed Edition."

"'Passage to India,' from whence E.M. Forster took the title for his novel. It was published in 1872. The last lines read, 'O farther, farther, farther, sail!' Whitman believed that democracy would spread like divine ivy to every dark corner of the world. He had embraced 'Manifest Destiny' since 1840 when the term was first coined in a New York newspaper. Should I go on? It's a ridiculous idea that is still alive in your American foreign policy."

Williams tried hard not to show any surprise or admiration. He picked up another book.

"*The Theory of Literature*, page 72."

"By Wellek and Warren. On page 72, they argue that it's impossible to visualize a metaphor. They're wrong. They should have said that it is impossible for some people, like them."

Williams scanned the page until he found the passage Francisco was referring to, and then he nodded and closed the book, still resisting the urge to show any expression. Williams was a man who, like Aguilar, viewed himself as superior to all other men, but he did not comport himself accordingly unless he had been drinking too much. Francisco continued …

"Or, well, they are only partly right. All images, not simply visual, are filtered through language."

"Ok, you can stop. With how many books can you perform your magic trick?"

"I don't know how many. I suppose, many. It depends on whether or not I thought it was important when I read it."

"Fine, then, we'll skip the books. Instead, I want you to memorize these maps, whether or not you think they're important."

Williams pulled maps out of a satchel. There were maps of Islamabad, Rawalpindi, Lahore, Karachi, Abbottabad, and a dozen other smaller towns.

"Use your God-given ability and pay special attention to locations that are circled. You can work on this here. Do you want me to put on music?"

Williams wasn't being kind in his offer. After the first few weeks of working with Francisco, he realized he could memorize things faster when there was music playing.

"Yes, thanks. I'd like to hear *Rhapsody in Blue*, by George Gershwin."

Williams put the music on and left Francisco alone with his studies. Francisco's mind hovered over the maps, working systematically, dividing larger areas into smaller ones, starting in the upper left corner of a map, like a Chinese character, and flying left to right and top to bottom, leaving long strings of mnemonic codes sewn into the core of his visual memory. The rhapsody rose up an octave, then another octave, like a bird rising and widening its circles, and from its heights the valleys and peaks below diminished in contrast. The farther we are from a thing, the more it greys. The colors bleed out. Francisco focused on a map of Rawalpindi, a city halfway around the world.

Chapter 7

Rawalpindi, September 2003

THE BODY'S OWN SALT mixes with other elements—whatever we swallow, the garlic, cloves, cardamom, rice, sweet breads—and the salts turn sweet and bitter and flow through the pores of our skin where the moisture ferments in darkness under the clothes, the armpits, between the legs, the hair and skin collecting a heavy, pungent oil. Most of the women only bathed once a month, and their bodies' odors had seeped into the fabric of their burkas, which also had gone unwashed. Francisco entered the classroom and his first thought was a memory of a workroom with poor ventilation, where his grandfather had accidentally tipped over a gallon of kerosene and where grease had fused with the dirt and sand. The odor stung his eyes.

Francisco walked down a long aisle that split the room into two sides with twenty-five women to a side. He walked to the podium in front of a blackboard, and as he did all of them stood up at attention, as if part of a brigade. *Good Morning, students*, he said. A chorus of one voice answered, *Good Morning, sir*. Many of them were dressed in bright subcontinent colors and their heads were covered with scarves, but a few wore brown or blue burkas and wore the *hijab*, making them look like nuns, or the way nuns used to dress. A few wore black burkas, covering their faces with veils so that Francisco could not tell if they were smiling or grimacing. He had worked hard for many years to try to read body language and facial expressions. He had even read books about this since he was fairly incapable of interpreting social signs instinctively. All the knowledge he acquired remained purely abstract, and now he was thinking, how is it possible to interpret body language or faces when they are undisclosed? Being in general is that way—undisclosed. Why should their clothes be any different?

Francisco called their names …

Samina Ahktar … "Present"

Serein Asad … "Present"

Humaira Kahn … "Present"

There was a second "Humaira Kahn."

Humaira Kahn … "Present"

Francisco paused …

"If it is all right with both of you, I will refer to you as Humaira No. 1 and Humaira No 2."

"Yes, sir."

"Yes, sir."

Francisco went on with the roll.

When he had called all fifty, he closed the folder and stood there looking at them looking at him. They were all bundled up in the heat in a long rectangular class with no ventilation and no air.

"I would like each of you to visit me individually. For a graduate course, there are far too many of you, and we must get to know each other as soon as possible. I want you to talk to me about your interests and your research plans for this term and for the foreseeable future. If you can manage it, bring me your thesis prospectus. If you don't have one, don't worry about it. Nadia has passed out the syllabus with my hours. Now … our class. American Literature. Maybe you have already formed some opinions about the Americans, so why don't you do me the honor of sharing. Who are some of the authors you know?"

Francisco waited on an answer for more than thirty seconds. Clearly no one wanted to speak. Finally, Humaira No. 1 raised her hand.

"Yes, Humaira."

"Well, sir, we already know that Walt Whitman was a sick degenerate. Pakistan has already formed the correct position, and it is supported by Edwin Haviland Miller's Freudian analysis, sir."

Miller had been one of Francisco's teachers, possibly the worst, but this had occurred at New York University, and Francisco was Bolivar Collins. He couldn't comment about memories of Miller, sitting through tedious, inane monologues in a seminar more than twenty years ago. He was, to be sure, absolutely the most dogmatic professor he had ever encountered. Barranca, or rather Collins, turned in a paper that was complimentary of Mallarmé's translations of Poe, hinting that they might be better than Poe's too carefully measured verses, lines written for a metronome—not bad if the verse is being written for small children. In the essay, Collins venerated Poe as the inventor of the modern short story and innovator of genres: horror, spy stories, detective stories, etc ... But Poe had written out his poetic theories first, and then set about to write an awkward sort of poetry that would try to fit his theories, an act akin to forcing the feet of young Chinese girls to fit into very tiny shoes. The feet had to be bound and the bones broken. The essay managed to position Collins in the crosshairs of Miller's contempt, which expressed itself in wrath and various forms of psychological torment, including public ridicule.

The war between Miller and Collins began with that essay, but it did not end there. The day that Miller wanted all of them to believe that Whitman was sexually aroused by wounds (a la the "attraction" half of attraction and repulsion in Freud) was the day that Collins got up and walked out.

"Are there any other thoughts on Whitman or Humaira's view?"

A student stood up in the back.

"Sir. I am Serein. I believe Whitman was the greatest of all poets and mystics in the English language after Shakespeare. I would compare him to Tagore. Do you know Tagore, sir?"

"Not in Tamil, Serein, but in English, yes. And I agree with you ... 'I release myself in lacey jags ....' It doesn't get more mystical than that. There are places, such as the middle of 'Song of Myself' where Whitman, as Whitman, simply disappears or vanishes into the world of spirit. The physicality and sensuality are there, yes, and the sexuality that Humaira refers to, but along with the British counterparts (Byron, Shelley, Keats—for example), Whitman believed the physical world was infused with a vast and cosmic divine spirit that manifested itself in freedom. He believed that spirit or democracy OR spiritual democracy would spread far west, as far as India, and in some ways, it has. Freedom is our natural born state. We are curious, like the 'child fetching the grass with full hands' to ask, 'What is it?'"

Francisco had become noticeably excited. A few of the students joined the conversation. It was a good beginning for Francisco as a "professor," despite the reality that he was not a professor. Nadia sat in the back of the class furiously taking notes, taking down every single word, even noting gestures, facial expressions, and inflections. Francisco never saw these notes, but others did—persons who had no identity, persons who were specters but who did not live in a spirit world.

Several of the girls followed him from class to the verandah, asking more questions. Francisco began to forget that he was not a real professor. It was easier to accept this role than that of a kidnapped victim and semi-trained spy for a Mexican drug cartel. He felt, too, that he was complicit. He wondered what his life would be like if he had just stayed in New York, written his dissertation—a book that was to be about Wallace Stevens—had taken a quiet teaching job at a small college in New England. Maybe he could have avoided some of the tragic, deleterious consequences of his impulsive nature to dash off to faraway places like a knight errant in search of an empty cup, to just "get up and go / and go ..." without the foggiest clue what direction to take. The young Francisco—or, Bolivar, rather—had never bothered to consult a compass, not until everyone he loved was taken away from him in the Congo, and then in Nicaragua. He was just beginning to learn, when living in Cuba with his wife, Renee, and their daughters, that most people lived more careful lives. Now Teodesia's safety was at risk, Teodesia's and Karlita's and Paco's, as a consequence of his impulsiveness.

The sense of helplessness to reverse the past is paralyzing. Time itself had passed away. The past and the dead were one thing, but he had gone on living his present in the wake, holding the deathwatch over them. Whitman understood these regrets ... "Vigil strange I kept on the field one night." Whitman knew a terrible loneliness and the feeling that one has sold his soul, but those fears, like Francisco's, he had managed to keep hidden from view. Only the best readers could find them.

Anyway, there were a thousand ways to sell a soul to one's demons. A good whore can convince herself of her own sweet lies. Her john will bankrupt his family only to be with her for a few moments, to lie with her and try to forget. Nature insinuates that somewhere inside ecstatic moments, moments of orgasm, whether sexually induced or by some psychological or religious means, no past or future exists, but a moment outside time that escaped the circles that constituted the earth's music. The rest of the time some people chase after this ephemeral experience. They sit in a dark room gripping a glass of whisky, or they try to lose themselves in bright lights and noise.

After class, there had been a ruction between two of the girls over Whitman's degeneracy, so now Nadia was bounding like a chivvying rabbit toward Francisco. Then she was upon him …

"The students have never heard the word sexual used in public before, but I think they covered up their shock very well. Anyway, they are all saying that you are very wonderful and that you must know a great deal."

"Shocked? I didn't notice that. Be that as it may, we have not finished discussing the 'sexual degenerate'."

Two cooks served lunch through a small window. Their kitchen was a concrete bunker that allowed no entrance into the university compound. It was constructed to insure the separation of genders. The window was only large enough to pass a plate through. Francisco could hear them talking, using Urdu …

"I tell you he is CIA."

"What would a CIA guy be doing at a women's university?"

"Are you stupid? The Chancellor and General Kahn are advisory members of Musharraf's cabinet. He has all sorts of access from here. And you think his being right here—Prince Edward's palace—is an accident?"

The women's college had been built originally by two Sikh brothers around the year 1900 to accommodate Prince Edward, but the Prince cancelled his visit to India. Francisco continued to overhear them, nodding to Nadia while ignoring her so he could listen to the two men talking in the kitchen.

"We're across the street from Musharraf's house. He is probably a sniper for the CIA! He could do it from his own office window!"

The cook was behind a grey concrete wall, so Francisco could only imagine him pointing up at the Victorian tower to his office.

"It can't be more than two hundred meters from his window to Musharraf's."

"You're paranoid. That's what you are. Ridiculous and paranoid. Put some lentils on that plate and give it to him."

Now Francisco was the helpless prisoner of Nadia's inquisition, without defense, with only a plate of lentils, a small piece of lamb, and some flat bread the Pakistanis call *rhoti*. Some questions are cute from little children, but from a grown woman, they made Francisco wonder what men felt when they stood before a firing squad. She was very pleasant to look at, but somehow her beauty only made her incessant questions even more ridiculous for being disproportionate with the face that uttered them. When he tried to answer, he would manage to reach the halfway point in a sentence when Nadia was beginning a new question. Many of the questions were formed from circular logic …

"You know, of course, because you are the professor, and professors must know, that our interpretations are pre-ordained because they come from Allah, and anything that comes from Allah must be true."

"Is there a question in there somewhere because to me it sounds like you are turning in circles?" Francisco asked.

Then he fell silent while she went on. When he finished his tea, Nadia showed him to his office. He could see into Musharraf's compound, just as the cook had said, though it was more like 300 meters rather than 200, just across the Pindi causeway. Finally, Francisco managed to shake off Nadia with the simple truth. He was tired from jet lag and now needed to rest. So Nadia left him alone. When she did, Francisco went back down the stairs and out to the rose gardens, which were spacious. He looked intently at the red spine-like blossoms of a bottlebrush tree for a long time. Without giving notice or speaking to anyone, he walked out of the gate and went to wander around in Sadr Market, thinking that he might go back to the bookstore to purchase some books that he actually needed.

Chapter 8

Sinaloa, 2003

OUT OF THE INSTINCT to survive, Carmelita Vaghina became a very well-paid prostitute and she belonged exclusively to Aguilar, who kept her bank account in his own control for her own good. But there was more to her than her job or good looks. During a fifteen-minute study break, Bolivar, now Francisco, had wandered outside in the sunlight. He noticed Carmelita reading a book. He knew the book. He even knew its author. Before this the two of them had never spoken.

"Excuse me. I am Francisco. What do you think of the book you're reading, *Snake's Nest ... Nido de Serpientes*?"

Carmen looked up at him through black sunglasses. Her expression was pleasant.

"I know who you are. You're the one they are sending to Pakistan."

"Yes."

"I did not know that General Vargas was so friendly with the Nazis. I am from Brazil, but this is all before my time, back in the 40s."

"Yes," Francisco said, "until a U-boat sank one of Brazil's ships just off the coast."

"Right," she said. "Then he declared war on Germany, but he never bothered to actually fight them. Seems he was a little busy fucking over Brazil to really bother with Nazis."

"Lêdo Ivo was lucky to survive the regime. Most of his generation either left, went to prison, or were executed."

"I'm impressed. You know something about this?"

"Lêdo was an acquaintance of mine. I translated the novel into English for a press in California. We met some years ago in Mexico City. Then he asked me to come to Rio, so I did, but just for a few days. He was a funny guy. He could never make up his mind what language to speak. When speaking, his sentences came out in bits of German, French, Portuguese, and Spanish, all cobbled together. But we could follow each other. Often his wife took that jambalaya of his and translated it into coherent Spanish."

Carmelita was suddenly aware that Francisco was talking to her as a person. She felt a little uncomfortable because no one ever talked to her as a person, let alone talk to her about something interesting.

"So you visited my country. And did you like it there?"

"Very much, but I was only there for a few days to see Lêdo. Ivo may be the first Brazilian writer to talk about homosexuality so directly."

"I wondered about that, too."

"What brings you to Mexico? Or is that too personal?"

"I belong to the man. It wasn't really my choice. Or, well, I had a choice back in Brazil, but I was too young or stupid to know I did. I was brought here—kind of the way they brought you here—but I was fifteen years old. He brought me here and this is where he erased me. Take care that doesn't happen to you. There are a lot of ways to be a whore. You don't just have to be a woman. He'll turn you into a whore before you know what happened, and then it will be too late. Did you read this novel in Portuguese?"

"I tried to read the Portuguese, but I confess, I relied mostly on the Spanish version you're reading."

Carmelita's eyes were wide open behind the black sunglasses.

"Can I call you Little Brother?"

"Sure. But, why? I'm older than you."

"The man took my little brother away. He took everyone away."

"How did you come by the book?" Francisco asked, trying to lighten the conversation.

"From the library. Aguilar has someone collect books from all over and put them on the shelves so people will think he's read them."

"Have you read many of them?"

"I've read a lot of them. They're the only windows I'm allowed to look through to the outside."

Carmelita pointed to the high walls of Aguilar's estate as she said this.

"It's the same way with some—not all—of his soldiers, too. They don't want to be here either."

There was a long silence between them, like one of those silent, uncomfortable prayers in church. A mourning dove cooed from somewhere beyond the wall. Then the peace was suddenly interrupted by Williams, who informed Francisco that his break was over while shooting a look at Carmen, in effect signaling her not to talk to Francisco or interfere in business. She knew the look.

Other than the relief she sought in books, cheating on Aguilar every chance she got was her form of rebellion, and she had managed to seduce most of his employees without getting caught, including Williams. She did not even like them. It was only physical. For a moment she could forget that she lived in slavery. Every time she got a man, always in a clandestine manner, she pretended that the man loved her. Each one of them was her husband who had come to rescue her from Aguilar the Pig. She took them wherever she could, in the blind spots of the cameras at two o'clock in the morning outside, or inside in a walk-in closet. Then she kissed the man on his temple and told him she loved him, but they could never do that again. It was fine, though. There were so many, and very often three or four of them were killed in gunfights with the federals or with other cartels. Replacements were in endless supply. Sex with the same man more than once, given her cause, was unthinkable. Sex with the same man meant Aguilar the Pig.

"Ciao, Francisco. We'll talk again," she said defiantly for Williams's sake. She wasn't sure yet if Francisco would be her next conquest.

"Yes, that will be nice," Francisco called back, enthusiastically.

Chapter 9

Rawalpindi, September 2003

As Francisco passed through the gate of the university, one of the school guards took out his cell phone and pressed a button. This call was supposed to set off a chain of calls to spotters on almost every other street in Rawalpindi. But just as the guard's call went out to keep Francisco under surveillance, a streak of reddish orange arched and screamed over the university, landing just outside General Musharraf's compound with a large explosion. For a moment, Francisco thought he was back in Nicaragua. People began running in the direction of the explosion, which, Francisco thought, was a very bad idea. The missile was small but it made a loud noise. Little bombs were often bait for bigger bombs, so Francisco went the other way, toward Sadr Market. The missile originated from the dry riverbed that snaked through rocks and shrubs. When the projectile exploded, a flock of storks rose out of the eucalyptus trees that grew along the river. The trees provided enough cover for the Taliban when a gun battle followed their initial attack. Francisco tried to shake off the shock of it and keep walking, gripping his cane firmly in his right hand. All the would-be spotters were rushing to see what had happened, so actually no one was looking for him, although he did not know, after only a couple of days in this new place, how many eyes were supposed to follow him. He just wanted to be on the outside of the walls. Like Aguilar's estate in Sinaloa, the women's college also had high walls and guards with automatic weapons. He wanted to explore; perhaps there was a place, a neighborhood, that had a park, or a café, or somewhere pleasant to sit; perhaps somewhere in Rawalpindi there would be something resembling "normal," a word which Francisco hated for its lack of any real meaning, but one that seemed appropriate now. However, Rawalpindi, like all of the large cities in Pakistan, was a militarized zone and nothing unnecessary—like a café—existed. Even vendors were cleared away from the roadsides so as not to invite suicide bombers. The two boys from a Pashto tribe who launched the small missile exchanged fire with Pakistani soldiers, but they were shot before they could make it back into the eucalyptus trees. Shot many times over.

Bombs, Francisco learned in short order, were so frequent that many had lost their curiosity unless the explosion occurred somewhere they deemed relevant to their own lives, such and such a street where someone's uncle lived. Mostly people became nervous if a bomb had not gone off for more than three days, and then they slipped into a state of anxious agitation. Francisco walked along the causeway wall that was plastered with photographs of "martyrs," soldiers who had died for Allah and Pakistan. Graffiti, too, was allowed as long as it bore a correct message: an artistic rendering of the word "Allah" in "divine Arabic," next to a Nazi swastika. Of course, the swastika originated in India. It was a symbol to ward off evil, and it dated back about 15,000 years. But this one was the Nazi version. Yet another message warned women not to be whores, leaving the definition of the word all encompassing. Yet another, "Allah hates Jews." This reminded Francisco of things he read that were going on in his own country—people carrying signs saying, "God hates fags." Since his 20s or 30s, Francisco had lost his adolescent hope for humanity's distempered world. Eventually he replaced the hope with a simple mission to value individuals. He was also aware of his selfishness, a character flaw that was intensified when he hadn't just committed suicide to save his family, rather than cave in to Williams's demands. It was hard not to think about the harm he was doing to countless "individuals" by assisting Williams and Aguilar. I *spare the lives of Teodesia, Karli, and Paco, but how many will die if I cooperate? Suicide would have been the best solution. Maybe it isn't too late.* So his thoughts went.

Francisco found himself outside of the bookstore in Sadr Market, but this was a Monday, not a Sunday, and not a prime number. He just looked around for anything that might help with the classes. There was a used copy of George Orwell's *1984*, so he bought it. *Everything about the book was true when he wrote it in 1946, and it was still true. The great tragedy of the work*, Francisco thought, *was that it wasn't at all fiction.* The bookseller was a very young man. He put the book in a brown sack and thanked Francisco, who thanked him in return.

Then Francisco walked back to his house—which was a "safe house" of sorts—in Chaklala. By around eleven o'clock in the evening, Francisco fell asleep reading. Sometime between 1 a.m. and 2 a.m., there was a hard rap on his door. It was one of the bodyguards.

"We go!"

"Why?"

"We go! Security. We go."

The bodyguard motioned for him to pick up his suitcase and come immediately. Francisco was in his pajamas. He started to pull on some pants, but the bodyguard said, "No. No, we go now!"

Francisco followed the guard to a car. Two other guards were positioned at the open gate and the car was running. Francisco got into the car behind the driver. Two of the three men jumped into the car with him and the car took off. Another car down the street had just turned the corner and turned off its lights. Francisco, the driver, and two of the three guards pulled away in the opposite direction. Their car was just reaching Chaklala Market, about three short blocks away, when a grenade exploded inside the garden walls of his residence. Someone had thrown it at the high window, but it hit the corner and fell back into the garden. An hour later, Francisco and his fellows arrived in the F10 Sector of Islamabad. *What a dehumanizing name for a neighborhood*, Francisco thought. He thought of the quaint old names of neighborhoods he'd known in childhood and early youth, *Forest Park, Kirkwood, Creve Coeur, Webster Groves. Real names. Not names laid out by the maker of a board game—Battleship.*

"You stay here now," one of the guards said.

But now Francisco couldn't sleep. It was four o'clock in the morning. In a couple of hours they would take him back to school to begin the class on literary theory. He stretched his arms back behind the pillow and felt something when he did. He got up and turned on a lamp. He turned the pillow over and there, hiding and waiting for him was a letter. He opened it:

Dear Francisco,

I love you. I see you and tremble. I love you so much it hurts like a thousand blows. I cannot eat or sleep because the sea of your presence floods my heart and mind. But I do not dare to reveal myself. I must keep myself hidden, anonymous … unless there is a way by a miracle of Allah you feel the same way when you see me. You do see me among the many. I wonder if you see me as the one, the only one. Yes, it is a mortal sin but I have decided to spend eternity in Hell if there is a chance to be with you. Your wife must be a very awful wife to not come with you. What sort of wife would abandon her husband like that, leaving him without comfort? I want to give you the comfort of a woman and I think when you see me you think that I am beautiful. There is a look in your eyes that tells me. Maybe you have guessed who I am. If you have not … if you wish to unveil me … then leave your copy of The Scarlet Letter *on the terrace tomorrow where you have your lunch. I will be the one who brings it to you. Until tomorrow …*

We'll be together soon, Inshallah,
Anon

Francisco folded the letter and put it back in the envelope. He did not want to think about the letter or how it got there. He knew it was part of a game, but he did not know the players, the rules, or the objectives. He was too tired to think about it, so he put the letter in his bag and lay back on his bed and closed his eyes, trying to remember the meaning of home.

Chapter 10

Jlalpan, 2001

Teodesia was up first and in the kitchen slicing bananas to put in the oatmeal. When she finished, she went to the backyard with her basket and plucked six oranges to take back to the kitchen. In the backyard, a flicker clutched the bark of a tall pine and was rat-a-tat-tatting its wood.

"Despiértense! Wake up, everybody!" she yelled.

Groans from her undead family were heard down the hallway as they slowly made their way to the kitchen table, to Bolivar first with his eyes barely open, then to Karli right behind him with her eyes a bit more inclined toward morning, and finally to Paco who just slouched his way to the table where he secured his forehead on the table's ledge.

Only Teodesia and Karli were talkative in the morning. Bolivar and Paco took their waking slow.

"Oatmeal! Again!" Karli whined.

"It's a big day, Karli. We're all going to Tequisquiapan for the day. We're going to go swimming."

Bolivar hated to swim and he knew this was Teo's excuse to get him to do his physical therapy. His injuries in Nicaragua combined with his sedentary lifestyle were beginning to wear on his range of motion and his energy. Teodesia had given up nursing to raise their family with him, but she had not given up on nursing Bolivar, nor would she ever. So Bolivar ate his oatmeal and drank his juice. Then he had coffee and listened to Karli and Paco bicker over who could swim faster. When Bolivar was fully awake, he leveled a challenge at them:

"Your mother is a faster swimmer and runner than both of you, I'll wager."

"Mom?" Paco said with disbelief.

"No one is faster than your mother," Bolivar affirmed.

"Or prettier!" Karli said.

"Stop now. Your father is exaggerating. Anyway, we're leaving at ten o'clock, so Karli you have time to practice your B major scale, and Paco you need to do a few more pages on your term paper for summer school."

"What are you writing about, Paco?"

"Ronald Reagan."

Paco's voice was always level. His voice was flat and dry, and he spoke through his teeth as though he was always ready to bite someone.

"What is your thesis about Ronald Reagan?"

"He was all right. Too liberal, maybe. But he's the kind of president who could set things right in Mexico."

"Don't you think he might have violated constitutional law by ignoring the congressional ban on selling arms to Iran and secretly waging a war in Nicaragua?"

"No. If the president does something illegal, then it isn't illegal."

This was the argument that Reagan's Attorney General, Ed Meese, had made in 1987. Meese was using the Nixon justification for Watergate a decade earlier.

"I see," Bolivar said. "Well, maybe I don't see. Your logic sounds a little more like a magic trick than logic."

"Lots of important people agree that Reagan was America's best president," Paco said.

"Boys!" Teodesia said. "It's too early in the morning to discuss politics. Paco, if you are finished, then go work on your paper. Karli, you get to your piano now."

Karli promptly went to the living room where Bolivar and Teodesia had decided to put a new baby grand piano. Still in her pajamas, she went up and down the scale of B major, sequentially hitting all five black keys both going up and coming down simultaneously with both hands. Teodesia and Bolivar leaned into each other and kissed good morning.

"Now play your first and second arpeggios," Bolivar called out to her from the kitchen.

"Ok! They're easy!"

Karli cycled through the arpeggios in B major. She was becoming more nimble-fingered with every passing week.

"Bolivar, could she really turn out to be great?"

"Maybe. She'd need a teacher. I can't take her very far. The problem is that we live in Jlalpan. All of us would have to move back to Mexico

City to find her a teacher on the faculty at UNAM. She does have the passion for it. Or … possibly, we could hire a master to come here, board with us, and coach her daily."

"That would be expensive," Teodesia said.

"It's worth exploring the options," Bolivar said softly, thinking out loud.

"Yet, she says almost daily that she's going to be a writer like her 'daddy'."

"And 'marry a great man,' like her mother," Bolivar said. "At least one of our kids likes us. What is up with this Ronald Reagan thing?"

"He's got this new teacher at school. I met him. He's a real firebrand leftist. Paco decided to be contrary to everything he teaches them in their history class because of something he said on the first day of class. I don't know what his teacher said, but whatever it was it really offended Paco. The one thing Paco sure about is that he looks like you and he wants to be an American. I think the teacher had some rather disparaging things to say about American foreign policy."

"Then he's probably a very good teacher. Maybe I should go have a talk with him. Maybe all of us together can help Paco get through this … this … what … onset of adolescence. What's his name?"

"Rosas. Marco Rosas. He's in his twenties or early thirties."

"I'll walk over on Monday after school lets out."

Teodesia looked thoughtful. Then she had an idea.

"If you do talk to him, maybe you could encourage him to bring up the topic of stereotypes. I know the other kids are calling Paco a 'filthy gringo' and picking fights with him during the free hour. He only has one friend—some kid who dresses in black and tries to scare everyone by wearing swastikas. I think Paco said his name was Raul. This Raul kid never speaks to me but when you are in your office out back, the two of them climb up to the tree house. I can't imagine what they talk about. They stay up there a long time."

"Well, next year Paco will take his entrance exams. If he does well enough, he'll be in a new place with all sorts of people."

Teodesia looked down, looking for words that might be lying around on the floor, words that might make sense of what she had to tell Bolivar.

"There's something I've been waiting for the right time to tell you, darling. And … there isn't going to be a right time. So I'll just say it. Paco wants to join the American army or Marines."

"What!? I won't allow that and he knows it."

"I know. I know. He came to me about a week ago and asked if he could borrow our marriage license in order to take it to the embassy and apply for citizenship."

"And?"

"I told him that I'd have to discuss it with you."

"Nothing to discuss, dear. I'll support him for college, not for the military. We've both seen enough of that insanity to last our family for the rest of time."

"I knew you were going to say that," she said, breathing a little easier.

"Anyway, the United States has made going to war their national pastime. There's no way I'll agree to it. To make matters worse, they've just elected a very loose cannon—this George W. There is no telling what sort of mess he'll get the country mixed up in."

Bolivar paused. He could see that there was something else. Teodesia could never hide her worries.

"What is it? Tell me."

"He is going to petition to change his name, too."

"To what? Reagan?"

"No, dear. He wants to drop 'Collins' and just use 'Segovia.' He says that way people won't associate him with a …."

Teodesia couldn't say the word, so Bolivar said it for her.

"A 'traitor.' Teo, technically I am a traitor."

"You are not a traitor to me or to your family. You are the finest man I have ever known. And remember that half or more of Latin America remembers you as a hero, at least the people who've heard of you."

"That's only in the yellow press, Teo."

"Still, you are a hero."

"Mexico will not hesitate to follow a US request for extradition if that ever happens. It isn't likely though. They would have to admit to their secret war."

"Who knows, Boli? Maybe under this new crazy person—Bush—they can find some other excuse—your articles in *La Granma*, for instance."

"I never once mentioned the United States in any article. I was always careful to use euphemisms like 'The West' or 'the capitalists.' Extradition, even under Bush, is probably unlikely. And even if they tried, we'd be on the next plane for Havana. All of us."

It was getting late in the morning. Teodesia called the children to get their swimming suits and get in the car.

"You, too, *mi amor*," she told Bolivar."

Chapter 11

Rawalpindi, 2003 to 2004

BARRANCA'S NEXT PRIME-NUMBERED Sunday visit to the bookstore in Sadr Market occurred on October 5, 2003. The author secluded behind the books would have a first name beginning with the letter D. "*Cycle through the alphabet starting with A, skipping two letters each time. Read it backwards to lift out the message from the typographical errors,*" Williams had said. Barranca felt behind the books and he reached behind the third shelf from the top. He pulled out a copy of D.H. Lawrence's *Sons and Lovers*. Standing there, he began scanning it backwards for the message he was obliged to deliver. In the space of ten pages, the typos amounted to the following: "The *Santana* leaving October 29 Stop." Francisco searched his head for "the *Santana*"—The *Santana*! It was the boat in *Key Largo* that Bogart piloted out to sea at gunpoint. He struggled, gained control over the bad guys, and bleeding from a bullet wound, shot and killed Edward G. Robinson's mafioso character.

Another courier would use his cipher to deliver the rest of the message. Barranca merely had to purchase a silk tapestry from Mahmood's rug shop and have it mailed to confirm his transmission. So Barranca passed the information to Mahmood, then picked out a rug and gave him an address for where to mail it. He did not know the extent of Mahmood's involvement and probably never would. He wasn't permitted to know much at all. He did not know that Mahmood personally sent his message to the Taliban, who, in turn, brought their truckloads of heroin across the border into Karachi and loaded it on onboard the "Condoleezza," an actual ship that belonged to a person by that name.

The third prime-numbered Sunday of that year was December 7. The author began with the letter G. *The Poetry of Gerald Manly Hopkins*. As he had before, Barranca stood in the corner of the bookshop reading the book backwards. In five minutes he had the message: "The Storm King December 15 Stop." *Where does Williams get this stuff?* Barranca knew the reference. It was the name of a boat in one of Hemingway's novels, *Islands in the Stream.* When this information was handed over to Mahmood, the cipher would be amended to identify the actual ship in the Port of Karachi. The name of Hemingway's clipper would be sent inside a tapestry as before, thus insuring the safety of his family. If his part of the cipher did not arrive in Mexico City, his family would be murdered. Or so Wayne Williams had said.

Francisco Barranca had never spoken to the young man in the bookstore. He didn't even know if the boy spoke English. But on prime-number Sunday, January 11, 2004, when Barranca came in and looked at the literature books, the young man introduced himself.

"Hello, sir. My name is Anoosh."

"Francisco." He reached out to shake hands.

"Excuse me, sir. I noticed that you always buy books from the same shelf and you always read backwards."

"Oh, yes. Well, Anoosh. That is the shelf where you keep the literature and I check the editions for accuracy by using a proofreading technique common to editors. They look at pages backwards in order to make sure that words are spelled correctly. That way their minds don't focus on content and miss the errors."

"And are they accurate? I mean the books."

"Sadly, no."

"Oh yes, I know this. In Pakistan we have a lot of pirated editions. You have probably noticed."

"I have," Francisco said. "Take this one, for example. It's the works of John Donne, one I need for a course I'm teaching in British Literature. There are three lines missing from the first page … here, here, and here. Also, there are seventeen typographical errors before you reach the beginning of page two. Whoever typed this edition was either illiterate or very drunk. Possibly both."

"It's a shame," Anoosh said. "It's broken like my country."

"Not at all, Anoosh. Don't despair. There is much beauty and grand history in Pakistan."

"I hope so."

"I'm very happy to meet you, Anoosh. I'm sorry that I did not introduce myself on previous visits."

As soon as he left the bookstore that day, he turned to the back to finish the cipher—*The Caine Mutiny. What a hideous juxtaposition,* Barranca thought, *putting* the Caine Mutiny *inside Donne's* Holy Sonnets.

Subsequently, Francisco Barranca did visit with Anoosh at the bookstore, and he made sure to buy two or three other books as well so as not to arouse any suspicion. He also went on days that did not fall on prime numbered Sundays. He suspected Anoosh might be the sort of person who could pick up patterns easily, someone like himself. Now he visited the bookstore more frequently and stayed to converse longer.

On Sunday, March 7, 2004, he took his cipher from a copy of Mark Twain's detective novel, The Mysterious Stranger *No. 44*. The message was *The* H.M.S. Pinafore *leaving March 20 Stop*. On April 11 of the same year, *The letter M. Skip two for P. Paul Valery, a French poet*. The message was *The* Pequod *leaving April 17 Stop*. By this time, Anoosh and Francisco had become friends. Anoosh always put on a pot of tea and asked Francisco questions about writers and books. Francisco asked him about his family. His wife had just had a baby, their first born. He and his family lived in the room over the bookstore with Anoosh's uncle.

"My wife apologized because the baby wasn't a boy, but I don't care about that. I think it's stupid to care about such things. But my wife is more traditional than I am."

"Mine, too," Francisco said. Of course, Francisco was thinking of his actual wife, not his fictional one.

It was true. Teodesia was very traditional in many ways. She ran the family like a typical Mexican wife and mother. She alone decided where things would be put, what pictures could hang on the wall, when it was time for the kids to do their homework. They had one of their worse fights when Teodesia wanted to put the baby grand piano that Francisco bought for Karli and Paco's lessons in their guest room. Teodesia had finally acquiesced, but only after consulting with the local priest, Father Sebastián, who told her that pianos belong in the living room and it was Guadalupe's will that pianos be in living rooms. Then there was Francisco's cluttered office in a small work shed in their back yard. Early in their marriage, Teodesia had tried to tidy up his office. It was one of the few times she saw him red-faced angry. "Never do that!" he yelled. He was sorry he yelled, but then he calmed down and explained that he knew where things were in his office the way that she knew where things were in the kitchen. She frowned and promised never to touch his papers or books again.

Chapter 12

Sinaloa, 2003

CARMELITA WAS BORN INTO poverty in a bad neighborhood of São Paulo. She attended a public school and worked every day for three hours in a dress store by the age of twelve. Her parents both worked hard, too, but had long ago given up hope of ever leaving their neighborhood. Often her parents worked at night, and there was no one except her little brother at home when she arrived from the dress shop at around eight o'clock. She made him something to eat and he watched television while she read books and did her homework.

When Carmelita turned fourteen she met an older boy of sixteen at school who had money like no other kid. He started giving her things, too. Carmelita was thrilled. She had never had anything so nice. A black lacey dress, for instance. She didn't have anywhere to wear it, but she liked to take it out of the closet and look at it. Then, this boy—his name was Adrian—gave her jewelry. Gold jewelry with rubies and amethysts. Finally, Adrian had maneuvered her into the willingness to go out with him at night, wearing her dress and jewelry.

"I want to dance with you," he said. "You are so beautiful. Everyone will be jealous of me."

And Carmelita was hooked. She kept the dress and jewelry a secret from her parents. She made her little brother swear to be good and stay in their apartment and not breathe a word to their parents about her going out.

Adrian picked her up at nine o'clock on a Saturday night and took her to a club called Pinheiros. For the next few months she kept seeing Adrian in secret, but when her father came home unexpectedly early from his night shift, he found his son, alone, in front of the TV and questioned him. Being ten, it was not hard to extract the information he knew. When Carmelita arrived after midnight, her father was sitting in his chair, ready to do battle. After that, she cried in her pillow. *They have taken everything from me and left me with nothing!* She wanted to get even. She was going to see Adrian anyway.

The next chance she got, she went with Adrian to Pinheiros, but it was the last time she saw her family. The club was noisy and the lights started to blur. She could hear Adrian's voice in her ear and feel his hand pulling her through the crowd. She could smell the alcohol on his breath. Then she could feel a man on top of her. After that, there were gaps in her memory. She remembered being on an airplane. She remembered getting out of the airplane and seeing a sign that said "Culiacán."

Her parents alerted the police, put up posters, talked to neighbors. Even the television news displayed her photo and provided a tip line to the police. Finally, they checked the city morgue, staring down row after row at the blue-lipped corpses. But it was no use. Her trail was cold the moment she was drugged and carried onto Aguilar's private jet.

For the first six months in Mexico, Carmelita was catatonic. One of Aguilar's assistants had to bring in a private doctor to feed her through tubes. She stared out of her bedroom window at the compound walls for six months, saying nothing and not understanding Spanish. She soiled herself. She could not be bothered to get out of her chair to defecate in the toilet.

When reports reached Aguilar, the news incurred a simmering wrath: "If she doesn't snap out of it soon, we'll have to dump her with the others," meaning that he would use her in his campaign of fear and terror over the people of Culiacán, letting her join a list of savagely murdered women whose bodies were left in the desert near the *fabrillos* that American businessmen built to cash in on the new North American Free Trade Agreement. Aguilar was sick but he had no interest in fucking a catatonic zombie, not even a fifteen-year-old zombie. He was about to issue the kill order when suddenly, a light went on inside Carmelita's head. Maybe it was a dark light, but whatever it was, Carmelita was suddenly up and walking—a little unsteady, but walking. She had wondered outside to look at the swimming pool. She began eating. In no time at all, she was beginning to gain back some of her previous weight and beauty. She was just a few months away from her sixteenth birthday when Aguilar sent for her.

By the time Carmelita had reached twenty, she had learned most of the security cameras' blind spots, both indoors and out, and had been forced to have sex with a dozen of Aguilar's men. She imagined a day when she could cut their throats.

Now nine years had passed since she was abducted. Carmelita was twenty-four and she had never been outside Aguilar's compound.

"Hey, Paco!" she called to Francisco Barranca in early August 2003, a few days after they first met and talked about the Brazilian writer. "Come take a break. They aren't around now. The Pig and Williams are both in New York! Come talk to me!"

"Hello, Carmelita. What are you reading today?"

"It's a novel by Saramago, *La Ceguera*. Of course, the Pig doesn't have it in Portuguese. It's about everyone in the world all suddenly going blind, except for one person who pretends to be blind out of sympathy or fear of being different or something. I haven't figured this out yet."

"I read it in English—*Blindness*. Truly great. And true. We are blind, and if we aren't, we will ourselves to be blind. True everywhere."

"I've not been everywhere. I've only been here. Tell me what it's like out there, will you?"

"Ok. Despite what you're reading, people can be very decent and good. Life can be wonderful, Carmelita. Before I was brought here, I was living a good life with my wife and kids. We have a house in a little town called Jlalpan in central Mexico. We are—unlike what we read in books—'normal'."

"Normal," she echoed, without comprehension.

"I mean that we enjoy really simple things and we love each other. Sometimes I stay awake at night just remembering the way my wife yells for us to get up for breakfast in the morning, or the way my daughter practices the piano in the living room. I was really living."

"Watching television with my brother … that was living," Carmelita thought out loud.

"Yes! That's living. I'm afraid the Aguilars of the world are beyond hope of ever grasping anything so simple."

"Or reading a book?"

"Yes! A book. Writing a letter. Having a conversation. Being mindful about how you are arranging some flowers. Noticing a bird. Yes!"

"I like you, Paco. Can I call you Paco?"

"Yes, but it's Williams's name for me. My name is actually Bolivar."

"Bolivar! Oh!"

"Carmelita, isn't there any way you can go home to your family? Can't you just runaway back home?"

"It's complicated. I suppose I have enough money to do whatever I want. At least I'm told I have money. I make a thousand dollars a week here. Problem is I've never seen any of it and I don't have any way to get it. I'm an employee like everyone else, but the Pig has López keep the money for me."

Carmelita paused to consider whether or not she should trust Barranca with a secret. She decided she would.

"I keep a little money that some of the soldiers give me. But I have never been let out of the compound. I don't know what they'd do if I tried. I don't even know what direction to go or if I could get on a plane."

"You can follow the road east to Culiacán and take a bus to my house. My wife, Teodesia, will help you get home—should you ever try. I'll write the address for you. Here, put it here in Saramago's book."

Francisco wrote his address in the back of Saramago's novel. Francisco commented as he wrote his address …

"I figure that we are about ten miles west of Culiacán in the middle of nowhere. You would have to go on a night with a full moon and take a gallon of water with you. If you tried to walk it in this heat, you would probably not make it."

"And you? Why don't you just run?"

"My situation is different. If I don't work for them, they will hurt my family. But if you can get away, you can tell my family I'm alive. They don't even know where I've been. One morning I went to buy a newspaper and the next thing I knew I was being tossed into a black car headfirst. They drove me the whole way here with a sack over my head. If we can help each other … if you can get out of here … you must tell Teodesia not to speak to anyone about this. No talking. No telephone. Understand?"

Barranca suddenly came to an abrupt halt.

"No. No … never mind. This is all too dangerous. No plan that we could make would keep both you and my family safe. We do not even know if you can get past the guard."

"Maybe. Maybe we should think it through. Every detail. Getting past the guard may be easy. I've learned some ways to get what I want from the soldiers."

"Oh, yes. I see. About that …"

"You want to know about my job here?"

"No. Of course not. I think I know. No, my curiosity is why you bother to take time to talk to me at all. None of the other women have ever talked to me. A few words of greetings—that's all."

"I noticed that," she said. "I thought about it. I think some of them were brought here when they were much younger than me, and the older ones, the ones about my age now—well—they just disappear. They are here and then one day they aren't. No one talks about it."

The sun was beginning to go down on the desert surrounding the compound. It stretched dark, blood-red fingers of fire on the salty barren landscape. Joshua trees cast bluish shadows. Tiny green intermittent lights from fireflies enchanted the grounds of the estate.

"I'm going to swim. Want to?" Carmelita asked. "The water is really warm."

"You swim. I'll fix you a drink if you like."

"A mojito?"

"I'll make it two." Francisco was feeling a little relaxed just knowing that Williams and Aguilar were away.

Carmelita was wearing a two-piece white bikini. She stood up from the lounge and towered over him at six feet. She was attractive, but Francisco averted his eyes from her.

"I'll just be a minute," he said, getting up to make the drinks.

Carmelita dove into the blue illuminated water and swam to the other side of the pool. Barranca returned with the mojitos and sat hers down on the ledge. Carmelita swam over to him.

"Give me your hand," she said.

Barranca thought that she wanted to shake hands, as if they had made a pact and were sealing it. So he reached out to shake her wet hand. When he did, Carmelita pulled him into the pool. Carmelita was laughing when Barranca's head emerged.

"What? What?"

"Wait, Bolivar. Stand still."

Carmelita pulled the strings on her white bikini bottoms and they floated to the surface to the water in front of him. From a distance someone seeing them would mistake them for the white belly of a dead fish floating on the surface of the water, perhaps a flounder.

"You can have me," she said.

She was undeniably the most beautiful woman he'd been this close to, with the exception of Teodesia. But Barranca could not bring himself to embrace her. He leaned into her and he gave her a small kiss on her cheek.

"No, Carmelita. We're friends. We're good friends. I hope you understand."

Carmelita stood still in the water. No man had ever said no. She didn't know whether she should feel angry or relieved. She just stood there.

Barranca got out of the water and took a towel. He was going to pretend the incident never occurred.

"If the bosses are still away, let's talk more tomorrow. I think I'll retire for the evening," he said, hoping to bring her thoughts back around to the idea of escaping.

Carmelita was still motionless. She had not even bothered to reach for her bikini bottoms. But she managed an answer.

"Tomorrow. Okay."

But that same night Williams and Aguilar arrived and Williams gave Barranca a list of things to pack.

"Be ready at six in the morning. You're going to the airport."

Chapter 13

Rawalpindi, 2004

ANOOSH PUT A POT of tea on a hot plate the moment he saw Barranca enter his shop. It was May 23rd, a Sunday, and the atmosphere outside was bustling and carnival.

"Hello, Anoosh!"

"Hello, sir. I have not seen you for some weeks."

"Yes, the job has me going most of the time."

"Maybe you would prefer my job?" Anoosh said with a smile.

Barranca laughed.

"Indeed, I would. I have always dreamed of having a little bookshop, perhaps when I retire. A little bookshop and a little tobacco. Maybe an old dog to sit by my feet."

"The students will be having their exams soon, and you'll have term papers, correct?"

"Correct," Barranca replied.

Bolivar pulled a book out from behind the books that were showing. *P skip two for S. Samuel Pepys' London Diaries*. The descriptions of London's Black Plague of the Eighteenth century reminded Barranca of the epidemics running up massive death tolls in the refugee camps just on the outskirts of Pindi and Islamabad.

"Tea-white with a little sugar, as you like it," Anoosh said.

"Thank you."

"Samuel Pepys," Anoosh said.

"British essayist. Eighteenth century. Very fine writer. I fear he is bordering on forgotten. Thought I would talk about him tomorrow in the British Literature seminar.

Bordering on forgotten. Barranca was suddenly struck by his own words, how applicable they were to him. It was almost two years now. He too felt that he was bordering on forgotten.

"I did not know that I even had this book. In fact, I often do not know that I have the book you're looking for—and then by some miracle of Allah, there it is!"

Barranca scanned the book from the back while Anoosh talked.

"I swear before Allah that I do not recall ever acquiring many of the books I've sold you."

"In my own little library, I too am often finding a book I didn't know I had, or that I forgot I had," Barranca said, hoping to make Anoosh think it was normal not to know what one has or doesn't have.

The Black Pearl leaves on May 30 Stop. Barranca thought, *A pirate ship. Appropriate.*

"I am glad I have books you like," Anoosh exclaimed.

"Anoosh, you are unique in all of Pakistan. I've never told you before—I am very impressed by you. You have a very good life. What's more, your English is almost without flaw. How is that?"

"Oh. My father, when he was still alive, had enough money to send me to Leeds University, but I was only there for one year. Then he died and I had to come back to take care of my mother. My mother moved in with her sister's family here in Sadr and I took over the bookshop for my uncle."

"Terribly sorry for your loss, Anoosh."

"I miss him. He was a good man who knew the difference between right and wrong. He only loved my mother. He never took a second wife, never. That would have killed her."

"And Leeds … I know the school. Very good place. I know a professor there who is writing a biography of T.S. Eliot. I wish I had had the fortune of just a year in England."

"Things are changing there, you know," Anoosh said, his demeanor turning dark. "When I was there, we were all chums. Brits and Pakis, it didn't matter. We played football—I mean what you call soccer—and afterwards drank pints at the pub. No one ever talked about religion or their stupid ideologies. Now, there are more and more skinheads just waiting for you around the corner, and conversely, extremists—the ones who think it's a good thing to fly an airplane into a building."

This was a subject that Barranca and Anoosh had never broached. Now Anoosh had opened the door.

"I sensed long ago that you were not much into dogmas," Barranca said, quietly, because another customer was just entering the store.

"No. You're right. I try not to be, in as much as it's possible. To tell you the plain truth, I do not really believe in God. I say 'Allah,' but in my heart I just use the word to stand for 'love'."

"That makes your theology pretty much the same as mine. My wife believes in God like He were an actual person. I suppose I'm an agnostic. If I'm with a group of people saying a prayer in unison, I generally say the 'be-good-to-your-neighbor' parts and mumble over the word 'Jesus' or 'Christ'—you know. We say that *God* is beyond us. A moment later we're trying to squeeze the idea of *beyond* into a tiny box. I suppose some need to personify God in order to grant themselves the illusion of understanding. I just can't put God into a linguistic box, can't personify, can't apply any pronouns."

"I wish I could be your student, sir."

"We can be each other's student—why not?"

"It's a deal!" Anoosh exclaimed.

"Anoosh, along these lines," Barranca said, seizing on the opportunity to ask a delicate question, "I have been curious since the first day I visited your shop last year: Why on earth do you have all these copies of Adolf Hitler's biography next to The Holy Koran?

Suddenly Anoosh looked embarrassed.

"Oh that."

"It's ok. You don't owe me any explanation. I ask only out of curiosity."

"It's not what you may think. I will tell you." Anoosh searched for his words … "I have a landlord. My uncle was not finished paying for the shop and so we are still renting. Our landlord often comes to check to make sure that we have plenty of Hitler, and he insists we keep his biography next to the Koran as if the former were a companion work to help with interpretation."

"I'm relieved to know that it was not your idea," Francisco said.

"Not at all. To make matters worse, they are the two bestselling books in Pakistan." Anoosh added, "Do you know a little book of poems that John Lennon published?"

"I vaguely recall that, yes."

"Once I had ten copies of his poems stacked on top of the Hitler. I put them there to try to ward away the evil, or maybe just the feeling of disgust I felt, but the landlord came in one day and saw this. He became furious and threatened to evict us."

"Most unfortunate," Barranca said.

"Still, I managed to escape his scrutiny. At any given time, I have here over a dozen books which are banned."

"I noticed! *Lolita, The Satanic Verses* ..."

"And many others," Anoosh said, almost bursting, "but the landlord is ignorant. He does not know one book from another. So it is my little rebellion—and, my little secret, which I have never told anyone."

"How do you come by them?"

"NGOs mostly. They drop them off when they leave the country. Once a Canadian even left what some people would call very salacious materials: books by Irving Wallace, a bunch of Playboy magazines, which I keep hidden in the back, romance novels, even a copy of the *Kama Sutra*.

"You don't say!"

"The landlord has no idea. I also have history books written in India, stories that paint a much different picture about our conflicts with them. Did you know that the many Muslims of India consider themselves to be Indian first and Muslim second?"

"I knew that, yes."

"To most people, that's heresy. Islam, they believe, is destined to spread to every corner of the world until every inch of the earth is 'holy'."

"Unfortunately, the evangelical Christians think that way, also."

"A lot of nonsense if you ask me," Anoosh said. "I wish with Lennon that religion had never been invented."

"Amen, Anoosh."

It was getting late and Barranca had yet to deliver the message about *The Black Pearl* to Mahmood. He looked at his watch and the hour startled him.

"Oh, I've got to go. Let's continue our talk soon. I'm running a bit late."

"Don't worry. I will always be here. Maybe I will get some tobacco and a dog for your next visit."

The two men said farewell and Barranca took his message to Mahmood, who was standing nervously in the doorway eyeing Barranca's two bodyguards watching from the car.

"Hello, Mahmood."

"You are late. Late can be dangerous where these matters are concerned."

"Yes. I haven't written it down. Do you have a piece of paper?"

Mahmood went to his sales counter and tore a receipt from its tablet.

"Any particular rug?"

"You pick it out, will you?"

"Of course. You can pay me next time. I'm just getting ready to close up the shop."

After writing the message, Barranca waved goodbye to Mahmood and then got in the back seat of the car that carried him and his guards to the safe house in F10 Sector of Islamabad. "The Captain" sat in the back with Barranca. Although he did not speak or read English, he was curious to see what Barranca had purchased from the bookstore. He kept pointing at Barranca's satchel. Barranca decided it would be harmless so he took out the book, *London Diaries*, by Samuel Pepys. The book had no illustrations, not even on the cover, nothing to interest the Captain, so he handed it back to Barranca and started a conversation with the other guard who was driving, both of the men unaware that he could understand Urdu.

"He always goes to the rug shop after the bookstore. Always," the Captain said.

"Yes, I have noticed this," the other guard said.

"We must inform ISI. We need someone to write down the titles of these books he buys and someone to watch the rug shop and the store."

"I was just thinking this, too." He was nodding.

"I will have Nadia send someone when he is teaching his class to write the titles of these books. It could be harmless, but I suspect he is up to something."

"He's a teacher," the other said. "He may just be using the books for teaching."

"Nadia can find out more," the Captain said.

"I agree. ISI may decide to put listening devices in both stores. The ones at the safe houses are useless as he is always alone."

Barranca noted every word they said as he stared out the window at the dilapidated shacks that families called their homes. He looked up at the kites flying their menacing circles that reminded him that he too was simply turning in the same circles, one day to the next. The whole world turned in circles under a blue sky that turned brown and grey from contamination. Circles without music was a kind of death, not the eternal life that some religions use them to signify. A circle without music is insane.

The other guard added … "He often takes the books to his office."

"In that case, Nadia can have someone look through the ones at his office when he is out of the house. Perhaps they can piece something together from his emails."

Barranca thought hard. He had been quite careful about email. He only sent emails to other professors. No. There wasn't a single email that would betray him.

"Maybe he has his wife resale our rugs in Mexico. I hear that they are much more expensive in the West."

"Possibly," the Captain said.

"And maybe he just likes to read these old books."

"Possibly. Professors are known for reading a lot."

"It's probably nothing."

"Probably. Still, I will make a full report to Nadia and let her decide how to present these activities."

Barranca listened and learned. When they had finished their conversation, Barranca said "Captain?" and rubbed his stomach to indicate that he was hungry.

"Sahib," the Captain said, bobbing his head up and down.

"Sahib, yes," Barranca said.

Sahib would make him something to eat when they arrived. On short notice Sahib usually fixed a bowl of bland porridge.

Chapter 14

Mexico City, 2003

When Karli opened their mailbox one day in the last week of August, the box's door flapped down and so did Karli's mouth. She stood and looked inside the box in disbelief for a moment, then she seized a letter addressed to "Paco's Tree House." She rushed to the house, not even stopping to close the mailbox door.

"Mother!" she cried. "Mother!! Mother!!!"

Teodesia was in her garden in the back and came running with dirt on her hands.

"Mother! Come with me to the tree house, now!"

"What's this about, Karli?"

"I will tell you in the tree house.

Teodesia followed her …

"Have you lost it, Karli? What is the matter with you?"

"Come on, Mother! It's important!"

Once they had climbed up into Paco's tree house, Karli began …

"He's alive! Daddy is alive!"

"What are you saying? How do you know this?"

Teodesia was dizzy and felt bewildered.

"Is it true? A cruel joke, Karli?"

"He sent us a letter! Look! Look!"

Teodesia took the letter in her hand carefully and looked at it.

"It's from your father."

"Yes! That's what I'm telling you. He addressed it to the tree house. He must have a reason."

"This letter is from your father," she repeated, stunned.

"Open it, Mother! Open it!"

The address was carefully printed so that a postman could deliver it, but inside Bolivar's handwriting was unique and few people could read it. Each of his letters was a bizarre deviation from its standard. The only word Teodesia could read was her own name; the rest was in that crazy scrawl that belonged only to him.

"Karli! I can't read it. What should I do?"

"Mother, don't worry. I know how to read Daddy's writing."

"How?"

"He taught me."

"Taught you?"

"Yeah, I asked him too and he did. Look, sometimes his a's are like Greek and sometimes Old English; his w's are just sea waves; the t's are never crossed and look like his l's except the slant is almost sideways for his l's … He uses something like an Arabic letter for g."

"Stop!" Teodesia yelled, impatient. "Read the letter … Wait! I better sit down. Wait! I am sitting down."

Tears began to seep into her eyes.

"Ok. What does it say?"

Karli carefully opened the letter.

My Darling Teodesia,

If you are in Paco's tree house, then proceed. If not, then go there immediately—the house may have microphones.

"Microphones!" Teodesia exclaimed. "Why?"

Darling, I am alive. On the day I went to get the newspaper, I was kidnapped. You have never received a ransom note because you and our family are the ransom. If I do not do as these men tell me, you and Karli and Paco will be in terrible danger. When you receive this letter, you will want to call out. You must not. You must act as if you know nothing.

"Do you understand that, mother? Daddy says you can't say anything to anyone."

"I understand. Keep reading."

I suspect that Karli is reading this to you now. I never dreamed that showing her how to read my handwriting could have turned out to be of such good fortune. My dear ones, you will never know how much I miss you. But time doesn't let me go into details. So the rest of this letter is instructional … I am sorry for that. I have an idea, but it will require care and attention to details. You and Karli must think very hard about what steps to take that can help bring me home to you safely. I have had a year to think about this, but the difficult part is that I am only now being taken out of Mexico and sent to Pakistan by Eduardo Aguilar.

"Eduardo Aguilar!" Teodesia nearly screamed.

"Who is that, Mother?"

"*El diablo!* Satan! Keep reading."

"Mother, I'm scared. You're scaring me."

"I'm sorry, Karli. But keep reading."

Tomorrow I will be changing planes in Mexico City. When I realized this I decided to risk sending this, posting it at Bonito Juarez International en route. There are three things I think may help. First, I want you to use a pay telephone in Querétaro to call Captain Tomás and have him meet you secretly in Mexico City. I want you to explain to him that I'm at a women's college in the Rawalpindi area of Pakistan and being forced to work for Aguilar, and they've given me a false name and both Mexican and American passports which bare a photo of me under the name of "Francisco Barranca." Added to my cover is the fake name of a wife—Barranca's wife—"Isa Aramara Barranca." Maybe that will be useful information for Tomás.

Tomás is resourceful and he may know a way out of this for all of us. Second, I want you to use the pay telephone to call Ms. Regier in New York. I want you to ask her if she will publish my unfinished manuscript posthumously!

"Mother, he underlined posthumously. What does posthumously mean?"

"It means he wants everyone to think he's dead."

If we can make enough people think I'm dead the safer I may be; however, this alone will not make you safe.

If you have not cleaned or touched anything in my office, you will find a manuscript in the top left drawer.

"Mother, you haven't rearranged his office, have you?"

"Not a thing. Maybe I dusted a little."

"Mother?"

"I swear, Karli. Okay, Okay, then what?"

Mail this to Ms. Regier after you speak to her and throw in some of those odd mementos from the past—just things lying around the office. The idea is to create a "specter" out of "Bolivar Collins," not to present the living one, so choose things like the medal Ortega gave me, that painting of me by Tomás, and whatever else you can find that you think might help. People believe more in actual things than they do people and we can use that. If Ms. Regier knows I'm alive and need to be dead, she'll know how to market this story. Ask her also to do an obituary for the Times. She'll understand that. And NO PICTURE of course, except for the painting, which is so expressionistic that no one can tie it to me very easily.

When you see Tomás, ask him if it is possible for all of you to get to Cuba. See if he can find out if the Sinaloa cartel can reach you there. Otherwise, Nicaragua is an option. But Mexico is not an option. I am sorry to tell you that. I suspect the CIA is involved in whatever mire they've put me in, which means that Nicaragua is probably not as safe as Cuba. As you know, the CIA is still running heroin and cocaine out of Nicaragua to sell in African American neighborhoods. Consult with Tomás.

Finally, when you are ready, you must make it look as if you are going on a short vacation. Do not appear to be moving. You mustn't draw anyone's suspicions for I fear that Aguilar has someone always watching you.

I wish I could tell you more, but as yet I have only just learned I'll be flying from Mexico City and as I have no idea what my situation will be like in Pakistan, I do not know how I'll be able to reach you from there, or vice versa. Pakistan is the greatest variable, the greatest uncertainty in all of this.

I realize this letter brings you relief to know that I am alive—it brings me relief to send it. I also know that this letter has brought you fear. You, Teodesia, are the bravest person I have ever known, and now you have Karli and Paco by your side. So do not be afraid. Just be the Teo I know and love. And, Karli, who I know is reading this, I love you, too.

There is just one more item. I do not know if you will be contacted by a woman named Carmelita. If so, please do everything in your power to see that she gets home to her family in Brazil. I will let her explain … though I have my doubts that this poor girl will ever reach you. We shall leave that story for another time.

Love,
Bolivar

PS. When this letter arrives, I will be in Islamabad or very near there.

Chapter 15

Rawalpindi, 2003

MOHAMMED JINAH AND HIS brother Ahmed owned a shop on the side of the market facing a mosque. Mohammed had purchased the shop soon after completing a PhD in Theoretical Physics at the University of Delaware. He had intended to return briefly to Pakistan only to get married to his childhood sweetheart, but as soon as he did, the door of immigration back to the United States slammed tightly behind him, despite job offers from several universities. This left him with two options: he could take a job with the Pakistani Ministry of Defense in their nuclear arms program, or he could open a small shop. Abhorring the first option, he chose the latter. His brother, Ahmed, who was rather lazy and less ambitious, agreed to the partnership because it meant having a job in which the two could take turns, thus allowing Ahmed longer hours for sleeping. Both of the brothers were in their early 30s, but that is where their resemblance ended. Temperamentally, they were almost opposites: Mohammed was a liberal thinker; Ahmed, theocratic. Mohammed wanted out of Pakistan; Ahmed wanted to join the army to kill Indians in Kashmir. Mohammed thought secretly that religion was best expressed in quantum physics; Ahmed took everything the Koran said quite literally but he was often conflicted over interpretations. Mohammed had friends; Ahmed didn't have any friends, apart from his brother. Mohammed's best friends were Nasir, Altaf, and Ayesha. The three of them tolerated Ahmed for Mohammed's sake; otherwise they would have had nothing to do with him or his pet falcon.

The shop that the Jinah brothers purchased was directly across the street from Barranca's second Chaklala safe house. The market had been only three blocks from Barranca's original quarters. Barranca was shuffled about between safe houses in Peshawar, Rawalpindi, and Islamabad. When he had to travel, there were additional houses in Karachi and Lahore. By October 2003, Barranca was alternating between a house in F10 Sector of Islamabad and the number two location in Chaklala after a grenade was tossed over the compound wall of the number one location.

In the evenings, he motioned to the Captain that he wanted to walk to the market to buy food, making a little gesture of two fingers walking—this was permitted since the market was only across the street. So when Barranca signaled thus this afternoon, the Captain picked up his shotgun, nodded, and followed behind him, placing himself between Barranca and a nearby mosque and a row of rooftops where they were likely to come under fire, if at all.

Scavenger kites drew dark circles over the Chaklala dump, which always smoldered, mixing smoke with the aromas of saffron, cardamom, cloves, cumin, and curry. Mohammed and his brother were sitting on the steps of their shop. The Captain positioned himself twenty or so yards away so that he could easily view the men going into or coming out of the mosque, as well as Barranca.

Barranca placed some items into a basket, things that weren't obscured by packaging covered in Farsi, Russian, or Arabic—necessities like lentils and rice, tea … He picked up a can and looked at it, trying to decide if he could make any sense of the writing. It was in Urdu, but he had not learned how to read Urdu. Mohammed saw this and came over.

"Chickpeas," he said.

"Oh, thank you," Francisco said.

"I am Mohammed. This is my brother, Ahmed," Mohammed said, extending his hand.

"How do you do? Very nice to meet you."

Ahmed nodded and took a sip of tea.

"What else can I help you find?"

Francisco looked at his list.

"Salt? Tomatoes?"

"Do you cook?" Mohammed asked as he went for the items.

"Not very well I'm afraid."

"May I suggest a few things you might try?"

"Yes. Please."

Mohammed plucked a few items and put them on the counter and explained how to prepare them. Boil this. Fry that. "With this, you can make *biryani*. I'll write down the steps." Barranca was impressed by his

English and noted the accent was American. Mohammed shared with him how he had come back to get married and how he'd gotten stuck there.

"Perhaps we will go home to the States when things calm down."

"I hope you can do that," Barranca said.

The wind changed direction and picked up a cloud of dust that blew through a long row of tall eucalyptus trees. Mohammed and Ahmed, as well as the Captain, covered up their faces with scarves until the dust blew by. Barranca covered his face with his hands.

"What brings you here?" Mohammed asked.

The question came from genuine curiosity. Why would an American leave the safety of America to come somewhere so dangerous, particularly so dangerous for an American?

"I'm working for the Commission of Higher Education."

Mohammed brought out a third folding chair and invited Barranca to have a cup of tea. Now it was between the afternoon and final evening call to prayer. The bullhorn on top of the minaret had not yet blasted its final orders. The words of the same prayer would spill from the tower louder than a rock band's music, bouncing off the cinderblocks, stucco walls and mud bricks—the echoes overlapping like a round. But Mohammed did not get up from his chair to close his shop. In fact, he blatantly refused to close his shop in full view of faithful Muslims.

"You should be very careful here," Mohammed said, nodding in the direction of the mosque, in the same direction the Captain watched with some concern.

"Oh?" Barranca said, inviting him to say more.

"There are Taliban at that mosque."

"And do you go there? Or to another one?"

"Me? No. I'm not religious. Nor is my wife. My brother, Ahmed, goes there sometimes."

Ahmed nodded to confirm this as he checked the thin leather helmet on his falcon that perched on his left forearm.

"That is how we know there are Taliban there," Mohammed said. "Anyway, I am sorry if you are religious, but I am not, or not so much.

Barranca changed the subject.

"Ahmed, tell me about your falcon," he said.

"We have used them for centuries for hunting. This one I just recently bought from a dealer in Islamabad. I have not yet taken him hunting. First, I am letting him get used to the sound of my voice."

"How very interesting. You know, it is the first time I have ever seen one this close. They're marvelous."

"Yes. They are great hunters, great assassins. I must keep his helmet on him. As long as he is blind, he won't fly."

"What do you feed him?"

"Baby rabbits. Mice. Lizards ..."

The bullhorn blew just as another gust of dust rose from the dry streets, blowing brown the white achkans of men walking along the street.

"Do you have a cigarette?" Ahmed asked Barranca, even though he already had his own.

"Yes." Barranca offered him one.

"Look, Mohammed. He smokes the Soviet Marlboros!"

"Francisco, friend! Do not smoke those! They are decades old and contain cyanide. If you must smoke Marlboros, at least buy the Persian ones. Some of the Soviet ones even contain high enough doses of cyanide to kill you if you smoke a full pack in a day. The Russians seeded them behind mujahadin lines back in the 1970s."

Ahmed pulled out a pack of cigarettes of his own and offered one to Barranca.

"Players. English. Ok to smoke it," Ahmed said. "Look, Mohammed," he said, pointing to the Soviet cigarette. "It has actually turned green!"

"Thank you," Barranca said, taking the English cigarette.

"Nasir and Altaf are coming," Mohammed said, waving to his friends who were still a few blocks away.

"Yes, and that bitch, Ayesha!" Ahmed said, motioning in the other direction.

"Ahmed, I have asked you not to call her that!" Mohammed said. "Francisco, Ayesha is not a 'bitch'. She is a very fine person. I will introduce you to her and to my friends, Nasir and Altaf. You will like them, I'm sure."

"Of course I will," Barranca said. "But, Mohammed, isn't it a little unusual for a woman to be out unescorted?"

Ahmed let out a laugh.

"Shut up, Ahmed!" Mohammed said. "Francisco, I will let Ayesha explain herself to you—if she ever decides to."

Chapter 16

Sinaloa

On Sunday morning, Eduardo Aguilar attended mass at *Nuestra Señora de Lourdes* with his wife, Martha, and their two corpulent little boys, Eduardo Jr. and Pedro, who were both approaching their thirties and were still not married. Sunday was the one day of the week when Aguilar was expected to placate his wife and present the picture of a normal family, though as for that, the four of them looked like a caricature or a painting by Botero. Martha wore the most expensive dresses money could buy and tried to cover up her age with so much makeup that she resembled a clown more than a woman. She had been very attractive, once. Now, no plastic surgery, no jewels, and no dress could restore her former glory. The same could have been said for her worthless brats—so called by Aguilar, who wanted nothing to do with them. Martha had spoiled them. When they were not out all hours drinking and snorting cocaine, they were sleeping it off. They only dressed and got up on Sunday mornings so as not to lose their significant allowance. Sunday was Martha's day and no son or husband was going to take that away from her. This was her day to waltz, or waddle, down the church aisle with her chubby hand on her husband's silk dress jacket, followed by her two petulant sons.

That the whole city of Culiacán knew they were a sham did not matter a bit to Martha, not as long as they did not say so publicly, and they didn't dare to speak. Martha's father was still a congressman in the Cámara de Diputados—the very reason why Aguilar had courted and married her in the first place. And Martha's father was also a business associate of Aguilar's industries. Adding to that, her uncle, also on her paternal side, was the governor of the state and also a close business associate.

Martha knew full well what Aguilar's business entailed and she knew about the secluded estate ten miles out of town. Everyone knew. Still, when photographers from the tabloids took their picture every week, leaving mass, the photo always appeared on the high society page where she wanted it. There had only been one occasion when their photos had appeared in a respectable newspaper, and, in an article that suggested Aguilar's criminal activities in innuendos. When the family picture appeared in this newspaper, Eduardo had the journalist executed within a day. "Say what they wish about me," he told one of his more trusted soldiers, "but they will not denigrate my family." At the governor's orders, the police investigation into the murder was merely for show.

The family had just squeezed into their pew, waddling in sideways liked overstuffed geese, and now knelt down on the prayer bench in unison, when their combined weight crashed through the wood, shattering it into splinters. The boys and Martha let out a roar of pain when their knees smashed through to the marble, and the priest came rushing down the aisle.

Chapter 17

Peshawar, 1983

IN 1983, HASAN JALIL was a very attractive little boy with creamy brown skin, large dark eyes, and long eyelashes. He was also very sweet, smiling at anyone who passed. But the loveliness of young boys, like the loveliness of young girls, can be dangerous.

Hasan's owner was Mustaf Asad, a wealthy man in the business of air cargo who paid little attention to details as long as he remained wealthy. He was far more distracted by his collection of women, though as for that, they had started to bore him and he was making arrangements to sell a few of them to other wealthy men, some in Saudi Arabia, some in Dubai, and one in Eastern Europe. When he sold the first one, he was delighted. Of course, he would miss her, but she had brought him a very nice profit. Missing her was only a little wave of nostalgia and it passed. And there were always new ones to experiment with for the very first time. Each new girl was a new present to himself he could unwrap and toy with for a while.

When the overseer of this separate enterprise brought little Hasan to his attention, Mustaf Asad's curiosity was piqued. A boy ... I have waited a lifetime for a boy ...

"A boy?"

"That can be changed, sir," the overseer said.

"Where did you find him?"

"I bought him for you at the brick factory. He's an orphan. His parents were killed by the Russians."

"Mujahadin boy or Taliban boy?"

"Mujahadin."

"Can you understand us, boy?"

"His name is Hasan. Hasan Jalil."

"Can you understand us, Hasan-boy?" Mustaf asked, loudly, as if he thought the boy might be deaf.

Hasan smiled at the man, but he did not understand Urdu.

"Pashto speaker, sir," the overseer said.

This specimen is the missing piece in my collection … Nay, in my life.

"We will have to change his name, of course," Mustaf said.

"Of course. I know a man who knows someone called 'the Knifer.' Shall I make inquiries?"

"Yes. Do so discreetly or you will be the one who needs a 'Knifer,'" Mustaf said.

"Of course, sir. Most discreetly."

About a week later, the man called the Knifer arrived at the residence of Mustaf Asad. Outside it was a cool spring day and a male peacock's array of eyes spread into a semi-circle of shimmering indigo and gold, assuming an imperious pose.

"I will require an assistant," he said to the servant who opened the door.

Hasan's little boy body was tied to a cold metal table of the sort used in restaurant kitchens. Tears were dried on his face leaving almost imperceptible trails of salt. Hasan was thirsty. But the operation required that he not eat or drink for three days before and three days after. Hasan had been shivering, but now he lay on the table seemingly lifeless as the assistant bound his thighs in gauze and the Knifer placed one of his blades in the kitchen fire until it glowed bright orange.

When his instruments were ready and Hasan's feet and hands were tied to the table legs, the Knifer was ready to begin the operation. Outside in the garden a peacock screeched. The Knifer grabbed Hasan's little penis in his left hand and brought a curved knife swiftly up from behind Hasan's genitals, severing both his scrotum and most of his penis. Blood gushed and splashed everywhere. Just as quickly, the Knifer inserted an inch and a half long urethral dilator into Hasan's urethra. Hasan was still bleeding badly, but his screams were muffled by a wad of rags the Knifer had stuffed in his mouth, put there so the screaming wouldn't distract him from the work.

The Knifer then took a urethral plug and slipped it into the dilator. The plug was about the size and length of a porcupine's quill and a three-inch long string was threaded through an eye on the end of it. This device would be used to prevent incontinence.

Now the Knifer took the bright orange blade from the fire and pressed it hard against the gushing wound. The room filled with the smell of Hasan's burning flesh, but the bleeding stopped.

"Do not let him urinate for three days, or the wounds will become infected."

"I understand," the attendant said.

"I'm paid either way, whether the kid lives or dies, understand?"

"Yes, no peeing," the attendant said to Hasan with a scowl.

"Most of these operations do end in death, you know." There was a vinegary-ness in the way the Knifer spoke.

"Yes, I know. The master knows, too."

"Give him the heroin for pain, but don't get him addicted. I'm sure your master doesn't want a junkie for a playmate."

The Knifer was saying this as he was covering Hasan in blankets to keep him from going into shock. Hasan's eyes slowly swirled around the room as if they were trying to follow one of the invisible jinn—one of those demonic little spirits that flit about the pages of the Koran, causing all manner of misfortune. Otherwise, Hasan appeared to feel nothing. The Knifer pulled the rags out of Hasan's mouth.

"Let him lie there for an hour and then put him in his bed."

The attendant nodded.

"I will be back when it is time to begin estrogen injections. He will develop breasts. Even his hips will become round, and he will never grow much of an Adam's apple."

The attendant nodded again.

Upstairs Mustaf Asad was contemplating what new name to give the boy. Then it came to him …

"Ayesha!" he said with excitement.

This had been the name of a little girl he was in love with when he was a boy. Now he could have her.

Chapter 18

Jlalpan, 2004

Jlalpan was too small to have a public telephone. In fact, most of the people who lived in Jlalpan did not own telephones. The Collins residence was only one of a couple of families who had both a telephone and the internet, yet every house had at least five televisions, except for the Collins residence, which did not have even one because Bolivar considered them useless. When Teodesia wanted to see the latest soap opera, she went next door to watch it with her neighbor, Francisca. As for phones, if someone wanted to talk to someone, they simply walked down the road, which was the length of a football field with little side streets. All of the roads were gravel. Smaller roads of dirt with deep ruts in them descended from terraced hills where farmers lived and grew mostly corn, milo, alfalfa, and carrots. The nearest paved road wasn't until halfway to a bigger town called Tequisquiapan, and after that a somewhat larger town than that called San Juan del Río. After that a driver could use the federal highway running north to the city of Querétaro or south to Mexico City.

In the middle of Jlalpan was something like a town square, with a small municipal building set back off the main street. Bolivar made a donation to Jlalpan to build a small public library but hardly anyone used it except for a couple of the public school teachers who lived there only when school was in session. When Paco was very little and Teodesia was pregnant with Karli, they made frequent trips to Mexico City, each time filling up their trunk with books they found in the used bookstores on Donceles Street in the city's old historical district. They also tried to get the primary school, middle school, and high school to hold book drives. All three schools had just one warmish old lady who held the title of "Director," the equivalent of a school principal. The high school's total enrollment was usually around eighty to ninety, but only half that number actually bothered to attend. The primary and middle school fared only slightly better.

The most prominent building in town was a church situated beside the municipal building, Nuestra Virgin de Guadalupe, where Teodesia took the children to mass every Sunday morning to listen to Father Sebastián. The priest was in his twenties and clearly not happy to have to be so mismatched in the assignment of his post: he was—with the exception of Bolivar Collins—the only intellectual person in Jlalpan. For one thing, he was from Mexico City, and for another, he did not know how to use ordinary words that average folks could understand. Collins was the only man in town who understood him, but Collins only attended mass on special occasions and only when Teodesia begged him. Meanwhile, Father Sebastián wrote his sermons specifically for Collins, peppering his homilies with references to Miguel de Unamuno, Óscar Romero, and Jorge Luis Borges—none of whom were known by the poor farmers of Jlalpan. Sagacious as he was, Father Sebastián was also strikingly handsome, so the women adored him. Attendance increased the week he arrived and continued to increase. The women came just to look at him and the men came to keep an eye on their daughters and wives.

The day after Bolivar's letter arrived, Teodesia packed a cooler with sandwiches, juice, chips, and whatever else she found in the cupboard, and she and Karli set out for Querétaro, leaving a note on the kitchen table for Paco in case he should ever get out of bed. It was a Saturday morning, so as the sun was just rising in Jlalpan, the sun was going down in Islamabad. Karli was aware of this fact because she made a point of studying all the world's time zones, and she pointed out the facts with frequency: "It's seven o'clock in 'you-know-where'," she'd say. "You-know-where" was Islamabad, but Bolivar had made it clear that they were to be wary of microphones—perhaps even the car had a microphone.

Father Sebastián was out for his morning walk, and he asked them where they were going when he encountered them leaving the house with their cooler. Karli couldn't speak. She already had a crush on Father Sebastián at the age of twelve. Teodesia answered him …

"We're going to Querétaro for the day to do some shopping. Is there anything we can bring you?"

"Oh, let me think … Yes, there is a new book by Carlos Fuentes. Here let me … Oh, I didn't bring my wallet."

"No problem," Teodesia said. "You're good for it."

"I know it's been a hard year for you, Señora Collins."

Father Sebastián wanted to engage Teodesia in conversation, but Teodesia wanted to go to Querétaro to telephone Tomás in Nicaragua and Ms. Regier in New York. Still, the people of Jlalpan were never in a hurry, so Teodesia could not let on that she was in no mood to chat.

"We're okay, thank you."

"And Paco? Angry still?"

"Angry as ever. Maybe angrier. Perhaps you could talk to him."

"I will. I will do that. A year … It's been a year now and still no word."

Karli still wore a funny look. *It's uncanny how much he looks like the actor Gael García Bernal—only more handsome.* So it came as a shock to her whenever Father Sebastián addressed her directly.

"And Karli, how are you?" the Father said, trying to make eye contact.

"Fah … Fah … Fine," Karli said.

"I am always glad to see you on Sundays, Karli. I know that you are listening. Maybe you don't know, but we priests are just people, too. It's important to me to know that you are listening."

Karli managed to nod. Teodesia put the cooler in the backseat.

"Speaking of Fuentes, Señora Collins, has he been up to see you?"

"Once, yes. He came to pay his respects not long after Bolivar disappeared. It was just before you arrived as our new priest."

"It astounds me, the visitors you have. Imagine, Octavio Paz would come right to your house and no one in Jlalpan even knew who he was."

"Well, Father, that is why we moved here. Bolivar doesn't like attention."

"And Alí Chumacero! He was Juan Rulfo's editor, wasn't he?"

"Yes."

"Of course, your husband was … Oh dear … IS a great writer, a great man in his own right."

"Yes, Father. I think so. He is."

"Saramago visited too, didn't he?"

"Yes, Father. But Father, while it is nice of you to point this out, I think my husband would appreciate it if you didn't mention these visits to anyone."

"He's too humble, isn't he …"

"It's not humility, really. He just doesn't like a lot of attention. He says it's distracting."

"Still, God will deliver him back to us soon. I pray for this. And he is on the prayer chain."

"Thank you, Father."

"And to think, an American, or rather he was …"

"Yes, Father. But Bolivar says that he really isn't very American. Only that he was born there."

"He has, I read somewhere, a sister in California."

"Yes. She's been here several times to visit."

"And my half-sisters," Karli said.

"Really? I didn't know that."

Karli was a little defensive when it came to her sisters. She didn't like it that the Church had called her father's morality into question. His other wives were in the past, and anyway she loved her older sisters, the one who lived in New York and the African sister who lived in Paris. She never knew her three Cuban sisters who were killed in the war in Nicaragua.

"My sisters come every year to see me. To see us," Karli said, correcting herself.

"That's very nice. Very nice," Father Sebastián said, stretching.

Teodesia was looking around nervously. An old pickup truck went by and raised the dust. *Safe*, she thought. *None of Aguilar's men would use an old pickup.*

"We'd better get on the road, Father," Teodesia said, finally.

"Yes. I need to get to my sermon, too. I'm going to name it after a song, 'Bridge Over Troubled Water.' Faith is the bridge. Well, have a very nice time in Querétaro."

Karli could sense, even if her mother could not, Father Sebastián's attraction to her mother. She did the math. *Fifteen! Mother is fifteen years older than him. I'm closer in age to him by two years! Damn!* Karli's puppy crush on the priest ended right there abruptly. When the two were finally allowed to leave, Karli was quiet for a while … Then she let it out …

"Mother! That priest is in love with you!"

"Oh, Karli! That's nonsense."

"It's obvious," Karli said.

"Karli, watch to see if anyone is following us, please."

Chapter 19

Rawalpindi, 2003

By October of Barranca's first year in Pakistan, the days had begun to cool down. On a Wednesday morning, Barranca finished lecturing the American literature class and walked through the weeds of chittering conversations. He put his books down beside him on the school's verandah and told the boys in the kitchen to make him a late breakfast of eggs and *rhoti*. Hasam, whom he dreaded talking with, decided to sit down beside him, presumably to have a conversation, although Hasam did not have conversations; he had monologues which always circled around to an unpleasant conclusion. Today he wanted to discuss a new book about Moses and Marx. The book was in Urdu, so Hasam felt it his duty to retell the whole book in English for Barranca's sake. The thesis was simple enough. Most of the world's ideologies eventually got around to claiming some grounding in the favorite sacred text, and this book claimed that Islam was communism's natural end, or so went the friable argument.

Hasam, who hardly ever looked directly at a person, stared up at empty space while he pontificated, subordinating clauses which he had already subordinated once or twice, using a kind of Urdu grammar to lace his English and muddy his points. Barranca pretended to listen by tossing an occasional "oh" his way and nodding in the space of his very brief pauses. As Hasam talked, Samina walked up to the short, three-foot stone wall of the verandah—women were not allowed to be on the verandah as it was reserved only for the male administrators, and the only foreigner on the faculty, Barranca.

"Sir, do we have a surprise quiz next week?"

"Hello, Samina. If I tell you, then it won't be a surprise."

Rafia had come along with Samina. The girls almost always traveled in twos, always to appear vestal. Sometimes in threes. Usually in twos. Rafia turned and twisted like she needed to use the bathroom, but her contortions were meant to exhibit discomfort should there be a quiz coming.

"Hello, Rafia."

"Hello, sir."

"Well," Hasam said, "you can see that if Marx had discovered Islam, then he would have freely admitted his affinities." Hasam went on, ignoring the presence of the students entirely. "The evidence is irrefragable."

Samina apologized.

"Are we interrupting you, sir?"

"No, Samina. Not at all. In fact, I'm just going to my office if either of you want to discuss your term papers."

"I want to write about *The Scarlet Letter*," Rafia said, through her veil.

Rafia was among the few who wore the entire veil—not the hijab, and not simply a head scarf. And her burkas were always black. All Barranca could hear was her voice and all he could see were her eyes, which were very pretty.

"What do you want to say about *The Scarlet Letter*?"

"I would like to say that Hawthorne is wrong to suggest that sin is not an essential part of human nature."

Barranca had almost forgotten about the anonymous letter left under his pillow just a few days earlier. *Rafia? It could be Rafia?* It was a simple matter of curiosity and no more. He had no intention of leaving *The Scarlet Letter* on the verandah to see who would retrieve it, who would reveal themselves as his would-be clandestine lover. Even if he were lonely, and he was, he could not risk so much—not his family and not the unknown girl, providing it was written by one of the girls. If caught in illicit relations, a young woman of Pakistan would be put to death by a member of their family—an older brother, the father, an uncle—as a matter of honor. If they were lucky, they would be arrested and spend the rest of their lives in the women's prison in Karachi. As for the man, he was blameless. If it were not for the woman's evil powers of seduction, handed down from the first woman, Eve, then men would not have to face such temptations. They were Satan's agents, as the logic went.

Nadia saw Rafia and Samina interrupting Barranca's breakfast and came bounding over to scold them.

"Off with you, both! Right now. You leave Dr. Barranca alone."

"Nadia, please. Ladies, you may speak to me whenever you wish."

"It's all right, sir," Samina said. "We will come to the office."

"As you wish," Barranca said. "Nadia …" Barranca shook his head. "Nadia, you must allow me to do my job."

"That is why I am here. The VC has sent me to ask you to join her and the Chancellor in the Chancellery to assist with an interview. There is a professor, Dr. Qadir, visiting. She is a prospective professor."

"At what time?"

"It has already started."

The interview was underway. When Barranca opened the door to the Chancellery, the Chancellor was talking about the school's accomplishments.

"Come in, Dr. Barranca, please," the Chancellor said.

The Chancellor turned to the candidate, Professor Qadir, or Professor Q, as she would become known later.

"Dr. Qadir, this is our most esteemed professor, Dr. Barranca, from America."

Dr. Qadir did not get up, nor did she offer her hand to greet him. Among academics, the Islamic gender issues regarding western greetings were usually ignored, but not by Dr. Qadir. The Chancellor and the Vice Chancellor, both women, shook hands with Barranca. Women in positions of power liked to show their western sophistication, especially in front of retired generals like General Kahn, who also stood up to greet Barranca. The Chancellor, the VC, and the General all settled back in their chairs. Dr. Qadir had not bothered to stand up. The Chancellor continued …

"Well, now that we have Dr. Barranca with us, I believe he may have some questions for you."

Barranca had already done some interviews for the Higher Education Commission, but they had been at Karachi University and the University of Punjab in Lahore. This was the first interview for the women's college. The VC commented before Barranca could formulate his first question. Barranca liked the VC—she was smart and she held a valid PhD from Stanford University, though she had not been to the United States since the 1960s and often said things that were clearly dated. The VC began …

"Before you start, you should know that Dr. Qadir comes to us from a university in South Africa. If hired, she would be teaching general literature courses for both the undergraduates and the graduate students, but her specialization is English drama."

"Excellent. Shall we start with drama?" Barranca asked.

Dr. Qadir did not make eye contact or acknowledge his question. This flustered Barranca a little. He expected someone who wanted a position to at least feign interest. He tried to begin with pleasantries …

"Dr. Qadir, what is something you loved about South Africa?"

Collins had lived in Africa but Barranca had not. Barranca caught and repressed his impulse to personalize his question with this tiny piece of biography. Dr. Qadir did not even so much as shift in her chair, lean forward, or acknowledge that a question had been asked. Then her mouth opened and something resembling an answer came into the room …

"There was really nothing of interest to me in South Africa," she said in a strange monotone.

"Oh," Barranca said, unable to hide his surprise that bordered on mild shock.

What else could anyone say? How is it possible to follow up after a statement like that? But Barranca had to continue anyway …

"If your assignment is to teach Shakespeare, and British literature in general, then let's begin with some general questions and we can talk specifics later."

As interviews like these went, the interviewer began with the broad questions and then got more and more specific as the hour drew on, much like the way a bloodhound makes mile-wide circles around a raccoon, but little by little, closing the circle.

"What is your favorite Shakespeare play?"

Qadir's expressionless demeanor did not change or register any question; nevertheless, she answered …

"I have never read a Shakespeare play."

Barranca was in shock. Was he face to face with Herman Melville's Bartleby? Would the answer to any question be a negation? He looked at the VC. The VC tried not to meet his eyes; instead she looked down at her lap. He looked at the Chancellor with a puzzled look as if to ask if there were any need to continue the interview. To his surprise, the Chancellor said, "Perhaps there are other playwrights more to Dr. Qadir's liking."

"Let's see, my next line of inquiry was to have you compare three Shakespeare clowns. Let's forget that. Maybe Shakespeare is overrated," he said, unable to contain the edge of sarcasm.

Qadir did not register his disapproval. It is possible that she did not possess the intellect to detect any form of irony. But if that were the case, how could she have been granted a PhD in British drama?

"Walk me through the Mystery Plays, please."

Qadir had no response.

"No? Fine. How about talking about the Italian influence on British drama?"

Again, no response.

"Oh, let's skip the Renaissance. Can you name one of the Cavalier poets? No? I suppose we won't be getting to John Donne or John Milton? Spenser, maybe? No? And let me ask, just for clarity, your PhD is in British Literature?"

"Correct."

"You attended a university in South Africa," Barranca said, looking down at her resume. "Alexandria University in Pretoria."

"Correct."

"South Africa … Well, then, we could discuss South Africa's Nobel laureate, Nadine …"

Barranca didn't finish her name, hoping that Dr. Qadir would fill in the blank. But there was no response. So Barranca finished her name for her …

"Gordimer. Nadine Gordimer."

"I have never heard of her," she said with a tone that revealed pride.

The Chancellor leaned in and spoke to the candidate, Q, in comforting tones.

"Don't worry, dear. I'm sure Dr. Barranca can fill you in on whatever you need to know to teach your classes."

I can do what? he asked himself, trying to hide an expression of incredulity. Then he suddenly realized the whole meeting was a formality and a farce. *Her new position with the women's college had already been decided, but by whom? She's a general's daughter. Or worse, she's another agent with ISI.* It did not take an intelligent person very long to figure out that these circus interviews were conducted so that a report could be filed. As long as Barranca conducted the interviews, evaluated university curriculums, and taught his classes, it did not matter how broken a school or a whole country was. His presence, via contract between the women's college and the Commission, netted his host, the Chancellor and her allies, the sum of two million dollars a year. Be that as it may, Barranca sent his reports to the Commission by the end of every week and he pulled no punches: every word was the truth. In this case, "Professor Qadir is not fit to teach. What's more, her university degree is fake. My research reveals that no such university called 'Alexandria' exists in the city of Pretoria." He restrained himself from cursing. He wanted to write that a ten-dollar whore is more honest, but he didn't. So, he finished this report and many others like it and gave it to Nadia to post it. Nadia always promised that it would be there by the next day, and then she went to the Chancellor's office where she preemptively shredded the report, thereby insuring the continued flow of two million dollars into the school's general account where it was divided four ways the following day and redeposited into personal bank accounts, accounts in Saudi Arabia in the names of four of the top administrators of the women's university: the Chancellor, the Vice Chancellor, the Director of International Affairs, and the Director of Finance.

Professor Q decorated her office in December, and started teaching Shakespeare to graduate students and general British literature to undergraduates the following spring term, beginning the 10th of January. After her first day of classes, students were lined up outside of Dr. Barranca's office, more than thirty of them, to express their concern about her. After her second day of classes, the line outside Dr. Barranca's office was twice as long.

"Dr. B! Dr. B! Today she said that T.S. Eliot was born in London, England, not in St. Louis! We tried to correct her and she called us insolent! What can we do?"

And …

"Dr. B! Today she said she doesn't understand anything on her British Literature syllabus—the one you provided her with—and she asked Serein to teach the class."

"Actually, that's a fine idea. Make it a seminar and let Serein chair it."

It was outrageous and Q's arrogance, her willful ignorance, was an abomination. The situation could only have been worse had there been an outbreak of measles or yellow jaundice. Then Q decided to get nastier, blaming the women simply for having attended Dr. Barranca's classes.

Serein and Humaira No. 1 were crying in his office …

"She has ordered us to 'unlearn' everything you've taught us."

When they left, Sidra came in followed by Simba and Tabina …

"She says American literature is invalid because it is written by infidels. Oh, Dr. B, we do not even trust her theology now. How can we trust her?"

Barranca thought about this.

"I'm not an authority on theology. My advice would be to think for yourselves, but I think that may run counter to some theologies. As for trust, given what I have learned thus far in Pakistan, trust issues here seem upside down, or at least the current of trust runs a different direction. We begin, here, with mistrust—as you read in many of the stories of Homer's *Odyssey*."

Barranca did not care about Q's opinion of him, but what she was doing to the young women was disturbing. It became difficult to sleep. This conflict which began as a simple interview was escalating and Q was raising the stakes daily. By the middle of the spring term, in 2004, Serein came to Barranca's office alone. She had something to say that she did not dare repeat in front of any of the other girls.

"Dr. B, Professor Q is going around to the girls in private, telling them that the women of the International Islamic University are whores and that it is up to us to do something about it. I am afraid that some of the students are listening to her."

Chapter 20

New York, 2003

THE AMERICAN AUTHOR, Bolivar Collins, was killed in a car accident near San Marcos, Nicaragua, while visiting friends. The accident occurred on November 30, 2003, according to a spokesperson for the Nicaraguan government. The president of Nicaragua, Daniel Ortega, and the president of Cuba, Fidel Castro, as well as president Fox of Mexico have issued condolences to his family. Bolivar Collins was born in St. Louis, Missouri, but spent most of his life in Latin America. Carlos Monsiváis, writing for *El Universal*, writes that "his loss will be felt all throughout Latin America. In the end," Monsiváis says, "there was no 'gringo' left in him."

Collins was the author of several notable books. His first novel *Winter Signs* told the story of the holocaust of the American Indian in such intimate and realistic language that American history teachers introduced the book in high schools and colleges—a phenomenon that caused a bitter controversy in education circles. His second book, *Four Years of Solidarity*, presented an economic plan designed to counter the imbalances created by the United States that became the template for economic planning in Brazil under president Lula, and later Bolivia under Jaime Paz Zamora. Subsequent to *Four Years*, Collins served as an economic advisor to numerous countries in Latin America. His third book, another novel, was *Vivaldi's Lovers*, an exploration of "active loving and the arts," as Portuguese writer Saramago described it. A year later, Collins published a small book of poems, *Psalms of the Forgotten*, earning him both the Pulitzer Prize and a second National Book Award, as well as the National Circle Critic's Award—none of which the author accepted. In Latin America, Collins received both of Mexico's highest awards, the *Premio Nacional de Literatura*, as well as multiple ConaCulta awards. His American press is planning to release his memoirs in the spring of next year. Three other novels may also be published posthumously by the same press, though no schedule has been established yet.

Collins is preceded in death by his wife Renee Chaurand Collins and his daughters Noelia, Sophia, and Melissa. He is survived by his first wife, Marie Ella Collins and their daughter Makeila of the Democratic Republic of Congo. He is also survived by his daughter, Marti SansSouci of New York. Collins remarried by the end of the 1980s to Teodesia Segovia Collins. The couple had a son, Francisco, and a daughter, Karli.

The details of Collins' life remain sketchy, at least in the United States. Collins left the US in the early 1980s, traveling and living in France, Spain, the Congo, and Cuba. In 1999, Attorney General Ashcroft's office publicly declared Bolivar Collins an American traitor and reports that his office was in contact with then president Zedillo to begin extradition proceedings, but the reasons for these actions were undisclosed. However, the Nicaraguan government has released a statement confirming that Collins did serve as a Cuban advisor to Nicaragua during their civil war with the CIA backed Contras. It is of the darkest irony that Collins suffered and survived severe wounds as a result of a terrible car accident near the town of Aleya in 1987.

By all accounts, both by American and Latin America presses, Collins shied away from public attention and never granted an interview.

The above account was written by Ms. Regier Toulet for the *Times Literary Supplement.*

Chapter 21

Rawalpindi, November 2004

SUMMER'S SEARING HEAT ROLLED over in its sleep and cold rain fell and clouds covered the skies for weeks. On Sunday, November 7th, Barranca went to visit his friend Anoosh. As usual, Anoosh put on a pot of tea and settled down in his overstuffed chair for a long and wonderful talk with his friend.

"Hello, sir!"

"Hi, Anoosh!"

"What sort of books are we looking for today?"

"Not sure yet. Going to have a look around."

Barranca altered his pattern, glancing at other bookshelves, picking out books that caught his attention but that had nothing to do with the message he needed. *Flora and Fauna of Pakistan.*

"Think I'll get this one: *The Taxila Excavation.*"

"Important book," Anoosh said.

"Isn't that where Alexander the Great last camped?"

"You've not been there? It isn't far from here. I can get my uncle to cover the store and take you there."

"I'd like that. Some think a wound he received in India was from a poisoned arrow and his death was slow. As for that, I've never been interested in the biographies of legendary men. There's something impure about it. I guess I'm uncomfortable when anyone starts mixing historical facts and fictional accounts."

Barranca's own fictional ships had been setting sail since August 31st, over a year earlier. Always the ship was sleeping as if at the bottom of the sea, and he could board none of them. They either never existed at all or once existed and then were no more. He had cycled through the alphabet skipping letters by twos. A, *D, G, J, M, P, S, V, Y and no Z but B, then E, H, K, N, Q, T, W, Z, then C, F, and I—I, November 7, 2004*. Barranca reached behind the third shelf from the top and pulled out The Principles of *Literary Criticism*, by I.A. Richards. *This will be useful for the theory students*. Barranca flipped to the back and started scanning.

"A lot of typos, I suspect," Anoosh said.

"There generally are."

The boat's name was the *Bellipotent*. It was the boat that Melville's poor Billy Budd was martyred on. Ironic ship name. Ironic use of the book, now. *The Bellipotent leaving November 25 Stop*.

Barranca sat down and took up his cup of tea. It was beginning to cool off. At this very moment, Nadia came into the bookstore.

"Hello, sir," Nadia blurted out with fake enthusiasm.

Barranca and Anoosh stood up and Barranca introduced him to Nadia as his assistant at the university.

"What brings you here today?"

"Looking for a book, *The Lord of the Flies*."

"Yes," Anoosh said. "I have a few copies."

Anoosh got up to get her the book. He was thinking it a little queer that she should be out and about unescorted. *Couldn't she get arrested?*

"Well, I've got to be going," Barranca said.

"Remember, Taxila!"

"Yes! I want to do that. Next week?" Barranca said.

"That will be fine. Saturday?"

"Done," Barranca said. "Now I've got to be going …"

"Wait," Nadia said. "I want to go with you. Have you ever seen the old quarters of the British lord? Lord Hudson governed this province. It's only a few blocks."

Nadia motioned to the chauffeur and bodyguards to follow them in the car, but one of the bodyguards jumped out and followed them on foot, making them that much more conspicuous in the neighborhood.

"Did you bring an umbrella?" Nadia asked. "It's starting to rain again."

When they arrived at the old mansion, Nadia told the bodyguard to wait outside. The house of Lord Hudson had lost its former grandeur. Clearly it recalled a time of luxury and splendor. But now its boards were falling off. It bore not even a fleck of paint. Ivy crawled over the broken trellises, clutched there for life, and then died, and were left to hang, brown, brittle, and now wet. Windows were missing. The door was gone.

They went inside. Even vines and limbs from a banyan tree had found their way into its musty shadows. Barranca looked around. *Like me, the British should never have come here. Their ways simply do not correspond to this world.* Barranca was lost in his thoughts. When he heard Nadia, say "sir," he turned around.

When various forms of coercion fail, enticements and temptations may be presented. But these may be quite outside the norms and mores of acceptable behavior, most particularly in Pakistan. Nevertheless, as if duty bound, Nadia had positioned herself very close to him.

"Do you like me? I mean, in *that* way?"

"What?"

"If you like me, it is okay."

For a moment, Barranca stood there, frozen. *To touch another person is to embrace death*, he thought. That is, in Pakistan, this sort of closeness usually ends in death and usually for the woman.

"No, Nadia. No."

Nadia took a step back and feigned a look of upset. Then Nadia, true to her character, started rambling. It was a moment that may have swung one way or the other, like a teeter-totter.

"But I'm a blackie like your wife," she muttered.

Nadia was too witless to know where she'd gone wrong. But she would try a new approach.

"I have something you may want, sir," she said.

Nadia pulled a white envelope from her purse and waved it at him like it were a white kerchief and she would drop it coquettishly if he promised to pick it up.

"Nadia, just go. I'm sure you have a report to write."

"It's from Mrs. Barranca."

This stopped Barranca abruptly. He couldn't speak. He looked at her, waiting for her next move.

"Wouldn't you like to hear from your wife?"

Even the heat of his anxiety froze at that moment in the dilapidated old manor house. *She got my letter from the airport*, he thought. *She and Karli must still have been safe up until then. Maybe something was in the works. Maybe freedom?*

"What does it say, Nadia? I'm sure you've read every word."

Of course she had read every word, or better to say that she "tried" to read it but couldn't. Not only was it in Spanish, it was in a bizarre script that was indecipherable. Not even her superiors were able to decipher the letter, but it was decided to let it be passed on to him so that ISI could watch his response and see if the letter changed in anyway his normal activities.

"I'm sure I don't know. Letters are private," she said, almost mockingly.

"May I have it?"

Nadia tossed the letter down and walked out in the rain. Bolivar picked it up off the filthy floor, a floor that was littered with dried condoms and contraband, empty bottles of alcohol, and the used needle of a heroin addict. The letter was addressed to Francisco Barranca, The Women's College, The Causeway, Rawalpindi, Pakistan. Hand printed. He recognized immediately the hand. It was Karli's. Barranca began to cry uncontrollably. His body shook and tears gushed down his face, holding the letter tightly in his hand.

Chapter 22

Jlalpan, September 2003

PACO SCREAMED DOWN THE steps that not only would he not go with them to Mexico City, he refused to return to that stupid school.

"Fine," Teodesia yelled back. "Leave your family when you are most needed!"

"Why would I want to help him? He's the very person who has ruined my life!"

"So then, what? How do you plan to live? You know your father forbids you from joining the military."

"He has his convictions and I have mine. I'm going to kill ragheads. I'm American and it's my duty."

"And you would kill Latinos if called to? Because I am your mother, a Latina!" Teodesia was burning with uncontrollable anger. They both were.

"*Estúpida*! Latinos are not Arabs! And I don't believe any of those stories about Americans in Nicaragua. A lot of leftist bullshit."

"Have you at least talked about this with Father Sebastián?"

"I didn't talk to him. He lectured me. He doesn't know anything about the war or why Christianity needs to be protected. If the Americans fail, imagine the fate of Mexico! Did you know that the Taliban is already doing business with the cartels? Death is too good for them. Anyway, I can join early and then neither you nor Father will have any say over me. And if I go as a Mexican, the Marines won't even care if I'm not old enough."

Teodesia stood at the bottom of the steps. She covered her lips with a finger and looked away, trying to find the words that would stop him.

"You are just like him, Paco!"

"Oh? How? That's impossible. I'm American by choice. He's a traitor."

"When he was your age, he was just as impetuous. That was his flaw—don't you see? He wouldn't repeat those mistakes for anything now, and you could learn that from him."

"You're right about one thing. He didn't consider very well whose side to be on."

"Where do you get this stuff? He was never on anyone's side but his family's, and he paid," Teodesia said, with tears in her eyes.

"You're talking about those bastard kids of his. That nigger daughter he keeps in France!"

"How dare you talk like that!? Where did you learn that filthy word?"

"The dyke kid in New York? And you! You put up with it? What does that say about you?"

"All right, Paco. That's enough! Karli and I don't have time for this right now. We are going on a trip to the city and if you aren't coming, fine. We'll see you when you get back!"

But Paco was not home when they returned from Mexico City. He had taken a bus from San Juan del Río to Nuevo Leon. From there he swam across the Rio Grande with an altered birth certificate wrapped in plastic in his pocket, and a week later he was at Camp Pendleton in California. In Nuevo Leon, he instructed the forger to delete the name "Collins" from his original birth certificate and the US consulate never noticed the original's alterations when they clipped the official translation to his documents. But Francisco bypassed green card status and went directly to the Marines, who didn't care what country you were from as long as you wanted to fight.

Chapter 23

Rawalpindi, November 7, 2004

Barranca got in the backseat of the car in downtown Sadr in front of the old Hudson Manor, holding the letter from Teodesia.

"Home?" the driver asked.

It was one of around 10 words the driver knew in English.

"Home," Barranca said.

Barranca stared at Karli's precise printing on the envelope. He took a small penknife from his pocket and carefully opened it. To his surprise, the letter was written in his own hand. *Karli, my Davincita, you've used my very letters to speak to me. You are the only one. My God, how I miss you.* Barranca added up the months ... *You're almost fourteen, now. You were ten when I showed you how to read my scrawl ...*

Mr. Barranca, K.K. is writing this for T. This is her talking to you now: I have met once with our old friend T ...

Barranca understood that she had met with Captain Tomás. He also knew that Karli and Teodesia, possibly with Tomás' help, were writing in flat tones and obscuring the references.

... and will be meeting him again soon. He wants you to make friends with the Department of Spanish at Islamic International U. We believe a contact there might provide a wonderful "outlet" for you academically.

Tomás had figured out a "way out"—an "outlet." Barranca could hardly contain his emotions. Tomás had a contact in Islamabad.

Look there for someone who is also a T. Meanwhile, we hope you are enjoying your stay in Pakistan. We hear it is a lovely country and wish we could see it with you someday. Until then, we continue to enjoy our meetings in the trees.

They were saying they received his letter to Paco's tree house and that they understood the situation.

Love,

Isa Aramara

PS So far, no news from C.

This meant that there had been no news from the woman, Carmelita, from Brazil.

Certainly, Captain Tomás had helped them with the phrasing. They could not refer to anything specific; they could not express strong emotions. The letter had to seem simply "normal," and simply using a letter for a name was common between two people who share another person in common. Still, Barranca wanted to hear Teodesia scream out her passion for him. He admired the courage it took both his wife and daughter to restrain themselves—not at all easy for a Latina woman or a half Latina girl who idolizes her "daddy". Barranca set in the back seat of the car that was taking him to safe house No. 2 in Chaklala and could not contain his joy.

"Captain!" he said, smiling. "My wife!" Barranca said, happily holding up his letter.

The Captain was never not smiling, so he turned to look at Barranca with his permanently large smile and tried to repeat the word "wife".

"Wwwweeeve."

"Yes! Wife! Yes, Captain."

Bolivar held the letter to his chest.

A few moments later, the Captain said to the other bodyguard in Urdu … "I think he is not a spy. I think he is only a professor."

But why had it taken the letter a year to reach him? It was postmarked November 2003 a full year ago, Barranca wondered.

Chapter 24

Mexico City, December 2003

Teodesia and Karli checked into the *Hotel Donceles* behind the Cathedral of Mexico and the grand Zócalo. They were tired from the trip and snapped at each other a little when Teodesia told Karli she had to stay in the room while she went to meet Captain Tomás. Karli protested, saying she had every right to be there and reminded her mother that she had proven herself useful before.

"It's not that, Karli. Of course, I cannot do this—any of this—without you. But we don't know where Aguilar has eyes. Especially here. I want you to stay here and do not open the door for anyone. I will only be gone for one hour. And there's a TV."

"Dad doesn't like them."

"You have my permission to watch it. I doubt an hour of TV will harm you," Teodesia said in her most motherly voice.

Karli crossed her arms and scowled.

"At least light a candle from me to Daddy."

"Of course, dear."

A few minutes later Teodesia walked into *La Catedral.* She dipped her fingers in holy water and crossed herself. Then she dropped twenty pesos into a collection box and lit two candles for Bolivar.

Tomás was not late. He sat down behind her and used the kneeler to speak to her over her left shoulder. There was something different about his voice, something she sensed the first time they met in September, three months earlier. The years had changed him. He seemed all business. There had been an innocence in Tomás that she couldn't hear in his voice now. But he was there to help, and that was all that mattered now.

"Do you think you were followed?" he whispered.

"We used back roads. Stayed off the *autopista* … I don't think we were followed. Karli is at the hotel. We registered at the hotel with the Nicaraguan passports you gave us in September."

"We're probably safe," Tomás said.

"Yes. I think so."

"I'm going to work on the theory that once you and the kids are out of the country, the safer not only you will be, but Bolivar also."

"Out of the country? Where? Back to Nicaragua?"

"At first I thought about that as an option, but the truth is that Aguilar has people in Nicaragua. The American CIA buys their cocaine just a mile off the coast. No, Nicaragua is out of the question. You will go to Cuba."

"Cuba?"

"I have already talked to Castro."

"You can do that?"

"Teodesia, I'm not just a captain anymore. Yes, I talked to Castro on a secure line and told him as much as I could. He says that you are all more than welcome—you, Karli, Paco, and Bolivar as soon as we can get him there. He stopped short of sending any of his own agents there, but I think we can handle things from my end."

"Cuba. Bolivar loved it there. Do you think we will?"

"In many ways, it is a wonderful place."

"Tomás, did you read the obituary from the *Times* that Ms. Regier wrote for us?"

"The translation, yes. I thought it was fine. Now Ashcroft and Bush can give it a rest. That's something. Anyway, they can't very well extradite a corpse. But Aguilar still has him. Something that does work for us is that Aguilar hasn't seemed to make any friends in Cuba, and the Cuban security has managed to block virtually all inroads the traffickers have tried to build to their island."

"God bless them. What will become of them when Castro leaves us some day?" Teodesia asked, with all sincerity.

"I can only speculate. I'm afraid for them," Tomás said, shaking his head.

"Tell me more about the Spanish professor, Tahmina Zara."

"Tahmina Zara. I've been sending her emails, posing as a professor at Ave Maria University, a Jesuit university in San Marcos. With all this, I've had to get help from my staff. She knows me as Professor Jorge Martinez Saracho. First we ran a check on the name 'Francisco Barranca,' but we searched in the old paper files. It turns out that he is—or was, rather—a real man who lived in the Washington, D.C. area and taught at Georgetown. His Spanish was fine, at least as good as your husband's. The bastard even fought in Nicaragua, but with the Contras."

"And he is dead?" Teodesia asked.

"Dead or underground. Impossible to say. He might be a ghost."

"So the real Barranca is a wild card," Teodesia said, frowning.

"Possibly, yes."

"And if so, this whole thing could blow up in our faces," Teodesia exclaimed, raising her voice above their whisperings. "What do you make of Tahmina? Will she come to Nicaragua?"

"Maybe. There's nothing definitive about that. It seems she focused more on Castilian letters, but I think we can get her if we create a major conference. We're inviting her to be the keynote speaker, so she probably cannot resist. It's my understanding that academic egos thrive on these things. They get a chance to walk around a five-star hotel and pretend to be important. She sent me a proposal to talk about the Moors of Spain. Anyway, I have to assess her in person to know if we can create anything like trust."

"You're playing a vanity card, then. It sounds like there are too many *what ifs* here," Teodesia said, still with the frown on her face.

"There always are, Teo. But let's stay positive, okay?" Tomás said, trying to assuage her anxiety.

Tomás was the only person other than Bolivar who called Teodesia "Teo." He had been like a brother to both of them. But hearing him say "Teo" caused Teodesia to think back almost sixteen years to when she and Bolivar first sat in these same cathedral pews. Teodesia had come to visit Bolivar in Mexico City when he was writing *Vivaldi's Lovers*. The war was finally winding down. They had fallen in love in Nicaragua but there was too much sorrow there. They had needed time. Then, when Teodesia began to visit Bolivar in a new place, faraway from war and farther from their pasts, they gradually began to open like a couple of flowers after a hard winter.

"So, Tomás, since when are you not a captain?"

"Quite a while. I'm the Deputy Director of Nicaragua's National Security."

"Holy Shit!"

"Shhh! Teo, you're in a church!"

"Why didn't you tell us?"

"We don't advertise much."

"Bolivar was right. You aren't just resourceful; you also have the resources."

"Let's not get overconfident. We still need to discuss how we're going to get you to Cuba without Aguilar noticing."

"I'm listening."

Chapter 25

Rawalpindi

In 1999, Mustaf Asad suddenly found himself broke. His lack of attention to his legitimate business affairs and his obsession with his toys caught up with him and ruined him. The government seized what few assets he had to weigh against his debts. One by one he was forced to let go of his staff, the accountants, the servants, the gardener, and—sadly—his playthings, the women who were handmaids, as well as his crowning achievement, his creation of the most exotic, the most alluring and most delightful miracle, Ayesha Jalil.

Frantically, Mustaf Asad searched the drawers through the rooms of his estate, looking for diamonds and pearls, gold and rubies—all those gifts he had purchased to adorn his pets for dress-up times. Where could they be? The wenches had seen this day coming and sequestered them away, perhaps somewhere in the walls. He ordered his last servants to break open walls before their last day, which they did, but they found nothing.

Asad was less concerned with finding the hiding places of the girls than with finding Ayesha's. The jewels he bought were trinkets and fakes and the outfits were of cheap cloth. But he had dressed Ayesha in quality silks and real gold, rubies, emeralds. He had circled her neck with pearls and hung real diamonds from her ears to sparkle when the moonlight spread over his bed.

Ayesha's hiding place was a trunk, which she had buried in the garden. Only she and the peacocks knew where it was. When interrogated, all of the women said the same thing: the first servants to leave had taken everything with them and the master was a little busy enjoying opium at the time to notice the wealth being carried out the front door.

Finally, Asad had no choice. The police arrived to evict him, thereby setting free his harem. They had brought trucks with them to haul away his furniture and his paintings, some of which were valuable. Asad had no knowledge or interest in art, but among his collection was a small painting by Rembrandt, which had been missing from the Rembrandt House Museum in Amsterdam for over fifty years. Ayesha often stared at the painting, a portrait of a young boy. She marveled at the way a golden light illuminated the boy from inside out. In other paintings, the light came from somewhere outside and merely angled into the scene. But this painter knew how to make things glow. It was, she thought, a divine source of light.

A week after the estate was vacant, Ayesha returned with a bolt cutter and a shovel and retrieved her things. For a while she lived with a few of the other girls. The women were helpless. They had never learned any skills to survive on their own and had no education. They did not have much of an option but to become prostitutes. One of them convinced the others that they should use fake names and advertise on the Internet. They all agreed. Even Ayesha agreed to participate, but insisted they target westerners, possibly diplomats, and that they confine themselves to only the best hotels, like the Marriott.

Although rich with jewels and silk, Ayesha also did not know any other kind of work. She naturally assumed that her new freedom meant that she could pick and choose the man who paid to feel her breasts and penetrate her rectum. Men began to contact them immediately, and because Ayesha was the most exotic, she was the most highly sought after and made the most money, but Ayesha was generous and she kept the other women afloat financially when they weren't getting enough work.

Above all, they would have to learn to be quite discreet. Prostitution was illegal and the punishment was execution. Ayesha, ironically, was shielded from that fate since technically she did not exist in Pakistan—that is to say, according to official record, there were no eunuchs in Pakistan. It was deemed a barbaric practice and outlawed decades ago. Ayesha could not be prosecuted for the crime of being changed from a boy to a girl since the practice did not exist, and if the practice did not exist, Ayesha did not exist. If caught, she merely had to take off her clothes for the inspectors and prove to them that she did not exist. There was no law against "not existing."

It did not take the police long to discover the nonexistence of Ayesha, and once they did, they left her alone. She was free to wander around on her own. Her favorite place was the center of Islamabad, with its lovely shops and stores that catered mostly to the diplomatic community. Among the shops was a very large bookstore with air conditioning. One could wander around its aisles and enjoy the cool air for hours, and Ayesha was keen on learning how to read. She never bought a book, but she would open the books for children and stare at them. It was on one such day that Mohammed was also looking at books. Ayesha did not observe any of the usual customs—much like Mohammed—so when she saw him looking at a large book with diagrams, she sashayed over and asked, "What's that about?"

"It's a book about accelerators," Mohammed said.

"Show me more of the pictures, please."

Mohammed noted that she had violated social protocols, but he didn't care. They began talking and didn't stop talking. He invited her for a pizza at a place just next door to the bookstore and she joined him. That's where Ayesha told him she couldn't read. By the end of the afternoon, Mohammed had volunteered both himself and his wife, Zohrai, to be her teachers. Mohammed and Zohrai had lots of books in their house, and many of them were for children since Zohrai had two daughters from a previous marriage who lived with them.

Before Ayesha agreed to let Mohammed and Zohrai teach her how to read, she had to tell him about her "uniqueness." She did not want to like them only to face rejection later, so Ayesha leaned in and told Mohammed in a soft voice that she had been born a boy.

Mohammed responded with a curious look. "It must have been horrible for you."

"Yes, it was at first, but one becomes accustomed. What can you do?" Nothing in Mohammed's questions or facial expressions suggested judgment. On the contrary, he seemed incapable of casting judgment on her. So Ayesha liked him immediately and the next day she accepted an invitation to meet Zohrai, who also passed no judgments about her. Zohrai brought out a pile of easy readers and the two of them sat at the kitchen table to read.

All of this was a few years earlier. Today, Ayesha was walking to the market in Chaklala to visit Mohammed, Nasir, and Altaf who were having tea with a foreigner. She saw Ahmed get up and walk away in the other direction. *Good,* she thought. *He makes me uncomfortable, too.*

She wore a white scarf and a white sari that left her ankles exposed. On her left ankle she wore a gold bracelet that circled around and flashed through little clouds of dust churned up by her sandals.

Ayesha was the tallest, and perhaps the most beautiful woman that Barranca had ever seen in Pakistan. His tea went the wrong way when he tried to swallow and he coughed, spraying the tea out through his nose. Ayesha made a joke of it instantly.

"I have that effect on men," she said.

"Sadly, not on me," Nasir said, snidely.

"Nor me," Altaf said. "But you are beautiful. No doubt."

The young men were being quite familiar with their language around her. It didn't go unnoticed on Barranca. *Since when could a woman be part of a circle of male friends?*

Chapter 26

Mexico City, December 2003

Karli was pushing the buttons on the remote control until she suddenly stopped and with intense curiosity paused to watch a man and a woman making a baby on the television. The woman was whimpering—perhaps it was terribly painful. But then she was crying out for "more" and telling him to do it "harder" and "harder!" She squealed and he moaned. Then she started uttering "Yes! Yes! Yes!" intermittently with the panting, so Karli decided that the woman wasn't really in pain. Of course, Karli already knew how a baby was made. Her daddy explained it. But his explanation did not cover some of the details on television. For instance, why did this man now bury his face between the woman's legs, which only made her scream "Yes" all the more. You can't get a woman pregnant with your face.

About this time, Teodesia swiped her key card and came in the room. To her horror, she saw what Karli was watching and leaped in front of the television. "You turn this off this instant."

"Ok, Mother. Sorry, I thought it was an education show."

"Your father is right. There will never be a television in our house."

"Channel 820 has music. Would you like that?"

"Give me that thing!"

Teodesia turned the television off, and sat on the bed, trying to process her talk with Tomás. Bolivar, too, had written that they would need to go to Cuba or Nicaragua. Now it appeared they would be moving to Cuba.

"Mother, are you going to share? You saw Tomás, right?"

Teodesia nodded slowly. Then she tried to put a smile on her face.

"Karli, you have always wanted to travel, right?"

"Yep. Where are we going?"

"Cuba, I think. The short of it is that the sooner you and I are not in Mexico, the better chance your father will have."

"Then we go. Can we take Athena? We can't leave Athena."

Athena was their dog, a yellow Labrador.

"Athena can come later. In the meantime, she can stay with Francisca. We can only take a small suitcase, like the ones we brought today."

"What about the rest of our things? What about my piano?"

"Things are replaceable, Karli. People aren't. But we'll see if some of our things can be shipped. But later."

"When are we going?"

"I don't know. As soon as Tomás can arrange it. Maybe next week or next month. I don't know."

"Do you want to get some books for the library since we're here?"

"Your father would like that, wouldn't he?"

"Yes, he would. And we can find some that maybe Father Sebastián hasn't read already."

It was still early and the bookstores were open. Donceles Street was bustling with activity. Vendors yelled at people to buy kitchen utensils. A man with an upside-down bicycle was sharpening knives. Plastic yellow and red tarps flapped in the breeze over stalls filled with men's boxer shorts and pirated movies. A fruit vendor had built a series of small pyramids of papayas and mangos on the corner, and beside him an indigenous Mexican was burning copal and cleaning someone's impurities by whacking them with thin branches of tule. The street continued on beside the ancient temple, *Templo Mayor*, where the Aztecs made their sacrifices, collecting still-beating hearts in large urns. Teodesia felt that someone had taken her heart and often wondered if the thief would ever return it.

Chapter 27

Islamabad, December 2004

Nadia made one final effort to seduce Barranca. Her job depended on it. She pushed the record button and dialed his cell phone on a Sunday night in late December.

"Hello," Barranca said.

At first, Nadia didn't say anything.

"Hello? Hello? Who's calling, please?"

"I want you, Francisco," Nadia's voice dripped with a pathetic desperation.

It was the first time she used his first name.

"My body is crying for you. I need you," she whimpered. "I'll tell you everything. I kept copies of my reports, only please don't shut me out."

Nothing about Nadia surprised Barranca, but he played along. He wanted to know what sort of things she put in her report.

"Okay, Nadia. I agree to let you share one of your reports. Let's hear it."

"Here? Over the telephone? Wouldn't you rather have it in person?"

"Read one of them to me. I'm curious to know what you think is important."

"It's not what I think is important. I have to include whatever I can."

"Start by telling me who you write the reports for, ISI?"

"No," Nadia said, lying. "The School. They are for the Chancellor."

"I'm listening. Read."

"All right. This one is old." Nadia cleared her throat and paused awhile before reading.

Dr. Barranca had three cups of coffee, black with one sugar, in the morning between six o'clock and six thirty. From six o'clock in the morning until eleven p.m. when he went to bed, he smoked seventeen cigarettes. This morning in his American Literature class, he discussed the lyrical structure of Walt Whitman's "Song of Myself," correlating the structure of this poem to the structure of his life's work, "Leaves of Grass," likening the structure to an Orphic journey, or the psychological equivalent of the mythic passage. The students appeared to be interested, although I found it difficult to understand. When I questioned Serein, she said it wasn't hard to follow and claimed that Dr. Barranca is a genius. Serein may have been the only student who understood the lecture. I questioned both Humairas—Humaira Khan and the other Humaira Khan—and neither of them had ever heard of Orpheus, and they were not quite sure what Dr. Barranca meant by "lyrical structure." After class, Dr. Barranca walked to the verandah and had a late breakfast consisting of lentils and rhoti with tea-white. Three students visited him: Tabina, Samina, and Rafia. They stood on their side of the verandah wall. They asked him what they should write about, and he told them it was entirely up to them as long as it pertained to the class. After the students, I attempted to engage Dr. Barranca in questions, which he dodged. For example, I asked if his wife would be joining him, and he answered only "maybe." When Dr. Barranca finished his breakfast, he went to his office and opened his emails. See the attachment …

"What's in the attachment, Nadia?"

"Your emails."

"Go on."

Five students visited Dr. Barranca's office: Serein, Maryam, Sidra, Humaira Kahn (the pretty one) and Humaira Kahn (the not pretty one). When I questioned them, they all said that they wanted to know how long the paper should be and what it should be about. Serein, however, stayed the longest and asked many questions about Whitman, but I did not understand his answers. I questioned Sidra who makes a point of knowing as much as she can about what other people say, and Sidra informed me that Serein wanted Dr. Barranca to know that she was secretly a Sufi. According to Sidra, the two of them talked at length about an eleventh century Persian poet named Rumi. At three o'clock in the afternoon, Dr. Barranca went to meet his chauffeur and the Captain at the gate and was taken back to his safe house in Chaklala. Sahib reports that he sat at his desk and read for several hours, forgetting to eat his dinner. At nine o'clock in the evening, he came downstairs to the kitchen and fixed a bowl of instant porridge. A little after ten o'clock, a bomb exploded five blocks from his safe house. Sahib reports that he came outside in his pajamas and said something to him in English, but Sahib does not speak English. The geology professor who is also residing at the residence told Dr. Barranca that it was merely a transformer that exploded and that such things were common. Dr. Barranca went back to bed.

"That's it. That was my report for Wednesday, September 3rd, 2003. Would you like to hear September 4th?"

"No."

"I'm touching myself, Francisco. Francisco …" She moaned.

"Go right ahead, Nadia. I'm hanging up now."

[*Click*.]

Chapter 28

Jlalpan, 2005

Teodesia and Karli had begun reading everything they could find about Pakistan as soon as they learned where Bolivar was. The place was frightening to them. "It's worse than having Zetas running around," Teodesia said.

"Look at this, Mother!"

Karli pointed at her laptop screen …

"This young girl had her face burned off with sulfuric acid. It's horrible. Why would anyone do that?"

Teodesia winced and read the article …

"It also says," Teodesia said, "that other women did this to her, claiming she was a prostitute. But she wasn't. She was just a student at school called 'International Islamic University'."

"And," Karli said, "there are lots of them! They do it for reasons they say are religious."

"Indeed! Religious! That's precisely the kind of thing your father hates about religion, how people abuse it or twist it to feed their own corrupted souls. Or maybe they don't even have souls."

"Do Muslims have souls, Mother?"

"If they're people, they must have souls, but you would have to ask Father Sebastián that. I don't know anything about Muslims. I only know that most of them don't like Americans, and your father is an American."

"Shhh. We aren't supposed to be talking about stuff like that, except in the tree house."

After that, Teodesia got a long cable and put their router in the tree house, so they could keep reading about Pakistan in the safety of Paco's fortress.

"This article says that a journalist was kidnapped in Karachi and got his head chopped off, like what happens up north," Karli said. "Same as here! Daniel Pearl."

"Daniel Pearl, yes, I remember hearing about that. In 2002, before your father was there."

"According to *El País*, General Musharraf used his control of the military to overthrow the state and name himself the president."

It was February 2005. Things were taking longer than anyone thought, including Captain Tomás. But finally, two airline tickets for Cuba arrived by special delivery. It was time for them to leave Mexico. Karli and Teodesia walked Athena over to Francisca's house next door. Karli had written out ten pages of words and sentences that Athena understood, as well as descriptions of Athena's gestures and bark-types for communicating her wants and desires. Teodesia carried Athena's bag full of toys. Their own suitcases were already packed. They had been packed for months and stored in an upstairs closet. Karli was allowed to take two books.

"We'll get you more books when we get there," her mother told her.

They asked Father Sebastián if he would drive them to the airport with their car and if he wouldn't mind keeping the car for them "until they got back," which was going to be never, but they didn't tell him that. On the way to Mexico City, they also asked him to go in the house and cover the furniture with sheets and lock up the house.

"But you're only going for a couple of days," he said.

"Well," Teodesia said, "we might decide to stay longer."

Karli could see that Father Sebastián was worried. She knew that he knew they weren't telling him the truth, but it was for his own protection. They didn't even tell him they were going to Cuba. They told him they were going to Cancún.

"It's a good time to go," Father Sebastián said. "The weather is perfect and you will be there in plenty of time before the American college students take over."

Karli wasn't the sort of person who could keep something to herself once she got a thing in her head. They weren't halfway to the airport when she blurted it out:

"You're in love with my mother, aren't you!?"

Father Sebastián blushed like a raspberry. You could see the color rise up from his neck to his forehead. Karli had never seen anyone blush as hard as that. But Father Sebastián gripped the steering wheel.

"Karli!" her mother shouted. "Wherever do you get such ideas?"

"Are you?" Karli asked the priest again, defiantly.

""To be in love,' well, no," he said. "However, I do admire your mother greatly. She is a very good Catholic and a brave woman. And, she has raised two terrific children."

"No," Karli said, "I mean that you want to make babies with her, don't you?"

"For heaven's sake! Karli," her mother shouted. "You're embarrassing the Father. And Karli, you know very well that priests aren't permitted to make babies."

"It wouldn't stop them from wanting to. That's all I'm saying."

Father Sebastián took a large breath, held it, and then let it out slowly.

"No, Karli. I do not wish to make babies, not with your mother, not with anyone."

"I thought priests weren't allowed to lie," Karli said.

"Karli!" her mother shouted again.

"Well, if you want to make babies, you can make them with me—that is, if you wait till I'm old enough—but not with my mother. My mother is spoken for, okay?"

Father Sebastián did not know what to say. He could wax endlessly about the great philosophers—like Unamuno—but in matters of teenage sexuality mingled with his pent-up desire for her mother, he found himself at a loss for words.

Chapter 29

Rawalpindi, October 6, 2005

PROFESSOR Q HAD MANAGED to reach some of the girls through a campaign of terror. Most of Barranca's first year graduate students were about to defend their theses and graduate, and Q was threatening to veto their degrees. Serein visited Dr. Barranca again about the problem, hoping that he would be able to stop her.

"She has reached some of them. I think Professor Q has recruited the girl who is to be the leader."

"And?"

"It's Sidra."

"Oh. Oh no."

Barranca remembered one of the first times he had heard Sidra stand and rally the women. Whenever Barranca tried to lead them out of their parochial darkness, Sidra was there to lead them right back to their caves. She led them in how to torture the poems, the plays, the novels until they said what she wanted to hear. Hemingway's Frederic Henry in A Farewell to Arms was a soldier in the First World War—perhaps the most senseless of wars. "He loves Katherine so much. He loves her with a love that is stronger and more primal than any arbitrarily determined allegiance to a state, so he defies the system and goes AWOL. The two of them row a boat across Lake Geneva where she can have her baby and they can lead normal lives."

"But sir!" Sidra had said. "He is a traitor and should be executed. None of our great soldiers of Pakistan are cowards. They do not run from their duty."

And Humaira No. 1 had been very quick to agree.

Then there was the day they discussed a story by Faulkner. Emily, in "A Rose for Emily" had grown very old. In her youth she could not bear to let her man leave her—so, in Hitchcockian fashion—she kept his dead body with her in bed.

"But sir!" Sidra Kahn said. "This cannot happen in Pakistan! No one is that sick!"

That was when Serein tried to counter her ...

"Sidra, maybe it is possible. I read an article about a necrophiliac in Rawalpindi. The police caught him digging up the body of a young girl the night after she was buried, and he confessed to the police that he did this because he 'loved them'," she said, making air quotes.

"Was it his wife?" Maryam asked.

"None of them were his wives and he confessed to dozens."

Sidra was indignant and reasserted her position amid much head nodding in agreement …

"That sickness exists in America; but it does not exist in Pakistan or anywhere in the Islamic world. It's a taboo!"

"Ah," Barranca said. "Let's explore this. Do you have a taboo that forbids you from eating cats?"

"Of course not," Sidra replied. "No one eats cats."

"Well, where I'm from no one eats cats either, and we have no taboo that says we may not eat cats. Do you see my point?"

Most of the class looked at him and squinted their eyes, so Serein decided to help them understand.

"The point is that if you have a rule about something, it means that someone is breaking the rule," Serein explained.

"That's right. And speaking of cats, you just read Hemingway's "Cat in the Rain" from the book *In Our Time*. What do you make of it?"

Humaira No. 2 answered …

"We have a saying. If a cat dies, the CIA did it."

Everyone laughed. Barranca smiled. Humaira No. 1 spoke up …

"Sir, it is difficult to feel any sympathy for a cat. The woman stands in the window shaking and feeling sorry for a cat, but what for?"

"She's projecting, maybe?" Barranca said.

But the conversation did not get much past this point. The girls had suddenly erupted at each other over theological divisions between Shi'ites and Sunnis with regard to the status of cats in Islam.

"Cats are filthy and bring evil!" Maryam said.

"No," Rafia said, "in the Hadith, the prophet interrupted his prayers to pet a cat. Therefore, cats cannot be evil."

It got very out of hand after that. Barranca had to raise his voice …

"Girls! Girls! Ladies, please! Tonight, I want you all to read the story again, but this time, I want you to change the word 'cat' to 'dog' and then write down how you interpret the story differently, the story 'Dog in the Rain'."

"But dogs are unclean, sir!"

"No, they aren't! Everyone knows that the Holy Prophet praised a prostitute for giving water to a thirsty dog."

It was clear they were on the brink of calling each other vile names, names such as "whore." One whispered something barely audible … "Sunni propaganda …" but Barranca could not tell who had said it. And he too was beginning to lose his composure, saying in a voice tinged with perceptible anger …

"Is there any text whatsoever in this …"

He stopped himself from saying "godforsaken."

"Is there any text whatsoever in this classroom that we might read and discuss without having to rely on Hitler's autobiography, the Holy Koran, or the Hadith?"

Suddenly the girls were silent. They could sense he was getting angry. Finally, Serein explained …

"Unfortunately, sir, there isn't. All books must be considered in light of the Holy Koran."

"It's fine, Serein. I want you all to forget about it. Class is over today, but I want to leave you with an idea, one that you read in Whitman. 'I am no stander above men and women or apart from them'."

Sidra spoke out again.

"But sir, we are all one percent inferior to men. It is written."

Francisco put his books in his satchel and said again …

"I am no stander above women." And he walked out the door.

Months passed. Barranca, some days, told himself he was making progress with them. He wanted his students to think independently, but now Qadir was on campus, preaching in the classrooms, lecturing them in their dorm rooms nightly where she lived as their housemother. By now she had simply become known as Q. She was not an isolated example either. Extremists had been infiltrating the universities since the 1970s. All of them were sympathetic to the Taliban or the Wahhabis. Some of them were sons and daughters of the Taliban warlords. Humaira No. 2's grandfather was a Wahhabi leader somewhere in Kashmir, and she was only allowed to attend school because her father sent her in an act or secret defiance of his father's iron fist. Q probably had similar blood ties to the extremists. Cycles of violence and vengeance had been playing out this way down through history.

When you want to defeat an enemy, you send in a Trojan horse, a corrupting influence. The Americans had allowed it to happen when they elected Ronald Reagan—immediately he appointed an anti-education department secretary to try to dismantle the Department of Education; an anti-environmentalist to "take care" of the environment, an anti-United Nations ambassador to obstruct progress with other nations, and so on down the list of government agencies. And, like Pakistan, he claimed to reduce the size and cost of government while his massive expenditures for the military sent the national debt to new heights.

Now Barranca was trying to think of the right words in response to Serein's revelation about Sidra. Serein was possibly the only freethinking graduate student, but Barranca was also aware that he was a strong influence on her and he knew that she might confuse his comments for directives.

"It makes sense that Dr. Q would go after Sidra. She's a natural leader and she's already inclined toward Q's turbid way of thinking, or rather the inverse of thinking. Have you spoken to anyone else about this? I mean, on the faculty?"

"No, sir."

"Other students?"

"Yes."

"What do they say?"

"Mostly they're afraid if they don't go along with Sidra, they'll be reported to Dr. Q and be expelled from school or fail their thesis projects."

"Most of you still have one year—that is unless you apply for doctoral studies."

"And we could lose our teaching assistantships."

By this time, some of Barranca's students had been hired to teach the undergraduate courses—among them, Serein, Maryam Haq, Humaira No. 2. On decisions like that, Barranca still held rank over Q, despite whatever dark forces brought her here.

"Sir! There's a scorpion on the wall behind you!"

Barranca calmly turned around and took off his shoe, giving it a heavy whack. When it fell to the floor he stepped on it with other shoe to grind it into a harmless state.

"These old boys sure have strong armor."

Nadia showed up at the door—supposedly with some papers to sign.

"Not now, Nadia … Come back in an hour."

The bounce in her step had left her. She had been defeated and ISI had taken most of her duties away from her, except that she was still to deliver weekly reports and shred Barranca's reports to the Higher Commission. Barranca barred her from sitting in on his classes. Now she wore a defiant frown but said very little. Not even "sir."

"An hour. Fine."

When Nadia was gone, Barranca and Serein continued.

"Does Sidra have a plan?"

"Sidra's plan—or Q's—is to … well, as they put it, 'punish the whores in Islamabad'."

"By that I take it they mean the students who attend the International Islamic University … why? Because it's 'coeducational.' What nonsense! They are among the most conservative Muslims in all of Pakistan. The professors lecture from behind silk screens. Dividers run down the middle of the class so the men do not see the women and the women do not see the men. The teacher doesn't see them. They don't see him. They're all blind, as blind as Ahmed's falcon!"

"Ahmed?"

"A friend. Never mind. Go on. Tell me what you know."

"Dr. Q has convinced Sidra to form … how do the cowboys put it? a 'posse' and 'punish them'."

"Who is inclined to join this posse?"

"Both Humairas, Simba, Hina, Tabina, Rafia, and the two Maryams … so far. Also Nadia. There are a few others. Only Samina has verbally resisted. She would rather be expelled than hurt someone. Me, too. I haven't opened my mouth, but I think Dr. Q and Sidra know where I stand."

"Good for Sidra. Good for you! Let's try this. First, you have not spoken to me. This conversation never took place. Type out a message, in Urdu, that says that the police are aware of these plans and assault charges will be brought against any person at the women's college who is planning to harm another student—any other student. You do that. Slip these under their doors when they're asleep, including Q's door. Don't let the message get back to you or to me. In the meantime, I have some friends who have contacts in the police. Also, I know some of the faculty over at Islamic International. I will work on giving them a heads up and have a talk with a policeman whom I think is an honest and decent man. Maybe we can prevent this."

Serein seemed relieved. Still, it was just a plan. Their countermeasures might not be enough to stop the frenzy Q had whipped up in some of the students. Sidra and Humaira No. 1 were clearly certain of their moral duty. The others were going along out of fear for the consequences if they disobeyed Dr. Q.

Barranca shook his head, remembering something that he could not share with Serein. *"All of them," Nadia had said. "All of the girls had had their clitoris removed by their mothers and grandmothers by the time they were eleven or twelve. We can't really feel a thing," she'd said, and "anyway, sex is for the husband." That was how it was "supposed to be." It was true for the women at the International Islamic University, too. It was true of women all over the country. "We were sewed back up with cat gut." Some of them had wiped it out of their memories. Others, some nights, would sit on the edge of their bed and look down at their mutilated genitalia. Even if a woman wanted to have sex with a man, she couldn't derive very much pleasure—perhaps she might form an emotional connection, but sexual pleasure had been literally cut out of her.*

Chapter 30

Managua, Nicaragua, October 6, 2005

By the autumn of 2005, Tomás had exchanged dozens of emails with Tahmina Zara—or rather, Professor Martinez Saracho had. For this Tomás had enlisted specialists in both Latin American letters, as well as Castilian, and he had to persuade Ave Maria University to hold a conference. Since Tahmina was to be the keynote speaker, he also had to find the funds to cover all her expenses and her honorarium.

The two biggest obstacles in his way were that he himself did not know enough about the world academics lived in or the world that Tahmina Zara lived in. In order to get her there, he had to create an actual academic conference, with actual professors willing to come to Nicaragua to pontificate for an hour and then sit around the bar at night, getting drunk, as they went on pontificating with bleary eyes. For every email Professor Martinez Saracho sent to Professor Zara, Professor Zara sent back an email with a dozen new questions, none of which he could answer on his own as Zara wished to "debate" the legitimacy of Christendom's claims on the Iberian Peninsula. "Get me someone whose an expert on Spain from the 11th to the 15th century," he yelled to an assistant. "This lady has more questions than an old man has aches and pains!" But Tomás persisted in nailing her down to a commitment and the conference would be held in January 2006.

In the meantime, in one of his *emails to her, he, or rather his helpers, put a little indirect question to her. We don't suppose you know of an English professor, Dr. Francisco Barranca? We heard that the esteemed professor was teaching in Rawalpindi.* To which a reply came back with a dozen new questions and a *PS, Yes, I met Dr. Barranca at a little get together in Islamabad just recently. How do you happen to know him?* "How do we know him? How do we know him? Jesucristo!" One of his assistants rushed into Tomás' office and handed him an article from a journal. It was a book review that the actual Barranca had written about a Chilean poet, Nicanor Parra, in the 1990s. It was not a very flattering assessment of his work—in fact, even Tomás could see that this actual Barranca was … *un pendejo* (an asshole).

After Tomás telephoned Teodesia in Cuba to let her know *He's alive! He's okay! Plans are shaping up!* He got his assistant to figure out an answer to Zara's Barranca questions. *One of our colleagues here at Ave Maria has read some of his articles and used to be in touch, but that was several years ago. He'd read something somewhere that mentioned he was teaching in Pakistan.* After that, Tomás worried, what if this real Barranca shows up? "Sir," one of Tomás' subordinates said. "He fell off the map sometime after the war. And we think he was CIA. If he's alive, he is probably working with an entirely different cover by now."

Tomás simply did not know enough about Aguilar's operation to probe very deeply. He would have to wait until he got Zara alone. When she came, he would assess whether or not he could trust her, and then give her only enough details necessary to help him get to India. Something like: *So, Dr. Barranca could be a little disoriented. It would mean a lot to the friends he made in Nicaragua if you could look out for him. Think you could at least convince him to take a break? Maybe take him on holiday to India? Our colleagues here remember him as a bit lost on his own.* Tomás knew virtually nothing about the Islamic world and hated it whenever one of his inferiors questioned his plans or pointed out the cultural differences. "She may be married, Colonel," an assistant pointed out to Tomás. By this time, the operation had become officially named *A Passage to India* and officially presented to president Ortega, who signed off on it without stopping to mull it over. "If you can," Ortega said, "pick up intel on the CIA's involvement with the cartels along the way, then it will be worth our efforts, and we will share it with Fidel and Hugo," by whom he meant Fidel Castro and Hugo Chavez, the president of Venezuela.

Chapter 31

Rawalpindi, October 6, 2005

AFTER HIS MEETING WITH Serein, Barranca cancelled his usual weekend trip, the trips he made to analyze curricula and interview faculty. He walked into Nadia's office and told her to telephone Karachi University and ask them to reschedule. Nadia did not even ask why, nor did she look up from her desk. She just affirmed his request with an abrupt nod and picked up her telephone. Then Barranca went down to find his chauffeur. The Captain and the driver were both pointing southwest on their prayer mats with their rumps sticking up in the air—it was the middle of the afternoon prayer. So Barranca got in the car and waited. When they finished, he instructed them to take him to Chaklala market before going home to the F10 Sector safe house.

There was Mohammed and, luckily, Ayesha too. They could see from the furrows on his forehead that something was amiss. Barranca didn't waste any time.

"There's a situation. I really don't know what to do about it. Some of the girls at the women's college are planning an attack on women who attend the International Islamic University."

"Acid," Ayesha said.

Mohammed nodded.

"Acid?" Francisco asked.

Mohammed explained …

"They steal sulfuric acid from their chemistry department and use it to burn away the faces of women they disapprove of."

Ayesha was looking down at her large feet, which were the only thing about her that wasn't especially feminine. She seemed lost in thought.

"Where are they planning this attack?" Mohammed asked.

"Near the mosque beside International Islamic, we believe," Francisco said, with his head down.

"Why there? They're really conservative over there," Mohammed said. "But I don't know anyone there who could help stop this. Ahmed might know someone there."

Ayesha interjected …

"I know someone."

They waited for her to continue but she was hesitant.

"Ayesha?" Mohammed asked. Ayesha was staring off into space …

"The Chief Constable sends his daughter there. He used to be one of my clients." There was a sense of resignation in her voice.

Thinking about what she would have to do with the Chief Constable sent a chill of regret up her spine. It wasn't so much him she detested but how they had met. She had met the Constable to answer some routine questions about her owner, Mustaf Asad. Ayesha had been a suspect in a crime involving him and so had to answer questions for a day and a night until the Constable was sure she was innocent. Now she was remembering the last time she saw Mustaf Asad. She could see his face in the dim lamplight, a face of horror and bewilderment, and she could hear his scream, delayed by the shock for a moment. As he opened his eyes, he saw her veiled figure holding his bloody penis just inches from his face. Its blood dripped and droplets coagulated in his unkempt beard. She made no expression, neither with her eyes nor under her veil. She had felt nothing. After she was sure Mustaf had had a good look at his penis between her thumb and first finger, she walked over to his apartment window, ignoring his screams, and dropped it. It fell like a plucked, wingless bird, and landed with a thump several stories below. When it did, it roused a pack of sleeping dogs.

"Can you talk to him?" Mohammed asked. "Can you reason with him?"

Ayesha was slouched over, still in her thoughts.

"Ayesha?" Mohammed asked again. Then she raised her head and answered …

"It isn't that easy. I've never contacted him before. He contacts me. I've never contacted him. And also he'll want something."

"No, Ayesha. Forget it," Barranca told her.

Barranca felt helpless. Now he had involved more people in a potential tragedy. By trying to avoid a tragedy, we often cause the tragedy. Ayesha would let the Constable "do" her for free if he promised to stop the attack. And that is what she did, only he did not stop the attack. Five women were brutally assaulted. The Constable's daughter was home "sick" for the week. The attack was the night of October 7th.

On Saturday, the 8th, Bolivar was sitting in his safe house looking out the window at the lonely women who were combing their hair by their windows, some of them just sitting and staring out of the apartments they were not allowed to leave. A few children were outside playing, some riding bicycles and some playing cricket in an empty lot. Many of the husbands who lived in the adjacent high-rise apartment had left their wives alone in their very small apartments to go walking in Islamabad Park with their friends.

Barranca could not recall exactly when it began, but suddenly the cupboard doors were opening and closing as if a poltergeist had entered his house. The floor was bouncing up and down. It was an earthquake. He tried to get up but fell. He got up again and reached his doorway. The middle of the high-rise had a huge crack zigzagging down its fifteen-story wall. So did another high-rise beside that one. The children who had been playing cricket were on their hands and knees. Both of the towers came down, first the one in front of him. The crash was so loud that Barranca could not hear anyone screaming. The air filled up with cement dust.

When both buildings were down, the living began to wander over to the wreckage in a daze. A few men had already begun lifting pieces of rocks and brick out of the way of faint cries they could hear inside. Francisco looked west toward the Afghani refugee camps and wondered if God despised this country so much that he willed it to be wiped away. Then he remembered that he doubted that God existed.

By the end of the month, the world reported that tens of thousands, possibly as many as one hundred thousand people were killed in those minutes. Whole villages disappeared in landslides in the mountains. What was one man who disappeared? Still, he wanted more than anything to tell Teodesia that he was alive. *Teo, I'm alive. I'm still alive.* He did not even know that she was safe in Cuba. He could barely remember how long he was away. He could not remember when he'd lost hope, but he had.

Then he heard sirens, but the emergency vehicles were blocked by debris. They were sirens with no end. Men with donkeys and carts were there to help with the broken cement. Someone had a generator that was able to power a jackhammer. Francisco tried to locate the faint little cries he was hearing from somewhere below.

Chapter 32

Managua, January 2006

As soon as Karli heard the news in *La Granma* and saw the horrible picture of earthquake wreckage, she tried to remain calm, though she was trembling when she went to tell her mother. Teodesia immediately picked up the telephone and called Tomás, but no one knew anything. They would have to sit and bite their nails. Teodesia began praying, constantly. Karli would find her in the middle of slicing a tomato, her body frozen all but for her hands that chopped methodically and her lips that were muttering a prayer for her husband.

In November, by happenstance, Tahmina Zara sent her paper topic and outline to Professor Martinez Saracho (Tomás) and just happened to mention that she'd run into their old acquaintance, Dr. Barranca, at a conference on Gender Studies and Islam at the Islamabad Marriott Hotel. (Both of them had managed to escape injury when a suicide bomber made it just inside the hotel lobby entrance, killing seventeen teachers—the same hotel, a year later sustained a more substantial, more "newsworthy" suicide bomb.) Only when Tomás called did Teodesia learn that her husband was okay. Tomás had written back, as the Professor, "Would you mind letting him know for me that Professor Emeritus José Espejo sends his regards from Nicaragua." So Tahmina Zara sent Barranca an email saying, "Professor José Espejo sends his regards," but she left out the words "from Nicaragua."

When Barranca got the message, he did not know what to think. He wrote back, "Thank you, Dr. Zara." He didn't say that he didn't know anyone by the name. It would be three long months before he knew anything about *A Passage to India* or that Teodesia and Karli were safe in Cuba and his son had left and gone to America to join the Marines. By this time, however, Paco had been wounded in Afghanistan and sent home. Ms. Regier had given him a job out of good will, a little pity, and her sense of allegiance to her friend, his father. Save for a handful of people—Ms. Regier, Karli, Teodesia, Tomás and his staff, Aguilar and Williams and some of their employees, and Fidel Castro—

most of the world believed that Bolivar Collins was dead. Teodesia did not even trust Paco enough to tell him the truth.

The conference went forward as planned. Academics from various countries gathered in Managua because the town of San Marcos and Ave Maria University were too small to house them all. Tahmina Zara had never felt such humidity, but the evenings were cold in the highlands. She was greeted by two professors at the airport, Professor Martinez Saracho and Professor Emeritus José Espejo—Espejo was enrolled to catch stray balls. Maybe Zara would go off on some obscure piece of Spanish literature, in which case Tomás (Martinez Saracho) could only nod his head up and down or side to side and Espejo (who had actually been a bona fide academic) could jump in and comment on the finer points of Cervantes, San Juan de la Cruz, Fray Luis de León, the anonymous poet of *El mío Cid*, or a hundred other Spanish writers. They were ready for her.

After the keynote address, Tomás and Espejo invited Tahmina to the hotel bar.

"We don't drink," she said. *We* meaning *Muslims*.

Espejo jumped in.

"Of course, we mean to have you join us for tea. We've much to learn from you. You know, our countries share a common enemy," Espejo said cajolingly.

"Right. The Americans," she said. Professor Zara expressed very little personality in her voice when she spoke. It was difficult to surmise her views from her tone.

"They fought us here in Nicaragua and now they are dropping drones on you," Tomás said.

"And yet you are friends with Barranca," she said, almost suspiciously.

Tahmina Zara looked at them blankly. Espejo answered quickly:

"Ah, but he was different. He cannot be blamed for the aggressions of America any more than you can arrest one man for another man's crime. The Barranca I know would never condone an attack on your country, or ours for that matter."

"I suppose you're right," she said, though reticently. "Mind you, I've only met him a couple of times, but he doesn't give off the impression of being the John Wayne sort. So tell me, Professor Martinez, what did you write your dissertation about?"

Espejo had coached Tomás on just this question. After meeting her, however, they had come to think she would not ask any question since her sole preoccupation was herself. Tomás answered: "I wrote about our national play, 'Big Daddy Rat.' It's a folk play that has just won the UNESCO prize."

It was the perfect answer because their research had revealed that Zara knew absolutely nothing about Nicaragua and her profile indicated that she would immediately veer away onto a topic she knew something about. Espejo quickly changed the subject: "Would you mind taking back a small present from me to Dr. Barranca? It's only a book I think he would like, and some cigars. We would like him to know that he's not forgotten. Will you?"

"Well, I don't really know when I'm going to see him, but I suppose I can tell him to pick it up."

"Splendid! You are very kind," Espejo said.

"Very kind, indeed," Professor Martinez Saracho said.

"And may I say," Espejo said, "your thesis is quite right. Spain should return Andalucía to the Arabs. It's high time."

Tomás wanted to know one more detail …

"What a pity it is that our two countries do not have consulates. How, if you don't mind the question, did you manage to arrange your visa?"

"I applied for an in-transit visa at the Indian Embassy. From your office in Mumbai, I received my visitor's visa for Nicaragua."

"I see," Professor Martinez said. "Well done."

"We have a gift for you," Espejo said.

"And your honorarium, too," Martinez said.

"And this is the gift for Dr. Barranca," Espejo said, pulling a box from his satchel.

Zara put Barranca's gift in her tote bag and opened her present: Café Premium Segovia.

"Coffee," she said.

"It's made especially here in Nicaragua for exportation," Espejo explained.

The next day, still tired from travel, Professor Zara flew from Managua for Mexico City. There she changed planes for a flight to Mumbai. Finally, in Mumbai, she boarded another airplane for Karachi. From Karachi, she took an hour flight to Islamabad. When she got to her home in Islamabad she promptly dumped her tote bag in a corner of her bedroom, opened her suitcase, removed her toothbrush and toothpaste, brushed her teeth and went to bed in the middle of the afternoon. By the time she woke up, she had completely forgotten about Dr. Barranca's present, what appeared under their wrapping to be a book and a box of cigars.

Chapter 33

Rawalpindi and Islamabad, 2005-2006

BARRANCA WAS CHANGING. He began to look older, much older. And he had fevers but did not yet know that he was in the early stages of typhoid. He did his work, all of his work, but nothing more. When he did not have to work, he slept. The summer months of 2005 had been quite busy. He taught only one class of summer school, but he had to make more trips to Anoosh's bookstore and Mahmood's rug shop. In June, July, and August of that year there were six Sundays that fell on prime numbers. June and July were the busiest. June 5th and 19th were letters K and N, respectively: Kate Chopin's novel *The Awakening* and the name of the boat was PT-109, JFK's boat that got sawed in half in the Pacific, recounted in his autobiography, *Profiles in Courage*. N stood for N. Scott Momaday, author of *House Made of Dawn*, and secluded in its pages was the message *Crusoe's raft with no name leaving June 24 Stop*. Barranca thought, *How fitting that I should be passing a ghost of a message regarding a raft that probably never existed, built by a man that was invented by Daniel Defoe who presents the man as "real" until gradually we realize that he was a storybook man, only to learn later that maybe he had been real and Defoe had based his version of Crusoe on the misfortunes of an actual lost man*. "Oh, how I doubt my existence." All those ships, boats, and clippers in Robinson Crusoe and Defoe leaves them nameless. July brought the 3rd, 17th, and 31st. The 3rd was Q for Quintilian. *What?* thought Barranca. Williams is taunting me. Quintilian's wife died very young, so says his work, *Institutio Oratoria. And anyway, his first name was Marcus. Marcus Fabius Quintilian. Now for the boat … The Queen Elizabeth 2 leaving July 9 Stop*. On July 17th, Barranca's hand pulled from behind the other books *The Complete Poems and Plays of T.S. Eliot*. He scanned it like a machine scans a bar code. *The Falcon leaving July 23 Stop*. Barranca thought, *I remember that the Falcon was one of Sir Walter Raleigh's ships. It left England in 1578 to engage the Spanish. Maybe. What does it matter?* On July 31st his hand found a book by the American poet, Wallace Stevens. It was *The*

Auroras of Autumn and it was the first edition. There were only a few of these and they were very expensive.

"Anoosh!" he called. "I have found a book I want, but I have to pay you a little more than the penciled price on the inside cover. It wouldn't be fair. This book is worth quite a lot more."

The message inside, which otherwise bastardized a perfectly good first edition, was the embedded name of a yacht owned by Francisco Franco, the dictator of Spain—*Azor. Azor leaving August 6 Stop.*

August and September followed. August 7th. September 11th. Each time magic carpets flew from Mahmood's little shop of tapestries.

Like Crusoe, Barranca was sick with loneliness. Like the late poems of Wallace Stevens, he too had become brooding and filled with regret. Like Quintilian grown old, he missed his young wife. So it was in this weakened state that Barranca became careless, dangerously careless.

In August 2005, after 10 o'clock at night, someone knocked on the door of his house in the F10 Sector of Islamabad.

"Hello. I am Masood. I am your neighbor."

Before him stood a man in his mid-twenties and well dressed. Barranca noticed that he was wearing a gold Cartier. His white shirt had wide lapels and the two top buttons were undone so that he could show his chest, which he had also adorned with a gold chain.

"Hello. Can I help you?"

"No. Just … Well, we would like to invite you to our party, next door."

"A party. Actually, I was just about to go to bed."

"Tomorrow is Sunday. Do you have to work tomorrow?" Masood's voice was insistent.

"No. But …"

"Come then. We have … you know … drinks."

Masood lowered his voice when he said this and looked side to side.

"Actually, Masood, alcohol is illegal in Pakistan. I'm not opposed to it, but I can't jeopardize my position, you understand."

"Of course, of course … We also have Coca-Cola."

"Some other time, perhaps? Thanks very much."

On the following weekend, he received another knock on the door. Again, it was Masood.

"We are having a party, Dr. Barranca."

"I don't recall giving you my name," Francisco said, eyeing him for the response.

"Oh, oh ... my girlfriend recognized you. She is your student Serein's friend. Serein says you are a wonderful teacher. So you will come? We are going to play roulette."

Barranca wondered to himself if everything Masood did had to be illegal—yet another invitation to do something that could get a foreigner deported.

"Well, Masood, it's almost ten o'clock and I'm not really the party type. It's kind of you to ask. Goodnight, now."

"No problem. But can I introduce you to my girlfriend? She studied in America at Princeton and now she goes to Wash U, a university in St. Louis. She really wants to meet you. You know, all the nice things people say about you." Masood's style of begging was surreptitious and fake.

"Oh really? Sure, bring her by sometime," Barranca said, but in reality he couldn't care less.

"Tomorrow okay?"

"Let's see."

"Tomorrow is Sunday. You don't have to work," Masood said.

"Fine, tomorrow afternoon? High tea?"

Barranca had mixed feelings. He wanted to be left alone, really, but something else inside him was crying out for company. Even a couple of young kids in their twenties. He needed to be distracted. He knew that he was falling deeper into loneliness and was beginning to be plagued by dark thinking. *Maybe I will just turn on the gas and go to sleep*. And very often he didn't feel well, physically. Some nights he woke up with a fever.

Barranca closed the door and for the first time looked at the unplugged TV sitting by the front window. Maybe just having voices in the house would help him snap out of this increasingly heavy feeling of darkness, heavy like a granite capstone on a tomb.

Barranca plugged it in. A fuzzy white noise filled the room and the TV emitted a white light that illuminated the cold pale-green ceramic floor. It was an old black-and-white TV, the sort he hadn't seen since he was a child on his grandfather's ranch. His grandmother would stop everything precisely at 2:30 in the afternoon to watch a soap opera called *As the World Turns*. When it finished at 3:00, she turned it off and jumped back up to continue her chores. It was the only time he ever saw their television on. At eight o'clock in the evening, she finished her work, and sat in her chair to read. Grandfather sat in his chair a few feet away, but he seldom turned on the television. *Black and white. We think things were simpler then, but they probably weren't.* Barranca turned the nobs until there was a picture. A local Imam was lecturing on correct interpretations of the Holy Koran. *Whatever*, thought Barranca, *he has a voice*. The lecture was in Urdu so Barranca understood all of it.

His name was Mohammed Al Dost, "Al Dost" meaning "your friend." Mohammed Al Dost cited surah and āyah, chapter and verse, presumably to drive to some interpretive conclusion. He had a deep voice, not a bad voice at all. That was all Barranca wanted anyway. He went into the bedroom and puffed up his pillows and sat on the edge of the bed. *Maybe I will let him talk as long as he likes*. It was a voice of authority. The sort of voice one imagines God would have when one is a small child. Barranca lay back on the bed and listened to the voice of "his friend."

The storage cupboards in the bedroom were high up over the closet. One of them was just a little bit open, so Barranca went back to the living room area to get a chair to stand on. With his bad leg he should not have been standing on chairs, but he thought *so what if I fall and break my fucking neck*. I'm going to close the storage door. Barranca dragged the chair to the bedroom and pushed it against the closet. Then he stepped up on it with his strong left leg, bringing his weaker right leg up next. Before he closed it he opened it wider. Oddly there was a bag inside. It was pushed all the way to the back where it wouldn't be seen and couldn't be reached. So Barranca went back to the living room to get his cane, which he only used when he absolutely had to.

Mohammed kept talking to him the whole time. Barranca did not know that his "friend," Mr. Al Dost, had a twenty-four hour a day show, every day, running in loops, like the evangelist Pat Robertson in America he watched for ten minutes when he was a kid. It was called *The 700 Club*. Robertson smiled though. He said the most horrible, hateful things, but he always said it with a big smile.

Returned to the bedroom with his cane, Barranca got back on the chair and gently pushed the bag to within his reach. *Too light to be concrete.* Now his "friend" was raising his voice and screaming, "Death!" *Yes,* thought Barranca, *Tomás has forgotten me. Teodesia has forgotten me. If the devil exists, I just keep on lending him a hand.* There was the letter from Karli, then nothing. And, as far as the world knew, Bolivar Collins was officially and most definitely dead if Teodesia got through to Ms. Regier and Tomás. And knowing Teodesia, she did. That much he counted as certain. Whether or not they were safe or whether anyone cared anymore was as uncertain as living in this tragic land of dust blowing and dry loaves, the distant thunder over the dead scrub that crawled over the dry Margalla Hills.

It can't be flour, whatever is in there. Barranca took the bag to the kitchen where there was better light. It was a powder of some sort in an unmarked brown paper bag, like a bag of sugar or flour, and the bag in turn was inside a clear plastic bag. Barranca took out his penknife and opened it. It looked like flour but it was somewhat more brown. He sniffed it. It wasn't flour or sugar, or salt or anything else. Barranca licked his finger and stuck it in the bag to collect a sample. "Death and purification!" screamed his "friend" on the television. When he touched the powder to the tip of his tongue, his tongue became numb. He rubbed a little on his gums and they became numb.

Barranca backed away from the bag and sat down in a chair. *This is a kilo of heroin.* What was it doing here? The only thing in the house was its ragged furniture, some kitchen things, bedding, and his suitcase, which had always to be packed. *What is a kilo of heroin doing in my closet storage? No one just ups and leaves a kilo of heroin lying around.* Maybe his friend on the TV wasn't his friend. Al Dost—"friend"—was drawing to his conclusion. "Death … purification … a pure and unadulterated Pakistan cleansed of all infidels and apostates … death to the Shi'ites … death to the Hindus … death to the Christians who live in their filthy ghetto. Allah commands you to destroy your enemies! Destroy them in the name of Allah!"

Barranca got up and turned off the television. *There are 130 million people in Pakistan. 8% of the population is Shi'ite; about 1.5 % is Hindu; and .5% is Christian. The Christians and Hindus live together in the ghettos, not unlike the Jews in Warsaw. 10% of the population.* Barranca's "friend" wanted to murder thirteen million people.

Barranca took the bag to the bathroom and poured out its contents into the toilet. When he did, a cloud of brown smoke mushroomed up from the bowl and covered his face. As Barranca turned the water on in the sink to wash his face, he felt lightheaded and the pain in his leg—the pain that was always there, that had been there for fifteen years—faded away. Barranca flushed the toilet again. Now quite woozy, he took the brown paper bag to the front door. Outside there was a trash can and … no guard. Where was the guard? There was always a guard. For three years there had been at least one guard, and usually two. Barranca took his lighter and set fire to the bag and placed it in the empty trash can and watched it burn. *Purification … Fire …* He was only vaguely aware that ISI had put the heroin in his safe house. *If they cannot get something on me, they'll invent something. They're not going to let me leave—not Williams and not the ISI.* Something, even if only defiance, passed through his bones … *I'm going to live. They may kill me, but I will do everything I can to live.*

Barranca made sure the gas line to the kitchen was turned off and then went to bed. In his dreams, he could see Teodesia's face. When he was awake, he couldn't see her face anymore. That night he dreamed that she was in Nicaragua and Captain Tomás had secured the three of them inside a fortress on top of a mountain with an army of Nicaraguans whose sole job was to keep them from harm.

On Sunday morning, Barranca woke up and couldn't remember Teodesia's face, the face he was just dreaming. He walked to the window. The Captain was sitting in a chair outside the door with his shotgun leaning on his leg. Barranca knew that if he opened the door the Captain would snap to attention and greet him. Instead, he looked for something to eat and a book to read.

Sunday afternoon, the Captain knocked on the door to announce his visitors. "Sir!" he said, which was one of the ten English words he knew. Barranca indicated that it was okay to let them pass.

"Hi! I'm Fatima Abbas. I love Americans," she said with a twenty-something year old's energy, which is just a little too much energy if one is not twenty-something.

"How do you do?" Barranca said, more reservedly. "Please, come in and be comfortable. It's another very hot day."

"I've been looking forward to meeting you for so long. I'm from Pakistan. Well, not really, now I'm from St. Louis. Do you know St. Louis?"

Masood stood back and let her work.

"I guess I do. I've had occasion to visit." In that moment Barranca nearly slipped; he nearly said that he was *from* St. Louis, but he caught himself. Bolivar was from there; Barranca was from San Miguel de Allende.

"And you went to Harvard, right?"

"No. Princeton. You don't have any accent at all," Barranca said. "And you shake my hand like an American girl."

"Yeah, St. Louis! Go Cardinals!"

"What part of St. Louis," Barranca asked.

"University City."

"No kidding," Barranca said. "I used to have friends there." Actually, Bolivar Collins grew up there.

"No, I'm not kidding," she said and gave him a playful slap on his chest.

Barranca noticed that she was wearing a brown cotton skirt that didn't quite reach over her knees, and she didn't have a scarf to cover her head. Any ordinary girl would be picked up by the police for the infraction.

"So," Barranca said, "the two of you live here in this house beside me. We share this same wall."

"We only come here sometimes," Masood said. "For parties! You know, I keep inviting you, man!"

"Right. Parties," Barranca said. "Well, come in and let me fix you some tea."

Very attractive couple. And she even wears a little makeup—also against convention but not against their civil laws, not expressly. Still, the police would pick her up … unless … unless she is ISI. She'd just wave them off with her ID.

"I will just put the pot on. So, tell me, will you be going back to St. Louis eventually?"

"I'm here to visit my parents, and Masood of course, but I'm doing my graduate work at Washington University."

She's good. Much smoother than Nadia. Nevertheless, ISI, Barranca thought. *Let them play their game. I've nothing to lose anymore.*

"Tea-white or tea-black," he turned to them to ask.

A few days later, because Barranca had given up any hope of ever going home, he fell in Fatima; to be sure, not "fell in love," just fell in. What's more, he knew that she wasn't real.

Chapter 34

Cuba, 2006

Teodesia was having a bad day wondering if the professor—"Zara"—had followed through. Karli suggested they get out and go do something. So Teodesia and Karli went to see the Museum of the Revolution. All the way, Teodesia looked up at grand Spanish facades and down the narrow streets and wondered if Bolivar had walked down this one or that. She wondered what his life was like those years he had lived here with Renee and their little girls. Karli saw that she was lost in her thoughts …

"What are you thinking about, Mother?"

"Only about how happy your father was here. How good his life was here in Havana."

"It will be again, Mother."

Teodesia sat on the seawall and looked over at the waves lapping against the brightly colored boats. She began to cry.

"I'm sorry," she said.

Karli put her arms around her.

"He's coming back, Mother."

"I really don't think so. I'm so sorry, dear."

Teodesia was crying so hard she was shaking and it made Karli cry, too.

"He's coming back, Mother. He's coming back," Karli said, sniffling. "In the meantime, we have to live—you know—the way Father would want us to. He would want us to be happy."

"I know … It's that I know him. He will only make it through this if he knows that we're okay."

Chapter 35

Rawalpindi and Islamabad, 2006

In September of 2006, Barranca began his third academic year. New students arrived each year. Some of the undergraduates were now beginning graduate school. Samina had finished her master's degree and replaced Miss Nadia as Barranca's assistant. She was soft-spoken and attentive, but if she were a spy she showed no signs. She never asked Professor Barranca personal questions and Barranca didn't ask her questions, beyond a polite conversational level. After his first class with the new graduate students, Samina stepped up and asked him if he would like her to order his breakfast. She could call to the kitchen boys from her side of the little stone wall of the verandah.

"Thank you, Samina. You are very kind."

Samina brought with her a strange calm. Bombs went off a block away, or two blocks away, and Samina didn't even duck, jump, or scream. Barranca had asked her why.

"I'm not sure. I suppose it is because it's not within my control or anyone's to decide when or how they will die. I choose not to worry about it."

Barranca had nodded to affirm that way of thinking about it. He only learned much later that her family was killed by a Taliban bomb that Pakistan insisted was an American drone attack. Thousands were killed by American drones, but such was not the case in that instance. Samina was Punjabi and the killers were Pashtos from the Northwest Territory. Whoever set off a bomb—Musharraf's ISI, the Americans, or the Wahhabis or Taliban—a bomb was a bomb. And her family was gone regardless of whoever's twisted ideology. Barranca could tell no one that he had also lost his family in the same way, in Nicaragua. Bolivar Collins had; Francisco Barranca had not.

The first day of school that year began on a Monday and Barranca went to park himself beside the bottlebrush tree. The sky was blue for a change and it was even unusually cool. A Great Gray Heron swooped over the campus grounds. Then Hasam came to drink a cup of tea. If only Barranca could sew up Hasam's lips or convince him to leave him alone … but no. Hasam began his usual drumbeats around a bush, spiraling in verbose circles to great heights until he was ready to set his bush on fire.

"I am working on a new project, Barranca."

"Oh? What's that?"

"I am going to write a book and maybe you can help me. You have some experience publishing?"

"A little. Not so much. What is the book about?" he asked, not really wanting to know.

"You!" Hasan exclaimed.

"A book about me?"

"The likes of you, I mean."

"And what would that be?"

"You know. The Cold Warrior. Ronald Reagan on a white horse charging around the world, picking on the weak just because they are weak."

"I think you know that I don't subscribe to that sort of foreign policy."

Hasam always began these fraudulent "exchanges," which he called "dialectical," with an up-tempo beat. He reminded Barranca of his happy waggly Labrador, Athena. But unlike Athena, Hasam suddenly changed his demeanor, like a dog with rabies, his sick grimace appearing. He turned and affixed a look of deep and terrifying hatred and spit his words through clenched teeth …

"I long for the day I may kill Americans. You will be the first one I kill."

As soon as he said it, his amiable demeanor returned as quickly as it had disappeared.

Barranca got up without finishing his breakfast of lentils and bread.

"Excuse me, Hasam. I've some handouts to write."

"Yes. Okay. To be continued, as your American televisions say."

After school, Barranca got in the backseat of his car with the Captain. The other guard was posted outside his house in F10 Sector. Some days, on the road back to Islamabad, they had to pull over. Musharraf's office was in Islamabad, but his fortress/house was in Rawalpindi, so they often crisscrossed one another along a narrow road that was heavily guarded. Nevertheless, it was a dangerous road, sometimes mined by the Taliban. Occasionally the Taliban launched mortars at Musharraf's motorcade. Other times, automatic gunfire broke out on both sides of the road and the heaviest casualties were always the commuting civilians. On this day, no fighting broke out on their road.

Bolivar said hello to the guard outside and opened his door. Fatima had music playing—contemporary jazz. Barranca was delighted: Keith Jarrett's *Köln Concert*. He adored that music for its spontaneous and rhapsodic surges. He was convinced Jarrett had listened over and over to Brahms and Gershwin. Fatima was moving about the house lighting candles, wearing only expensive panties and one of Barranca's white t-shirts.

"Did you have a hard day, my darling Paco?"

Fatima put her arms around Barranca and kissed him passionately, moving her hands around his hair and down his back. She smelled so good to him. She wore just a little perfume. She was beautiful and needed very little makeup to accent her dark brown eyes. She had no blemishes except for a tiny scar over her left eyebrow. She was taller than most women, though not as tall as Teodesia. As he kissed her, though, he imagined that she was Teodesia and he pretended that he could see her face, only it was Fatima's face now.

"Do you want me?"

"Yes," Barranca said. "You know I do."

"Do you want me right now?"

"Yes ..."

Fatima took his hand and pulled him and unzipped him and sat him down on the edge of the bed where they made love and where they continued to make love as often as they could on Mondays, Tuesdays, Wednesdays, Thursdays; in the morning and after work; and Sunday nights when Barranca returned from Peshawar or Lahore or Karachi. But she was not Teodesia. She moaned differently, moved differently. She even screamed when she climaxed, and she wouldn't lie there with him quietly afterwards. She always jumped up and went to the kitchen for a cigarette and then came back in the room and started to talk, sometimes about things she read in the news.

"Do you want a cigarette, too?"

"Okay," Barranca said, sitting up.

"You smoke more than I do," she said, "maybe more. I want some wine. Do you want some wine?"

"Yes, bring me a glass, too."

Fatima walked around naked after sex. She came back to the bedroom with two glasses of wine.

"How do you know I'm not poisoning you?" she joked.

"I wouldn't care if you did, Teo."

"What? Whose Teo?!" She put down the glasses of wine.

"I'm sorry, my mind was drifting … I was just remembering a time in my life years ago. It's nothing. Fatima, forget it."

Fatima faked a frown.

"Don't let that ever happen again. Understand? Or I'll put a knife in you, right here," she said, with her stiffened index finger over his heart.

"It won't. I'm sorry."

"Drink your wine. I added a potion to make you love only me."

On Sundays Barranca even took Fatima along to the bookstore. He no longer cared if ISI literally wanted to fuck him. Fatima's body felt good and she was tolerable, or perhaps it is more accurate to say, that she was able to play her role as well as the best actresses. She was a mirage. She was the water Barranca could see in the desert and he knew it wasn't real, but he didn't care. He thought about his assistant, Samina. So easy going despite chaos. *Samina's way is the right way. We shouldn't try to control so much. We should just live.*

On one particular Sunday in September—it would have been the 17th—Fatima asked him why he hadn't taken her to Chaklala to meet his friends there. Barranca had to think quickly. He hadn't wanted to involve them in this affair with an ISI agent.

"You wouldn't like them. They're only interested in physics."

"What are you saying? You don't think I'm smart?"

"I think you're very smart. I just didn't think you were interested in physics."

Barranca did not want his friends put on ISI's watch list, but he realized that it was probably too late to prevent that. In fact, they were being watched since the first day he met Mohammed and his friends, including Ayesha.

"So, what's the book you bought from Anoosh?"

B for Bernard. Bernard Malamud's The Natural. *The ghost ship in typos floating backwards through the pages is Nellie leaving September 23 Stop. Nellie is the name of the boat in Conrad's* Heart of Darkness.

"*The Natural.* Do you know it? It's by Bernard Malamud."

"Didn't they make a film out of that?"

"Yes, but they messed it up. Hollywood has Robert Redford, a baseball player, hit a homerun on the very last swing of his life."

"Yeah! I remember that. Hits all the lights and he runs around the bases in a blaze of glory. Typically American. Very upbeat. I like it," she said.

"The novel is better. He swings and misses."

"How better? That would be awful!"

"Because Malamud wanted to say that in the end the thing that mattered was the player's wife and family. All his life he thought that baseball was all there was. Staring him right in the face the whole time was love and he didn't know it. When he swings and misses, he finally gets it."

"I still think it's better to swing and hit the ball. He could have his family, too."

"Okay, well, we have both versions," Francisco said to placate her.

"So, what do you need these books for anyway, especially if you've already read them?"

"They're for the students."

"And the rug?"

"Oh, I always get two birds so to speak. My wife ..."

"Isa."

"Right. Isa likes them. Some of them she keeps and some she gives to friends."

"And she lives in Mexico."

"That's right."

"What's life like there?"

"It can be very lovely. Maybe when you're back in St. Louis you can fly down. It's not too expensive from the States."

When they got home, Fatima acted like she wanted to have sex. Just once in the morning wasn't enough. When they got inside the door she started to rub him and press her thigh hard against his pants.

Barranca let her but as he did his mind started to drift into memories. Carmelita was a little drunk that night. She'd made up a little jingle, *whores and spies and everyone lies*. And there were times when Barranca could see a blank look on Carmelita's face, like the real person inside her were dead. Now he could see the same look on Fatima's face. He was a job to her. Her affections were no more real than Carmelita's were for Aguilar or his foot soldiers.

The following Sunday, the 24th, was Ramadan and Fatima was moaning and moaning until she let out her little climax cry. When she was having her cigarette, Barranca asked, "You aren't exactly religious, are you?" Although, it was more like a statement.

"Of course I am. Why do you think that?"

"Because today is the first day of Ramadan. Don't you want to be with your family?"

"I will be."

"The sun will be going down soon," he said.

"Really? I wasn't watching the time."

As she was dressing, Barranca started to ask her questions. Subconsciously, he wanted to "out" her. He wanted her to know that he knew.

"Did you ever eat at Talayna's?" he asked.

"Where?"

"Talayna's. It's an Italian Restaurant."

"Really, where, here?"

"In St. Louis."

"There are a lot of restaurants in St. Louis, babe."

"There's only one Talayna's. You know. You lived in University City. You said you went to Wash U. Come on, tell me where it is."

"Are we playing trivia?"

"You go to Washington University. You're taking time off, but you go there, and you don't know where Talayna's is … Hmmm."

"What are you driving at, Paco?"

"I'll give you a hint. It's just off Forest Park Parkway … on …?"

There was a seriousness in Barranca's eyes, not playfulness.

"What difference does it make?"

"Forest Park Parkway … on …what avenue?"

"I gotta go. No more time to play. Ramadan and all. See you later."

She gave him a peck on the forehead and left.

"DeBaliviere Ave!" Francisco shouted as she got into her car.

Barranca wanted her to know that he knew she was ISI, but she probably already knew he knew.

On October 29th, Barranca went to the bookstore and stayed awhile to talk to Anoosh. *E for Edmund Spenser's "The Fairy Queen." The boat is the African Queen, leaving November 1 Stop.*

Chapter 36

Nicaragua and Cuba, October 15, 2006

Teodesia was having breakfast when her telephone rang.

"Tomás!"

"We have news. Finally, we have some news. There's an email on my computer from Tahmina Zara."

"That's the Spanish professor."

"Right. Let me read it to you … She says, *Dear Professor Martinez Saracho, I'm writing to apologize to you and to Professor Espejo. I changed my email after I got home from Nicaragua and forgot to inform you. Anyway, I have just found your emails and I so want to apologize. I completely forgot to deliver Dr. Barranca's present, but this morning I have rectified that. I sent it immediately to him in care of the Women's College. He will probably have it by the time you read this email.*"

Teodesia was quiet. She was trying to process what this meant.

"Teodesia, it means that he will know you are okay. He'll know to go to India. We have even sent him the documents he needs and we have sent him the letter from Karli, as well as yours."

"You mean, he might be home for Christmas?"

"If he's careful, and he is, he may be home for Christmas, yes," Tomás said.

"Oh, Tomás!"

Tomás could hear her crying and he heard Karli in the background.

"Mother, what is it?"

There was something of the old Tomás in his voice, or Teodesia imagined there was. Before he said goodbye, he said …

"I understand, Teodesia. Love you. Give Karli my best."

"Wait," Teodesia said. "Is it safe to write to Paco now?"

"No. You should wait on that. Soon, though."

"Thank you, Tomás. May God bless you, Colonel Tomás, my little brother."

"Okay. I better think about what to pack. I'll be going to India soon."

"God Bless you, Tomás. God Bless you! I love you!"

Chapter 37

Pakistan, November 14, 2006

In Islamabad, a courier with Dr. Barranca's present from Nicaragua forgot to make his delivery on October 15. A month later, he had to be in Rawalpindi and decided to deliver it then. Samina signed for it at the gate and took it to his office where it was sitting when Barranca returned from his morning class. He looked at it. It puzzled him. *I don't recall anyone named Espejo.* Barranca almost dismissed the package as some sort of mistake. *Sent over by Professor Zara.* Then he read a note inside an envelope taped to the outside.

Greetings Dr. Barranca,

We in Nicaragua hope this package finds you well. We hope that you enjoy the enclosed packages. And we wish to meet again soon.

Slowly it dawned on him … *Nicaragua! This is from Tomás! Oh my God! This is …*

He carefully opened the packages. *Cigars from Cuba? I don't smoke cigars … Wait. Why wouldn't he send cigars from Nicaragua? Cuba! They're in Cuba! Oh my God, they got out!* He opened some of the cigar cylinders and began breaking them up in his hands. They were cigars. He opened more cylinders. One on the bottom felt empty. *What's this? A letter!*

Samina knocked on the door.

"May I come in?"

Flustered, he put down the letter. The broken cigars were in plain sight.

"What is it, Samina?"

"Just a memo from the Chancellor about your trip to Lahore on Thursday morning."

"Thank you, Samina."

Samina looked curiously at the broken cigars on the table and then pretended not to notice.

"Is everything okay? Do you need anything?"

"Ah, yes," Barranca said. "Would you call my chauffeur for me? Tell him that I would like to go home early today."

"Of course. The fevers again?"

"Yes."

This was true. His fevers were back. He had typhoid and still didn't know it. But it wasn't why he wanted to leave. He wanted desperately to know what was in the letter, but there was no privacy at work. Barranca brushed the broken cigars into the wastebasket. He rolled the letter up and put it back in its tube and put the tube in his pocket. The other package, a new paperback that was sealed in cellophane—*La Poesía de Rubén Dario*—he put in his satchel. Then Barranca shuffled together the papers he needed to grade and placed them in his satchel. He took his cane and went down to find his driver.

He beat Fatima back to his house in F10 Sector. Once inside, he immediately opened the letter. It was three pages. Page 1 … Barranca had not read or spoken Spanish, which had become like his own native language, for almost four years.

My Dear Bolivar,

Rest assured that we will get you home, finally. First, as you will read from them, your wife and children are fine. Our concern is you. You will have what you need to come home, open tickets from Islamabad to Mumbai where I will be waiting for you. It's important for you to let me know that you are coming. You can do this with the following email address, which you should use at a cybercafe. Write to me at Martinez.saracho@avemaria.edu. *Write this from an account we established for you in gmail,* passagetoindia@gmail.com. *You can access the account using the password teopacokarli1960. When I receive your email, I'll leave for India and find you at the Gateway Hotel. Register as Francisco Barranca. I will be registered as Tomás Martinez Saracho. Once you get there, just trust me to take care of the details. Now I'm sure you want to read the letters from your wife and daughter.*

Just one more thing. We've had to change all your names. We're using Teodesia's last name … So, start getting used to being called Segovia. We're letting your kids keep their first names. Yours we've had to change for your documents in Cuba—Bolivar Collins may wish to write more books, but if so, they'll all be posthumous now, ok? Your name is Roberto, or Robert if you insist.

Page 2 … dated, January 1, 2005

My Dear Bolivar,

When you get this, your ordeal—our ordeal—will be nearly over. As you realize now, Karli and I are in Cuba. Paco isn't but he is okay. I will simply tell you now that I think your son—in his own way—went off in search of his father, albeit in his troubled, misguided way. He is okay now. He went to America. For a short time, he was in Afghanistan, but now he is living in New York. Ms. Regier gave him a small job working for her. Oh! Your posthumous memoirs were published! It's a great book. Stuff in there I didn't know about AND we're going to have to talk about that when you come home. But congratulations on getting the world to believe you died. (You died in a car accident in Nicaragua.) Yes, another car accident in Nicaragua! And this one was bad enough to actually kill you.

Cuba is wonderful. The people have been wonderful to us. President Castro had us come visit him. His health has been failing lately, but he wanted to meet us. We didn't stay long. He only wanted to tell us that he was happy that he could help. He said to tell you "anything for his friend" and to say "farewell to arms"—he said you'd know what he meant. Also, he personally had his secretary find our house. It's smaller than our house in Jlalpan, but it's fine. Karli's piano arrived. It takes up most of the living room. Some of your books—sorry, not all—made it. Karli and I try to stay busy. I've gone back to work at a local hospital. It's about the same pay I was making eighteen years ago in Aleya.

Tomás has been wonderful to us, and to you—if you only knew what he had to go through to make this happen. So be safe and don't be stupid or you will ruin all his hard work.

Bolivar, I love you. I will always love you. Some days, I have strange feelings about living here in Havana where you and your lovely family before us lived and were so happy. But sometimes, good things circle around again. We hear the same songs again, only they sound different—still good, but changed. Sometimes the song even sounds better. At least I think so.

We won't ever give up. Tomás says that when you know we are safe you'll do whatever you can to find us.

I'm holding you, dear …

Love,

Teodesia

Page 3 … dated January 1, 2005

Dear Daddy,

I really really really miss you. I'm going to have my quinceañera! All I really want is to see you, so even if I'm sixteen or seventeen, you have to promise me to throw me another party! Daddy, we're all fine, even Paco, even though he isn't here and swore in a postcard that you ran off with a new woman (like your dad did) to make another family. He called you a "pathological family maker." But he only writes these stupid things because he wants to be closer to you and doesn't know how. So, he goes off to fight in a war! Can you believe that? And there he was, right across the border in Afghanistan. He got what soldiers call a lucky wound, his shoulder, but it really messed him up for fighting.

Did you get my letter to you written just like you write, like sheets in the wind? Pretty smart—eh? You're pretty clever too, Daddy—"Paco's Tree House." I know you're asking … and YES I do my homework. I like most of the subjects. I don't always like the books they choose. Did you know that Cuba has censorship? It totally sucks! But president Castro told me I can read anything I want as long as I don't pass the books around. Just now I'm reading your book, Vivaldi's Lovers. It's not too bad. But boy, that guy sure was one horny dude—relax Dad, I'm a little older now. I even know some things you forgot to mention regarding how babies are made, etc … Anyway, relax, Daddy, I'm just trying to tell you that I'm not a little kid anymore—I want to prepare you for that so you aren't shocked when you see me.

Athena is here! She barks her love. Remember our neighbor Francisca? She took Athena to an airplane in D.F. She had her very own ticket. She did have to stay in Dog Jail for a month, though, and Cuba never charged her with any crime.

I can play Rhapsody in Blue, now. Got it nailed. You'll see. Or "hear" rather. Did you write any new books over there? Guess we'll find out. Come home as soon as you can. There are lots of seagulls here—I assume you are still goofy for birds.

Love,

Karli

PS. Here's Athena's signature, too.

The letter ended with a big splotchy paw print.

Bolivar … Barranca … Bolivar … Robert … whatever his name

was now, he was laughing the laughter that turns swiftly to tears and back again to laughter. The laughter of funerals and weddings and when babies are born.

Barranca grabbed his cell phone and dialed Fatima. He didn't want to see her. She answered …

"Yeah, I'm on the way. I'll be there in about five minutes."

"I'm sorry, Fatima. I'm not feeling well. I'm just going to go to bed. Do you mind if I cancel?"

"Did you take any medicine? You need me there to take care of you."

"No. No. I'll be fine. I just need to go to bed. Really."

"You sound funny. Everything all right?"

"Fine. Do you mind, please? I'm sorry, but I'd like to be alone tonight. Maybe I'm just getting old."

"Oh. Oh. I get it. It's the ol' 'I-have-a-headache' excuse. I thought only we women used that one."

"Fatima, please."

"All right. Whatever. Tomorrow then."

She hung up. Barranca put on his jacket. There was a wet chill in the air outside and he did have a fever. He stopped in a shop to buy some aspirin and then went to a cybercafe in F10 Sector to answer. He logged on to the internet with the account Tomás provided and kept his message short.

Dear Professor Martinez Saracho,

Message received. We owe you our lives.

Yours,

Robert Segovia

When he got home, he took the aspirin and went to bed, but it was impossible to sleep. He kept hearing his wife's voice and he tried to imagine Karli's fingers playing Gershwin. *How was it possible? She could barely get through the simplest pieces by Chopin and Erik Satie … the last pieces he had heard the week Aguilar's men threw him into the black suburban. Paco in a war? In this war, here? In the middle of this mess? Here … in the militarized zone … we were just on the edge of it, not in the heart of it. Oh, Paco … what did you do?*

Barranca's mind was racing out of control. He got up out of bed and paced around the house. He wanted to pack a suitcase and go to the airport. His tickets, a new passport with a visa for India, were inside a small rectangular hollow cut out of the book with a framer's knife, an Exacto knife. Probably by Tomás. Before the civil war, Tomás had been a painter. Maybe Tomás had taken it up again.

Barranca tried to go back to bed, but five minutes later he was up again. He got his needle and thread and took his corduroy jacket from his suitcase. He unstitched the inside lining and put his new passport and the letters inside the jacket. Then he wanted to turn on his own laptop but stopped. No, he couldn't do that. *Get a hold of yourself or you'll end up blowing the whole thing.* So, he tried to go back to bed again, but he couldn't close his eyes. It was the first time he could picture his wife's face in a very long time.

At three o'clock in the morning, his cell phone rang. *The VC? Why would the VC be calling at three in the morning?*

"Hello?"

"Dr. Barranca, we're going to have a visitor this morning. We need you at school by five o'clock."

"Most unusual."

"I'll explain when you get there."

Chapter 38

November 15, 2006

BARRANCA'S CAR DROVE THROUGH the gates of the women's college a little before sunrise. Samina was already standing beside the circle drive.

"Hi Samina, what is going on?"

"There's a meeting in the Chancellery. The VC told me to direct you to join them there."

Barranca shook his head in disbelief. The sun was barely up and there's a meeting. When he opened the door to the Chancellery, the VC shook his hand and explained: "We received a call just before I called you. Prince Charles and Lady Camilla are paying us a visit at eight o'clock. You're our most senior faculty member, so you'll be having the honor of being their guide. They'll be meeting some of the students and visiting classes as soon as they arrive—between eight and nine—then you'll bring them here to the Chancellery for some cakes, coffee, and tea. The press is already starting to arrive. Whatever you say to them, make us look good."

"Me? Not Q?"

The Chancellor looked embarrassed and said …

"I have asked Q to stay at home today. It seems that MI6 views her as a threat."

Then the VC began her instructions …

"After our little rest and conversation, the Prince is going to give a speech in the auditorium. You'll be seated on the front row with the rest of us."

"Such short notice. I suppose that's the way they do things," Barranca said.

The VC shook her head *no* and told him the reason they were coming to the women's college.

"It seems your president decided to drop a very large bomb on a madrassa near Peshawar, very near to where the royals had intended to go. Only America forgot to mention this to England."

"George W. Bush."

"That's right. The dead number over fifty and none of them were over the age of eight," the VC said.

"Why?"

"The Americans claim it was a terrorist training camp."

"Oh my God."

"They also believed that Bin Laden was there or thereabouts," she said.

"He is," Barranca said. "It's not a secret in Pakistan."

"He is, yes, near there. But not there, not at a boys' boarding school. Anyway, there are ways of doing things," the VC said, and it was clear that she had nothing more to say about it.

"What else do you want me to do today?"

"When the other faculty arrives, I want you to tell them to line up in the rose garden. The Prince and the Duchess, Camilla, will be greeting each of them. Have them tell their students to behave properly. Miss Nadia's class can gather around and sit in a circle in front of Jinah Hall. After their visit to some classes, the Prince and the Duchess would like to talk to them informally. Here's an itinerary in case you forget anything. They'll be tired, so they'll be leaving as soon as the Prince gives his address. Where they are staying is only on a need-to-know-basis, and we don't need to know."

The royal motorcade was on time and the administrators and faculty were in a perfect queue. Members of the Pakistani and British press who had been properly vetted were ready with their cameras. The moment Prince Charles emerged from his bulletproof limousine, hundreds of cameras began batting their shutters like an oversexed teenager batting her eyes at a movie star. Camilla was next, wearing a yellow silk scarf over her head to show her respect for Islamic custom. They moved slowly through the line—trained diplomats—asking each person a question. Charles was personable; he seemed so by nature. When he arrived at the Chancellor, the Prince said …

"And may I extend an apology on behalf of the late Prince Edward for standing you up. I've been informed that this palace was built to receive him."

The Chancellor laughed a little, nervously. She was obviously starstruck. The cameras didn't stop shuttering.

Dr. Barranca was standing beside General Khan, and when the Prince reached him he exclaimed: "By God, if it isn't Bolivar Collins!"

At this moment, Barranca was suddenly aware that the press cameras were also photographing him. He instinctively tried to shadow his face with his left hand while shaking the Prince's hand with his right.

"Oh, no, sir. I'm Dr. Barranca. I've been told I resemble him."

"Camilla!" Charles said, turning to his wife who was asking General Kahn a question. "Doesn't this chap look like that author you like so much? You know, Collins?"

"I get that a lot, Your Royal Highness," Barranca said.

"So, Dr. Barranca, what do you teach?" the Prince inquired.

"English."

"Any Shakespeare?"

"Yes, sir."

"Oh well, don't believe everything you read. You know, Richard III wasn't as bad as Shakespeare made him out to be. And you know the work of Collins?"

"Yes, sir."

"Let's have a chinwag later, shall we?"

"Yes, sir. I think we're having tea after your visit with the students."

"Splendid. It's really uncanny, you know."

Camilla shook his hand.

"You do, you know."

"Yes, Your Royal Highness."

"Good to know his likeness lives on."

Then the moment had passed. A journalist for *The Times* of London zeroed in on Collins' face and snapped the photograph that an editor published in the following day's paper. The editor called Ms. Regier Toulet in New York—at 4:30 a.m. New York time—to ask her if it could be him. Her first response was: "Don't you read the papers in London? Bolivar Collins died in a car accident in Nicaragua. I have a copy of the death certificate."

But the editor kept pressing. Then Ms. Regier decided to confide in him.

"Look, yes. It's him. But if you publish a picture it will sign his death warrant. Do you really want to do that?"

"But how?" he wanted to know.

"It's a long story. Publishing anything about it could get him killed and probably his entire family. I urge you strongly to resist."

"So, you knew he was alive and willfully lied to the world?"

"I have no comment and *The New York Times* is off the record. It's 4:30 in the morning here!"

But the next day in London, *The Times* ran with the story anyway, under the headline, "The Prince Meets with Bolivar Collins."

"An anonymous source at *The New York Times* has confirmed that the American writer, Bolivar Collins, was fraudulently declared dead by their paper in order to protect his identity and whereabouts ..."

But by the time the news became public, Collins (Barranca) was already on his way to Lahore to meet with faculty members at the University of Punjab about some curriculum changes there.

Before the news had broken, when Prince Charles and Lady Camilla had finished talking to dozens of the students, the VC escorted them to the Chancellery and servants brought out tea and cakes on silver platters. The Prince and Lady Camilla asked General Kahn and the Chancellor if they might be allowed to sit next to Dr. Barranca.

"Don't get up, Doctor," the Prince said.

"Your Royal Highness," he said to the Prince and then to the Duchess.

"Camilla and Charles," Camilla insisted. "We prefer to drop the titles now. The film's not rolling, you know."

General Kahn, Hasam, the VC, and the Chancellor were the only others in the room, which appeared much larger, lined with full length mirrors that the Sikh princes who built it for Edward were inspired to model after the hall of mirrors at Versailles. It made the four surprised functionaries' open mouths seem all the more gaping.

Prince Charles ignored them.

"Say, Dr. Barranca. I'm terribly sorry if I caused a bit of theatre this morning. Let's forget about all that. Tell me about yourself."

"Well, Your Royal Highness, with all the photographers out and about, maybe you could set them straight? I am just an English teacher working in Pakistan. The writer you took me for was killed in a car accident in Nicaragua."

"Indeed. We'll do what we can."

Camilla nodded. "You took us quite by surprise. I am really a fan of that Yank's work. I could never understand why the Americans—

the government that is—was making such a fuss about him. The extradition … all that."

By this moment, Charles was becoming increasingly cognizant that he'd really stepped into someone's mine field—this was Collins and he knew it. Now he would try to undo whatever damage was done inadvertently …

"So, the Americans pretend not to be impressed by royalty. Are you?"

"Sir?"

"Impressed."

Barranca smiled.

"Well, sir, I guess I've never given it much thought, or I suppose I imagined Prince Hal. You aren't hiding any tennis balls, are you?"

"Camilla! This chap Barranca could make a decent Englishman."

Prince Charles leaned in close to Barranca and whispered in his ear. "I don't know the situation, but we'll do what we can to throw them off."

Then he spoke in a normal voice for everyone to hear.

"Do you hear that? Tennis balls! *Henry V*. Dr. Barranca does know his Shakespeare. Well, I suppose I have made a blunder or two. Perhaps William will fare better. What do you think, Chancellor?"

The Chancellor did not know how to respond because she did not know the reference to Henry V. But she tried to fake it …

"I agree," was the only thing she could say without stuttering.

The VC, however, who also held a very high post in the ISI, was wondering what an agent for the CIA was doing in her women's college. By her logic, if he wasn't who he said he was, then he was CIA. In Pakistan, this would be true in almost every case, not at all a matter of paranoia.

"Charles," Camilla said, "they've arranged a place for us to rest before your speech."

"Momentarily, Camilla. Dr. Barranca, you're a humble, obviously intelligent fellow. I hope we can meet again."

"Yes, Doctor," Camilla said. "It's our pleasure to meet you, to be here, to see all of you. And the students are wonderful."

Everyone stood up. Before Barranca could get to the auditorium, the press was all over him, asking him if he were Collins. He assured them that he was not. Extant photographs of Collins were dated, anyway, at least by 10 or 15 years—perhaps that would dissuade them. And the Prince had whispered the promise to him that he would try to throw them off his scent.

The Prince gave an inspiring speech on the need for governments to spend more on educational infrastructure and said that the United Kingdom was committed to continuing its unwavering support. The trouble was that much of the money flowing into Pakistan for such purposes was diverted into Musharraf's military budget. Barely a quid ever saw a school. The Prince also said Islam was a profoundly good religion that brought comfort to millions around the world and that England acknowledged this.

Before Barranca could get halfway to his car, he was again surrounded by journalists …

"What did you and the Prince talk about?"

"Shakespeare," Barranca answered.

"Did he talk about politics?"

"He's the Prince, not the Prime Minister. What do you think?"

Barranca made it home that day and collapsed on his bed. He called the VC to tell her that he would miss class the following day due to his fever, but he agreed to go to Lahore if he felt better.

Chapter 39

Lahore, November 17, 2006

By the end of 2006, getting Francisco Barranca's itinerary was as easy as walking into a shop and picking up a newspaper, and the security was pretty loose in Lahore, so, while Barranca sat and listened to the professors argue among themselves about better ways to document research papers, a busy young woman, a secretary in the Journalism Department at the University of Punjab, was dialing someone on her cellphone to disclose the afternoon location of Barranca at a restaurant where she had just made reservations for his lunch reception. The Taliban had hundreds of sympathizers at the University of Punjab.

After the morning session that Friday, Barranca ate a sandwich while some students from the Noam Chomsky Center for Media Communications interviewed him about education throughout the land, an occasion that Barranca used to draw out some particular strategies from Prince Charles' more sweeping and inspirational speech. While he was doing this, a trash truck was placing a large bin beside a restaurant on the causeway.

At 2 p.m. or so, Barranca and two English professors left the university to go to lunch, bringing the total to five men in his car—the driver, the Captain, and three in the backseat. One of them gave the driver their location in Urdu. Then one of the professors continued to talk about trends and movements in postcolonial literature. They talked as the car honked its way through traffic on the causeway and talked as they got out and went in. They even talked with their mouths full about the importance of emerging "ecopoetry," whatever that meant. The driver got out of the car and sat in the shade and the Captain joined him.

No one noticed the trash truck return and set the large trash bin back down a few feet from Barranca's car.

It happened like that, at 3:33 p.m., on a Friday afternoon, just as the primary school was letting out early and just as people began to gather at the bus stop in front of the school, which was beside the restaurant that Barranca and the two professors were just leaving.

"Ecopoetry ..." Language is a lot like chemistry that way: some elements could bond and form a new compound; others might try to join and set off a bad reaction. Francisco thought maybe the two English professors could simply use the words "nature poetry," instead of the typical academic dance of hiding behind neologisms to obfuscate in order to appear elite. Francisco sympathized with their need to hide, but he did not suffer fools easily when they started to bloody a language.

A boy on a rooftop—the boy the secretary called—put down his binoculars after he verified his target and picked up his cellphone as Barranca and the other men got into his car.

There are lies of necessity, Barranca told himself, *and lies to save a life, and there are the opposite kind of lies, those that harm someone, but we are all so good at lying to make reality more palpable, how do we know when we're lying? A controlled hysteria replaces reality with a circus where everyone is cast in a role—freak, fat lady, magician, acrobat—and no one knows anyone differently as long as the new reality is deemed official.*

The boy on the roof across the street and down a couple of buildings took out the piece of paper with the number he needed to push with his thumbs.

"You're going my way; can you give me a lift back to school?" one of the professors said.

The driver started the car just as the boy on the roof, whose hands were shaking very hard, punched in the number. As soon as traffic cleared, the driver backed out, forming a backwards crescent.

The boy had misdialed the number to a cell phone deep inside the trash bin. He realized his mistake and quickly redialed the right number.

Barranca's car was some twenty feet away now going west on the causeway.

Contact. The call went through.

A small girl was tugging at her mother's black burka. A street vender was grilling spiced meats. Men in white achkans were trying to get home from work. Little kids from the primary school were all bunched together waiting for their parents to arrive and pick them up. In an instant everything was rearranged. Everything, pandemonium.

A circular wall of air like iron slammed outward picking up cars, bicycles, boxes of fruit, children along the way. The restaurant and everyone in it was gone. Half the primary school and several buildings on the other side of the restaurant were gone, too. The concussion lifted Barranca's car through the air and flipped it some seventy feet and sat it down on top of another car, sideways. Then, suddenly there was a deafening silence. It seemed like a very long time, but it was probably only a couple of seconds.

The driver and the Captain were both dead, but the Captain was still grinning. The professor of ecopoetry had a large hole in his head, and he wasn't moving. The professor who had been sitting beside Barranca's right was now grotesquely curled up and twisted into something like a fetal position on top of the driver and the Captain.

Barranca made very slow movements. He wasn't yet sure what had just happened. Oddly, an ear was resting in his lap. Without even thinking he picked it up and put it in his pocket. *Ears are important*, he thought. Through the broken passenger-side window, a thick and caustic acrid smoke entered, choking him and stinging his eyes, which blinked like camera shutters. He could hear screaming and moans and he could feel the heat of fires.

Through twisted metal and twisting smoke, shattered glass, broken bricks, streamlets of blood—he slowly crawled out of the window and down to the street. *Arms are important*. He picked up a small arm. He wanted to find the person it belonged to. He wanted to tell the person he was sorry. Then he found another arm, somewhat bigger. He held them up in the smoky air. They didn't match. Maybe someone would claim them. But then he saw a little girl who was on fire. Quickly he laid down the arms side by side, rushed to her, and frantically tried to pat out the fire with his bare hands. She wasn't even crying.

After that Francisco Barranca could not remember what happened. He did not hear the fire trucks or see them using the water cannons to wash the blood and viscera into the canal.

Chapter 40

Managua, Thursday, November 16, 2006

Colonel Tomás received the second email from Bolivar (aka Robert Segovia) and called his secretary to book a flight to Mumbai.

My Dear Professor Martinez Saracho,

Arriving the afternoon of December 2.

Yours,

Segovia

Barranca knew when he mailed this that he would not even have time to say goodbye to his friends. Of course, he wanted to go home, but he had also come to love Anoosh. He loved Mohammed and Ayesha, Nasir, Altaf, and even Ahmed. He even liked the old man Mahmud, the rug dealer, and he was certain that someday birds were going to make a nest in that ratty beard of his. He did not yet know how he was going to elude the smiling Captain, but he figured that he would just wait till he went to the bathroom and hail a taxi. November 19th, and December 3rd, 17th, and 31st, authors H, K, N, and Q would go the way of most authors and their books—to join the forgotten. Their secret ships would sink to the bottom of the ocean. Clandestine ports would, temporarily, receive a few less kilos of heroin, a few less weapons, and a few less sex slaves.

But Barranca worried still about the newspapers. *The Times* agreed to retract its story after receiving a call from Prince Charles. But there had been other journalists there, too. Barranca purchased an Urdu newspaper, which by this time, he could read. The story didn't have a picture, but it stated that Francisco Barranca, a professor at the women's college, was a spy for the CIA. His name, they thought, might be "Balthazar Colon"—a name that a non-English speaking journalist had tried to sound out phonetically from "Bolivar Collins." Some of the journalists returned to the college on Thursday to ask for an audience with the Chancellor or the VC, but they were stonewalled.

The VC wanted ISI to handle it—she had been in charge of investigating him since his arrival in August 2003, anyway, so it was a matter of pride to her. She didn't want the entire country mucking around in her business, nor did the others—General Kahn, the Chancellor, and Hasam—all of whom were benefiting financially, evenly dividing the two million dollars from the Commission earmarked for Dr. Barranca's research. It was enough incentive to tolerate an infidel and a male professor mixing with students of an all-women's college.

Colonel Tomás had about two weeks to prepare for India. The first thing he did was call Teodesia, but Karli answered the phone excitedly and told him she would have to relay the news. Mother had begun prescribing sedatives to herself and she was sleeping for the time being.

Chapter 41

Lahore, November 18, 2006

"You are in a hospital," a voice said. "You've been hurt, but you were also amazingly lucky. Can you hear me?"

Barranca could see a bright light surrounded by a large circular metal dish. The light was buzzing the way colors do in a painting by van Gogh.

"Lucky?"

"You saved your ear. You put it in your pocket, remember? I've just finished stitching it back. It should be fine, but it's going to hurt a lot when the anesthesia wears off, so we'll give you something for that."

"Ear?"

"Yes, your ear."

"The arms?"

"Your arms are fine. I noticed that you did sustain some pretty bad leg wounds, but you've had this problem for some time."

"Yes."

"You're groggy from the morphine."

Barranca could not make out the face belonging to the mouth that was talking to him. The light was directly in his eyes. The man talking was a shadow.

"What do you do? What brought you here? You are obviously not from Pakistan."

"Teacher."

"Splendid! Education is the first line of defense against this madness. I see you are coming around. You're going to feel nauseous. We need to roll you on your side. You still have some shrapnel in your back. Nurse … a bit of help, please. We also removed a nail from your shoulder."

"A nail," Francisco echoed flatly.

"Your hands are bandaged because you burned them. What's your name?"

"Francisco."

"I'm Doctor Waqir."

"Thank you for helping me."

Barranca did not realize until they were checking him out of the hospital that his conversation with the doctor had been entirely in Urdu. He also felt remorse for lying to the doctor about being a teacher. He wanted to hobble back and say it: "I work for a drug cartel and perpetuate the madness. I'm a fraud. I do it to protect my family, but I'm thinking now that it isn't a good enough excuse. I should have died. It would have been the best thing I could have done."

Dr. Waqir's words were true and now Barranca felt a heavy wave of guilt. "The first line of defense is education …." Probably the doctor's words would stick inside him like a rusty knife for the rest of his life, which he hoped would be short. *Perhaps … Just perhaps … if he did survive, maybe he could change his life—maybe become a real teacher.* In Cuba, he might see about working as a teacher, although he was stuck with a new name, "Robert Segovia." *Who can we be if we aren't who we are?*

Barranca's things were in a brown paper bag. His clothes, his wallet, and even his satchel were still there. His cane was not. But he mentioned to one of the nurses that he often needed a cane, and she wheeled him to the dispensary where he could purchase one. At the door of the hospital, he thanked the nurse and wandered outside. It was night but he didn't know what time and his wristwatch was smashed at 3:33. In the distance there was a bright orange neon light that said "HOTEL," so he followed the light to the building.

In his hotel room, he looked in the mirror. *I look like van Gogh, only he didn't get any morphine and he gave away his ear.* He sat down on a chair. He was having a difficult time remembering anything that had just happened. He could not even remember that he had booked a flight to Mumbai. He got up and poured the rest of the contents of the bag out on the bed. His clothes were soaked in blood, so what was he wearing? Gym clothes. Someone at the hospital dressed him in gym clothes and a sweatshirt. *I need to go out and buy some clothes.* The clock beside his bed said that it was after midnight. There was also a bottle of pills wrapped in a sheet of paper with instructions. *Change the dressing every day. Apply the ointment on the back of your head, your back and shoulder, and around your ear—gently. Take two tablets of hydrocodone every four hours.* The other pills were antibiotics—Cipromycin. *Take one with food every eight hours.*

The Sunday newspapers reported that more than twenty-five people were killed on the causeway in Friday's bomb, mostly children, and seventy-five others were wounded. But doctors feared for the more critical, and the number might be greater. *Wallace Stevens had written something like "It is equal to living in tragic land / To live in a tragic time."* Now that his watch was stopped forever at 3:33, the tragic land would vanish or be frozen, inimical to time.

Sometime after November 18 or 19, Barranca felt something in the lining of this corduroy suit coat. When he pulled out the stitches he found his airplane tickets and remembered he was supposed to go to India to meet Tomás, so he stayed in the musty hotel in Lahore for the rest of November until it was time to go to the airport in Islamabad. He was vaguely aware that he could not remember things—who, exactly was "Tomás," for instance—but anything that had ever been written he did remember. He could not recall faces, except for the little girl's, the one who was on fire. Faces were now just vestigial states of mind. Hers was the last face he could remember.

Chapter 42

Mumbai, December 2, 2006

WHEN HE BOARDED THE Pakistan International airplane in Islamabad, Bolivar did not notice the boney-faced skinny man behind him. And when he changed planes in Karachi, he did not notice that the same man also changed planes. And he did not notice that the unattractive tall skinny man got into a taxi directly behind his in the airport queue in Mumbai. But Tomás was there and did notice. He saw Bolivar check into the Gateway, as Robert Segovia, and he saw the tall man who checked in right behind him. And Tomás noticed the way he gave Bolivar a quick checking glance over his right shoulder as he turned to take the elevator to his room when Bolivar came limping over to the bar with his new cane. Bolivar could not even see his own shadow because he was looking ahead now.

Bolivar Collins had never been a man to show very much emotion. His family descended from stalwart Englishmen, and later New Englanders. But when he saw Tomás in the Gateway Hotel bar, he remembered him and tears formed in his eyes. His four-year-long disappearance from the world of friends and family came to an abrupt end. Tomás was older and his face had lost its quizzical nature but he'd have known him anywhere—as it turns out, even in Mumbai, India.

"Oyé, Viejo!" Tomás said, taking his friend, Bolivar, in his arms. "Oyé … Oyé … It's going to be okay."

Bolivar wiped his face and nose with the sleeve of his corduroy jacket.

"Let's get a beer," Tomás said. "And maybe you're hungry."

"That's how we met those years ago. You were a kid in a bar having a beer. You asked me for matches and the numbers in the matchbook matched with the guy you were there to get."

"I barely remember that," Tomás said.

"Do you still smoke?"

"Sí, *por supuesto.*"

"Good," Bolivar said.

The two men sat down at a table. Tomás situated himself so he could keep an eye on the lobby area.

"How did I get here, Tomás?"

"India?"

"No … No … I mean how did I come to be thrown into this … what … this existence?"

"You know as well as anyone that it's futile to try to make sense out of things that don't make any sense."

"Yes. That's right. I suppose that is why I write, or why I 'wrote.' In a story we make up we can live inside a momentary illusion that chaos somehow pulls itself together."

"Bolivar, I see you've been hurt. The bandages?"

"There was a bomb. I was in Lahore. About two weeks ago."

"Are you okay?"

"Yes, I think so. But I get these fevers almost daily. I can't seem to shake them. I've had them for almost a year now. At first they were on and off, now mostly on."

"You have always bounced back, Bolivar. It's what I admire about you."

"This is really happening, isn't it? We're really here, the two of us are here. We're alive and something about this is normal."

Tomás took a drink and paused, gazing at the lobby. He was quiet for a moment.

"What is it, Tomás?"

"I don't think we are completely in the clear. I think you were shadowed. Do you happen to remember a tall, boney guy, about my age on your airplane?"

Bolivar thought for a second.

"No. I didn't even think about it. I've been watched for over four years. I think I've just begun to block it out."

Tomás heard a noise, a ping coming from Bolivar's satchel.

"Do you mind if I have a look in there?"

Tomás rummaged around inside Bolivar's bag and pulled out the cellphone that Nadia gave him the day after he arrived in Pakistan. It pinged again. A series of binary numbers ran across the small caller identification screen: *010011100101010001010101010* …

"Would you mind if I got rid of this?" Tomás asked.

"No, get rid of it. In Pakistan they are only used for spying and detonating bombs. I don't know why I still have it."

Tomás took the telephone outside and across the street and threw it into the bay. Then he came back to the bar and sat down.

"That was a tracking device, which means they know you're here. I think they have also sent along a chaperone, but I have to make sure. Tomorrow morning, I want you to go for a little walk around the neighborhood at around eight o'clock. Then I'll know. Okay? I don't want you to worry about it. I will handle it. Just go for a walk."

"So … we should wait to call Teodesia?"

"We aren't going to do that from India anyway, no," Tomás said.

"Tell me about them, Tomás."

Tomás leaned in because a couple had just sat down next to them.

"Call me Saracho, okay? They're all okay. You remember their letters from Cuba?"

Bolivar nodded.

"We also did everything we could to make it appear to anyone that they went to live in a town called San Marcos near Managua," Tomás said. "They and later all your things were flown there first. They took an unmarked airplane to Cuba from Nicaragua. Castro made it happen."

"Good. Good. Better than I could have imagined. And you? Your life? I know you probably aren't a captain anymore."

"Intelligence. I work for Ortega."

"Oh? How do you like your boss?"

"He's a prick. You tried to warn me, remember? Left wing/right wing. 'Leave wings to the birds,' you said. You were right. Anyway, I'm part of it now. I know too much about our stuff for them to ever let me go. Jesus, a lot of our current bullshit is stuff I dreamed up myself."

"I understand."

It was getting late, but Bolivar and Tomás talked on and on. Outside they could hear the car horns gradually become less frequent as if they were crickets slowing their chirps as the night grew cool. At the bar sat a silvery brown boy wearing a Santa Claus hat with a large gold jingle bell on its tip that flopped to one side. His face bore a blissful, silly look. There was a red dot on his forehead. Bolivar focused on the red dot for a moment, *the bullet hole of enlightenment* ….

Chapter 43

Mumbai, December 3, 2006

FRANCISCO WOKE TO THE voices of shivering denizens, but they were of his own delirium and the chilling vapor that is loneliness. His body was pale and as white as a Weeping Cherry Tree or a white flag of surrender. Outside, smoke from small cookfires all over Mumbai drifted up into the trees, where in his fever Bolivar imagined people lived and built nests. The smoke drifted from branch to branch and swallows darted through a cloud leaving a trail in the fog and smoke like the wake behind a ship. *The sky is an empty nest*, his mind said. *There is a pure life in the sky and we can dig a fine and spacious grave that would be large enough for such a life.*

It was almost eight o'clock, time to go for the walk to let Tomás see if he were being followed. The bomb in Lahore was still very much with him, and the noise in the streets, the gibberish of the vulgate, frightened him. He thought he could feel the bomb ticking in his stomach, and it turned his breath sour.

It was a birth, a wet and sticky birth … it came into existence crying and covered in blood … it was the answer to someone's prayers … when it exploded it changed the sacred geometry of air … it crouched all heavy in its lead, but when it leapt up into the air it turned like a chameleon into something invisible … Then it left us and it didn't leave us … ravaged, hypnotized, confused … clinging to us in the ether or in essence … the way we hypnotize ourselves with fire … We danced circles around the flames and the busy streets all sang their hymns to the day and night—who knows what is human and what is not? Thoughts flew through Bolivar's mind as swiftly as swallows and disappeared. *What if the Word were Flesh and a bomb destroyed the Flesh?*

A scissored-tail flycatcher hovered off the ground, cutting Francisco's thoughts into pieces as he edged over an ancient cobbled path. Pigeons scattered themselves in the air, making ambiguous undulations. Bolivar hobbled on his delusive path. What was his story about? Had he actually lived it or was it lived for him by some external life force that merely dragged him down some street? He supposed there was a separate story for everyone, but that it was just one sticky string in a universal web. Existence was immanentistic, after all, as *the Upanishads* described: substance spewed from the bowels of a massive cosmic spider. Then we became conscious. We saw the spider as it crawled across our faces. Now there was an extraordinary nonchalance in the presence of horror.

In the sweaty teeming millions of Mumbai, is there one who will volunteer to be a character other than himself or herself—a volunteer to step forth and replace the old protagonist? Maybe there is a soul that exists in stasis, lingering trapped in the ocean of fog and smoke diffusing from the curbside fires or stuck in the wheel of the hotel ceiling fan turning in circles, unaware of the Body it knew, unaware of its transcendence from the Body it knew and despised for so long, the pallid sack of skin and loose assemblage of bones, the Body left staring out a pair of eyes opening them to look into the circles of hazy mandalas where greens turned red and back to green. What would it change, anyway, if after all this eternity, it were a meek and tiny mouse powering the cosmic wheel?

If his life were a book, Bolivar thought, it lacked a setting. Rest assured, he told himself, this is Mumbai. Not Pakistan and not Cuba. Barranca did not look behind him to see if he were being followed. He just walked.

It might be anywhere, or somewhere that is absent of weather, somewhere where the air is as heavy as crude oil. It's winter and not cold, but the Body is cold. The Soul remembers its Body shivering through the night's nausea, searching for warmth under a sweat-soaked sheet and that terrible heat that comes to the eyes like the shade of yellow on the signs along the ocean warning of jaundice: stay away from the beaches, the smoldering piles of rubbish, stand inside the circle of impending death made by the scavenger kites.

Bolivar felt devoid of any plan or destiny save for a dumb persistence to exist as he tried to find his way back through the streets to the hotel like a drunken snake trying to navigate the massive banyan trees and bougainvillea vines and the intense collage of dark shadows and bright sun. There was incense so sickening sweet that it caused him to start vomiting again.

But the Soul must have shouldered its Body, dragging its legs, which scuffled through a crowd of Hindus … Humaira 1 or Humaira 2 yelled out: They worship cows and we EAT them … A girl, no, half of a girl was yelling up from the curb “Hello Friend! Hello Friend!” She had a head and torso and two arms that propelled her forward on a small wooden board with skateboard wheels.

There is an Eastern mythology of friendship—one encountered by Odysseus, now written on the handbills for tourists, *Hello Friend.* Clouds of black flies tried to block the wretched body that only barely belonged to Bolivar Collins. He tried to give some children a few rupees and they descended upon him … No, I don’t have anymore … No, I don’t want to have sex with you. No, I don’t want to buy opium … They were tearing at him. One of them held on so hard he ripped Bolivar’s pocket … Please let me pass …

Cholera swept through the wooden crates in the tent camps along the central railway line. Sig*ns said “Clean water is available,” but they cannot read in Hindi or in English! Now they are dying and turning into the shadows that burdened the sun.* But the sun was burning through the morning haze *seizing the ghosts and beckoning them to return, to eternally return. A ghost, like the insane, cannot move except in circles.*

Bolivar did not want to die here because he knew he would come back as a fly for his sins to buzz about the wounds of the sick who were sleeping on sidewalks.

What day is it? December something. What year? Aside from the rickshaws and skyscrapers, it is probably the 2nd century BCE. How could I know that? These are the Koli Islands. Their jungles grew out of the pavement and covered the worn Victorian facades. The long legs of palm trees surrounded and cordoned off all memory of the British. The British will not arrive for another two thousand years. A silly princess in Portugal gives King Charles these islands that don’t belong to her for her dowry, but the banyan trees slowly take it back. The banyan’s grey vines drape over the streets, over the centuries, over the indigenous peoples who have adopted the same silvery brown color in order to hide from foreigners. Their giant leaves are supposed to be green, but they are silver and brown from the dust and pollution.

The soul of Bolivar told him to sit down at a juice bar and ask for orange juice. The boy behind the counter had a bullet hole painted on his forehead—just like the boy at the hotel bar.

British architects used utterly nonsensical notions of neoclassical proportion. Nature has drawn the trees too tall and the people too thin. Doors should have been made narrower. Homes should have been left to hang like the nests of Baltimore Orioles. It is December again and there was frankincense and myrrh, but they are for sale now, like people, like himself, like Tomás and Carmelita and Nadia and Fatima and Ayesha … and the balm that passes for air avails no star at night. If a direction should suddenly manifest an avenue, then the Body should feel compelled to rise and go, turning blindly at the corners.

Chapter 44

Mumbai, December 4, 2006

In the Colaba district of Mumbai, purple grackles cawed in the banyan trees outside the Gateway Hotel, and seagulls swarmed over the murky waters splashing against the seawall where thousands of plastic bottles and dead fish huddled together, floating on the surface, covering the inlets of the ancient port. Inside a room at the hotel, Tomás stood over the bruised and bleeding body of the stranger who had shadowed Bolivar. The stranger bore a defiant look and cursed at Tomás. Tomás tapped a message into a translation application on his cell phone from Spanish to Urdu. "Speak in a low voice or I will tape your mouth closed, too, and the interview will be over." The man said, "English," and Tomás wagged his finger … "I don't speak English very well, but you can tap your answers back to me on this with your free finger for as long as I let you keep it, that is." Tomás held his cellphone within reach of the man's right fingers—his wrists, ankles, and torso were taped to the chair.

"Who sent you?" Tomás showed him the question.

It took awhile but the man had tapped back his answer. He only had a couple of unbroken fingers left.

"Protect him from *fatwa*."

Tomás went back to tapping.

"You work for Aguilar?"

"Who Aguilar? PK send me protect Dr. B."

"We seem to find ourselves in a conundrum, you and me. What are we going to do with you?" Tomás did not translate this. He sat on the bed and thought for a moment. Then he got up and cut a length of tape to cover the man's mouth.

"No! Please!" the tall boney man said.

"Shhh!" was Tomás' reply as he taped the man's mouth shut.

Then Tomás retrieved a gun that he'd picked up at the Nicaraguan consulate. He screwed a silencer onto the barrel, pointed it at the man and fired it once at his head and once at his chest. Then he put the gun back in his bag. He took off the surgical gloves he was wearing and put these in the bag, too, along with a pair of scissors and two rolls of surgical tape. Before he went to collect Bolivar, he tossed the gun, the scissors, the gloves, and the tape into the waves of trash drifting on the water outside. He left the man lying on a plastic sheet.

Bolivar was waiting in his own room when Tomás came in.

"We're checking out right now. Are you ready?" Tomás said, all business.

Bolivar nodded.

"Was I followed?"

"Yes."

"And now?"

"The problem is solved. Don't worry yourself about it. Let's go."

Tomás and Bolivar needed to board an airplane before the authorities had time to review the hotel's cameras. This would take them, Tomás figured, until the next day if they were lucky. The stranger's room had already been made up, and Tomás left the "Do Not Disturb" sign on his door when he left.

Tomás and Bolivar went to the lobby where Bolivar checked out first.

"Oh, Mr. Segovia. You have a fax."

To Robert Segovia:

Return to Pakistan and resume your work or Teodesia and Karli will be joining Renee and Melissa and Noelia and Sophia—and your lovely Carmelita.

Eduardo Aguilar

"Come on, Mr. Segovia. Let's go," Tomás said.

"Wait … maybe we should think about this," Francisco said, not budging.

"Mr. Segovia, please, not here. Come on."

Bolivar followed Tomás. He sensed no warmth in Tomás—just a man who was all about business. The two got in a yellow and black taxi. And Tomás used an English word …

"Airport."

Then Tomás asked the driver a few questions—such as whether he had a family—in Spanish to verify that the driver couldn't understand Spanish. Then he turned back to Bolivar …

"Bolivar, it's not a decision I can make for you. I could swear to you that Aguilar doesn't know where they are—that he's bluffing—but not knowing what your enemy knows has always been their wild card. I do not know how he got the 'Segovia' part. This does trouble me."

Bolivar didn't say anything. He was thinking *If I die, maybe this could end, and maybe Aguilar would leave them alone.*

"Who is Carmelita?" Tomás asked.

The taxi slowed down behind a large white ox pulling a cart filled with silage.

"A friend, sort of. I didn't know her well. She was one of his girls. Years ago, I gave her our address in Jlalpan in case she wanted to go there for help. Aguilar just took her from her home in Brazil. Just up and took her because he wanted her."

"So, she was a fellow prisoner …"

"Yes."

"He's a real piece of work, that one."

"He is that," Bolivar said.

The taxi pulled up in front of the airport.

"I can't go with you, Tomás. I'm sorry. I'm sorry for everything. Sorry I got you into this."

"If Aguilar has a man in Havana, we'll find him," Tomás said. "The first thing I want you to do is see a doctor. Will you do that? You're sweating again."

Bolivar nodded. He was starting to choke up again.

"We were so close, weren't we?"

"We aren't giving up so easy, Bolivar. Use the account I gave you … Martinez Saracho … Keep the papers. Keep everything out of sight. I'll get word to you as soon as I can."

Tomás was thinking …

"How long will it be before your next job for Aguilar?"

"December 19th."

"I suggest you hide until then. Is there anyone you trust? Someone they won't know about?"

"It's like you said … I also don't know what they know. But maybe … There is a woman named Ayesha."

"Call her from a public phone. Have her meet you. Can she hide you until the 19th?"

"Maybe she can. I don't know."

Barranca bought a ticket for Islamabad, which was leaving a little earlier than the flight they were going to take together to Buenos Aires where the two men would have said goodbye. Tomás would be flying from Buenos Aires back to Nicaragua and Barranca was booked to fly to Cuba from there. Now they shook hands and embraced each other, and Barranca then went to board the airplane for Islamabad. On the airplane, Barranca took out his wallet and removed a small white piece of paper with Ayesha's phone number and placed it in his breast pocket. The next day, a maid at the Gateway Hotel knocked and knocked on the stranger's door. She called the manager and the manager came and knocked on the door, too.

Chapter 45

Islamabad, December 2006

It was evening when an unmarked white jet was setting down at a military base outside Islamabad. Its door opened and Sen. Hillary Clinton descended the stairs to the tarmac where President Musharraf was waiting to greet her. Clinton's entourage included a detail of secret service men; Musharraf also had a detail of guards, as well as other high-ranking officials on hand, including the VC of the women's college, a woman of approximately his same age with whom he had enjoyed a long standing personal and professional relationship.

Clinton's security detail consisted of three Secret Service agents and a fourth man whom she did not know. Just before leaving Washington, her office received a call from the Pentagon asking if one of their Force Protection agents could accompany her. It was a little irregular and she wanted to know why. The caller had replied, "As a courtesy. He's one of our experts on Pakistan and Afghanistan. We can send over a copy of his redacted file."

Clinton merely asked for his name and then approved his inclusion in her detail.

The Senator served on the Senate Armed Services Committee, but now she was about to announce her run in the Democratic presidential primaries, so her primary objective for the trip was to pad her foreign relations vitae and get to know Musharraf, this US ally in the "War on Terror" with whom she would have to be on good terms once she was the President of the United States.

On the airplane, she had tried to engage Special Agent Robin Ward, but found him diffident.

"Have you made many trips to Pakistan, Agent Ward?"

"Yes, Senator."

"And?"

"Senator?"

"How do you find it?"

"How do I find it?"

"I'm told you're an expert on the region."

"That's correct."

"Can you tell me a little about your mission here?"

"I'm sorry, Senator. You would have to petition the DOD. My mission is classified."

"I see."

After that, she backed off.

The motorcade filled with ISI and Secret Service agents—along with Musharraf, the VC, and Hillary Clinton—arrived at the Marriott Hotel where another detail of agents had finished their security sweep and taken up positions everywhere, since a suicide bomber only recently had made it as far as the revolving doors when he blew himself up along with seventeen other people. Some of the security personnel looked like tourists. A couple sat at the bar, a little area set aside for foreigners, a sort of free zone for anyone who wanted to order an alcoholic drink. But the two agents there were drinking Cokes.

After a desk clerk checked Robin Ward into his own room, he was free to come and go as he pleased. He had several tasks: Aguilar wanted him to find out what he could about what Clinton was doing in Pakistan and whether she had a clue about their operations there; the Pentagon wanted to make sure she didn't find out how they operated there; and there was Francisco Barranca to attend to.

Barranca made it to a telephone and called Ayesha as soon as his plane landed at Islamabad International. She came at once and lingered in the shadows beside one of the concrete pillars where the taxis come in and go out. But as soon as Barranca cleared customs and made it to the airport lobby, two men grabbed him by the arms and escorted him to their car. Ayesha saw this but was helpless to intervene. She watched them push him into the backseat, hard, with no regard for his leg. He had managed to keep ahold of his cane. She noted the direction their car went and then called Mohammed to tell him what had just happened.

The two men told Barranca to behave himself. They were taking him to a very nice place to meet an old friend. In other words, they did not wish to manhandle him when they reached the lobby of the Marriott Hotel. They wanted him to walk on his own. It was night and quite cold. The cold caused Barranca's leg to cramp. Sometimes his cane wasn't enough.

"Do you think you could help me?"

One of the men took Barranca's cane and handed it to the other. Then he grabbed Barranca's arm and pulled it around his neck.

"Walk."

Downstairs in a meeting room, refreshments were being served to the Senator and others around a table. President Musharraf was gregarious …

"Vice Chancellor Siddiqui has briefed me on your illustrious career. I admired very much your national health initiatives. I believe as President you will have more power than you did as the First Lady."

Sen. Clinton loathed obvious commentaries, but she also bore a political poker face. She turned to the VC …

"I'm sorry. I should know this. What position do you hold on the cabinet?"

"Special Counsel, Senator," she replied with graciousness.

"I see. It wasn't in my briefs. Please forgive me."

"Madame Siddiqui attended Stanford," Musharraf said. "She holds a PhD in International Policy."

"That was a long time ago. In the 60s," said the VC said.

"We were in school about the same time then," Clinton said. "We were all so idealistic, weren't we?"

"I know what you mean," VC replied.

Loathe to be on the sideline of any conversation, Musharraf interjected: "You will have no problem beating Obama. Americans will never elect a blackie."

Clinton pretended not to notice the racial slur.

"I'm pleased that you think I will win, but I cannot afford to take him for granted."

Upstairs the two men who had brought Barranca to Robin Ward's room now stepped aside and gave him his cane. Barranca took it and leaned against the wall beside the door of Room 209. It opened as soon as the other man knocked. Bolivar stared in disbelief at the man who had opened it …

"Surprised to see me?"

Robin Ward was Wayne Williams, or Williams was Ward.

"Come in, won't you?" he said to Barranca.

As soon as Barranca cleared the doorway, he was surprised again. Fatima Abbas was sitting on the bed with a drink in her hand.

"Hi Paco, dear," she said mockingly.

Barranca didn't answer her. He just looked at her for a moment. Then he nodded to himself that this all made perfect sense.

"Who was the Nicaraguan you saw in Mumbai?" Williams or Ward wanted to know.

Barranca didn't answer.

"Not talkative today? That's fine. We can talk later. Or we can avoid unpleasantries. You know, waterboarding is officially legal now, not that we care."

"You have good taste in books," Barranca said to Williams.

"All in a day's work. Now, the question is what are we going to do with you. Fatima? What should we do with him?"

"I've always believed in tidiness … in taking out the trash," Fatima said.

"Is that what I am to you, Fatima?"

She didn't answer. She lit a cigarette, tilted her head back, and blew the smoke upward. Ward or Williams continued …

"The VC wants you to continue your work at the school … Your presence there makes them eligible for a little grant that they consider to be a lot. There is more than one arrangement in place and we've gone to a lot of trouble for you. A lot of people have gone to trouble for you."

"Yes," Fatima said. "Who do you think was keeping you alive all the time you've been here? Do you really think a school could do that?"

"And," Ward or Williams said, "my colleague in Mexico has his money to consider. Of course, if you refuse to cooperate, I may be inclined to influence Aguilar to go with a new plan."

"His fax to India didn't exactly put me in a cooperative mood," Barranca said, resigned.

"Granted, he has a flare for the dramatic. But he follows through. He has scopes on your family in Nicaragua right now. You think we wouldn't know that?"

Nicaragua! He thinks they are in Nicaragua! He doesn't know … He doesn't …

"Well, do what you are going to do, Williams. I'm finished," Barranca told him.

Wayne Williams or Robin Ward turned to Fatima.

"Use the VCs men and call that guy … What's his name?"

"I know who you mean. What do you want to do with him?"

"Hold him. Find out what you can. I don't care where. Right now, I have a reception to attend."

Fatima put her arms around Williams's neck and kissed him and then turned to look at Barranca to see if this brought a response, but it didn't. She had only been a body, and bodies are dead—the skin and the hair, all dead. And anyway, Barranca was trying not to cry or laugh with relief because he now knew that Teodesia and Karli were safe.

Chapter 46

Rawalpindi, Sadr Market, January 2007

THE SHI'ITE MEN WITH their swords passed by Barranca who was hiding in a dark alley, shivering from the cold. Slowly he went on, dragging his right leg. His face was puffy from the inquisitor's fists, and weeks of having water poured down his lungs made him frightened to even look at a glass. The beatings had torn some of his stitches and blood was seeping from his ear. Something inside him felt elated. He sensed he was free but he was disoriented. He had turned the wrong corner more than once before he finally collapsed on the doorstep.

When he came around, he could make out Mahmood's big ratty bird's nest beard and smell his bad breath.

"You are alive again? Good. You have visitors."

Ayesha and Mohammed were there. Ayesha brought a chair to sit beside the couch. Barranca felt as if he were dying.

"I want you to take these tablets," Ayesha said. "It's cipro. I'm pretty sure you have typhoid. You were looking peaked months ago, and now it's worse. Maybe stage three."

"Good to have you back with us," Mohammed said. "You had us all pretty worried."

"You shouldn't be here. All of you. You're in danger," Barranca suddenly realized.

He tried to raise himself up.

"Lie still," Ayesha said. "Of course, we are all in danger. This is Pakistan. Everyone here is always in danger."

"How did you find me?" Barranca asked.

"You had Ayesha's number in your pocket, so Mahmood called her," Mohammed explained.

"Thank you, Mahmood."

Mahmood nodded once.

"Mahmood is fond of you," Ayesha said. "We are all fond of you."

"Mahmood," Barranca asked, "how is Anoosh? How is his family?"

Mahmood lowered his head a little …

"Mr. Barranca, I am sorry to tell you that the Taliban blew up his shop one night when they were sleeping. There were no survivors."

"When?"

"A couple of weeks ago. December the 19th, I think it was."

"Why? It doesn't make sense."

Referring to the Taliban, Mahmood said: "They didn't know you needed his store to help them, and they thought Anoosh was an apostate. But I have only heard rumors."

"And your allegiances, Mahmood? Isn't someone waiting to catch a boat or get a rug?"

"For now, I don't have any allegiances. When you are safe, I will have to go back to work. For now, my wife has prepared some chicken broth and a little rice for you."

"How long was I asleep?"

"Since last night when Mahmood found you on his doorstep," Ayesha said. "All of today. It's evening again. If you're strong enough, we're going to take you somewhere safe. Are you up to it?"

"I think so."

"Then Mohammed will call Altaf and Nasir to tell them to bring the car."

Chapter 47

Abbottabad, January 2007

MOHAMMED AND NASIR SAT in the front and Altaf and Ayesha sat with Barranca in the backseat. On the outskirts of Abbottabad, a smaller city near Peshawar, Mohammed told Barranca to get down. Ayesha put his head in her lap and Altaf spread a blanket over him.

"No one can know you are here. I'll let you up when we are inside, okay?" Ayesha said.

Mohammed's uncle Jinnah opened the garage door to his house and the car pulled inside. When the door closed, Ayesha told Barranca that he was safe now. Uncle Jinnah could not turn down Mohammed's request to hide his friend—he felt it was his duty to Allah to help a person in trouble. But he did have one condition, which he made clear to Barranca and to his nephew, Mohammed. He had two daughters about Mohammed's age who were still unmarried and living at home, and a younger wife, too. Under no circumstances would Barranca be allowed to know his daughters or second wife.

When Uncle Jinnah's conditions were made known to Barranca, he remembered a day in his American literature class. The students were reading Eugene O'Neill's *Desire Under the Elms*. When he asked them to comment, Sidra was the first to raise her hand.

"We do not see what the big deal is. It's just normal to separate the oldest son from the second wife," she said.

Barranca's frustration with the students had been mounting for weeks and his patience was wearing thin. The parochialism that infested their minds and shrouded their ability to think for themselves was a force like death, the force of institutions over individuals. Adding to this, Tabina's house had just been bombed. She and her family were dead, leaving a gaping hole in the seat she always used. Barranca threw up his arms and revealed his outrage, but his emotions blinded his ability to reason with them and made the onslaught of his verbal assault rather difficult to follow.

"You, and by *you* I mean you plural, are not worthy to be called graduate students. You have yet to grasp the meaning of a single book. *The Scarlet Letter* sides with nature, not with silly, arbitrary, lopsided Sharia laws. You outright dismiss *Leaves of Grass* because the author was a homosexual. Do you actually believe that Emily Dickinson rejected Christianity because she secretly yearned to be a Muslim? Maybe the family in O'Neill's play is just a little dysfunctional and if you call that normal, that makes you dysfunctional! You think that's normal? You are even more tragic than the play itself! You have no sympathy for Frederic Henry—Why? Because you think that war is ordained by Allah? Okay, so Frederic Henry is a traitor to God and country. You think Faulkner was mentally ill, so there you have all of his books neatly tied up with a bow. You have no sympathy for the woman in 'Cat in the Rain,' a woman who has just suffered an abortion so her boyfriend can go on living life as an adolescent, I suppose because that's so very Pakistani. My God! You can't even sympathize with the poor cat! And, yes, I know that most of you have suffered. I know that you have been mutilated and raped—you think for a minute I can't see through your first-person pronouns replaced with the third person? Do you think you have eluded me, always hiding behind the third person: 'I have a neighbor who knows someone who . . .' instead of 'This happened to me.' Try to say it sometime, 'Me! I was raped by my cousin!' Try to be honest at least with yourselves for once. You have to ask me to explain why the boys in *Lord of the Flies* revert to tribalism because you yourselves have never been anything other than tribal! Have you ever asked a fish 'Hey fish, how's the water'? What does he say? He says 'What's water?' Mark Twain had you in mind when he wrote 'To the Person Sitting in Darkness!' You! And in our Shakespeare seminar, remember? No, 'The Dark Lady' does not mean that Shakespeare was writing to 'a blackie'—which is a disgusting word, and I don't want to hear it ever uttered again, not from one of you. And Geraldine Brooks' new novel *March*! It was illegal—illegal!—to teach African Americans how to read. A good-hearted northerner visiting Virginia doesn't know that, and what does he do? He teaches someone to read, and reading—at least in theory—is supposed to lead you out of the darkness and into something like freedom, which is in no way just an abstract word. Freedom is lived and you aren't living as long as you do and say only what a handful of judges decided in the

16th century. In the meantime, you happened to miss out on a little thing called the Enlightenment and the Age of Reason. Kate Chopin was not wrong to leave her husband! She was right! If anyone ever treats you the way her husband treated her, you need to leave him. And do you want to know what bothers me—what really bothers me the most? Put your hand down, Humaira! It's a rhetorical question. What bothers me the most is that half of you are teaching the undergraduates! What can they possibly learn from you except how to endure misery and embrace ignorance?"

Barranca had come to a full stop. He stood at the window and looked out. The room was stunned into silence. Barranca stood looking out the window and did not stop looking. Rafia's sad brown eyes were crying and her lips trembled under her black veil. Serein had closed her eyes and was trying to meditate. Maryam Haq bit her nails, nervously hoping that Dr. Barranca was finished being angry. Nadia continued fastidiously to write in her notebook. The two Humairas looked at each other, both hoping that the other would give them a sign they could interpret. There was, then, a full half hour of class still to go, but the clock itself had decided to stop ticking.

Barranca finally turned away from the window and returned to the desk beside the podium. He gathered up his books and prepared to leave. Suddenly he stopped and said to them very softly: "I'm terribly sorry. All I really wanted to say was that I miss Tabina, too."

He looked at them. They looked at him. Perhaps it was the only moment in those few years that any of them ever saw a man, a person, in front of them, rather than "a professor."

"On Monday we'll talk about some of the modern poets—Eliot, Stevens. The class is dismissed."

Mohammed's uncle opened the door to Barranca's new room. There were stuffed animals on the bed and a poster of Brad Pitt on the wall. There was also a small writing desk. Barranca asked Uncle Jinnah if he could use the paper if there were any in the drawer. Ayesha promised to be back and reminded him that he was not to go outside. "The whole town is under Taliban control. If you go outside, you'll get us all killed." Barranca assured her that he understood and would stay inside.

Chapter 48

Abbottabad, January-February 2007

Mohammed's uncle made sure Barranca ate regular meals and took the medicines that Ayesha left for him. In a few days, Barranca had begun to feel a little better. He had not written anything in more than four years, with the exception of typed handouts, syllabi, carefully printed letters on the class blackboard, and emails about school matters. Williams forbade him to write anything in long hand, fearing his handwriting would be matched to Bolivar Collins and compromise his work as their courier. He had not written freely since the summer of 2002. Before, he had written daily for most of his life. Now he was not sure if he could.

Barranca took out a sheet of paper from the drawer belonging to one of Uncle Jinnah's daughters and tried to write. In the back of his mind, he was sure that whatever he wrote would be the last thing he ever did. He wanted to say goodbye to Teodesia. He had always been a man made of words, not a hero or a man of action, just words. He sat down at the desk of Uncle Jinnah's daughter and wrote. This is some of what he wrote:

for Teodesia
In heaven there are no churches, mosques, or synagogues.
—Iqbal

1
Walk with me on the Avenue of Mysteries,
Walk with me on the causeway in the full light of day,
Walk with me in the widening circle of kindred spirits,
Give your breath to the gathering clouds.

Regard the Stations of the Cross, the Stations of the Metro,
The stops along the way where
Time has worn away the face of Christ.

Faces in the crowd have passed beside the traffic and gone down
To gather in the trains.

The headlights bend
from the weight of bodies ferried to the other side.

2
Teodesia,
I dreamed …
That first you
Removed your finger
And gave it to me.
Then your left eye.
Then your left ear.
So I might touch, see, hear, and understand
Just a little bit of what you knew.

I wanted you to stop
And also I didn't want you to stop.
Your leg from the thigh down.
Your arm.
Then you pulled out your other eye
That contained a distant city in a fog.
It is a gift, a crystal ball to guide me, an ornament,
An oracle.

Then you gave me your ear, which was filled with voices.
Some pleasant. Others low and brutal with pronouncements.

Last, you gave me your vagina, the primordial nest
That fell from a tree in the wind.
It was torn and its stitches were crude.
I came so close to your soul,
I could almost hold it in my hand
Yet it was so far.
You had given me yourself, a rose, infinity

That lives in you. Petal after petal I took
To see your soul
And I didn't see it.
You were lost in the crowd.
With one hand, you gave me your hand
And I let it go in the crowd.

3
Walk with me on the Avenue of Mysteries.
Walk with me in the widening circle of kindred spirits
Through the torch light blue, dark blue darkening
The dormant fields to the end of each furrow,
Through the storm's dark blue and shudder of sudden wind—
This is my body, to have and to hold,
White as a Weeping Cherry,
The white flag of surrender,
White as a sheet or a ghost, so light
It is no burden at all to have and to hold.
Here, east of winter, where you have opened
This letter, I wake from a long sleep.
As you read, I turn into wind
Changing course toward home … with a poem
About silence and time:
The old man reaches a river, tired, and lies down.
Across the river, he sees the village
Where he was born.
It is a poem about dying
Only when we have lived, and about
Circles, or
The other way around.
It's not about the words.
The prayer beads of the sun and moon
Are hot and cold to the touch—
We chase after the thing with a word,
Follow it into the dark, and sometimes
The person we love feels lost.

That is what I meant to say.
I give you this. My shell.
I don't need it anymore. It was
A labyrinth, a house made of shadows.
Walk with me in the aisles
And into the valley where there is no king,
No certainty,
No light
But a dark red peony.

4
Smoke floats up lightly
From the cook fires and into the trees
Where we lived
--drifting from branch to branch
    with a swirl of swallows—
the pure life,
a life of reaching and twisting toward the light
reflecting the vast and empty nest of the sky
where we lived
and also where we could dig a fine and spacious grave
that would be large enough for such a life.

5
That was
A child playing with matches, playing at kissing.
The fire in fits and starts.
That was
The sun sinking like a ship on fire,
Auroras or enchantment, a young girl
Before shadows could converged
and a kiss dissolve in the end of August.

My heart sank like an anchor through the deep
And a bird cried from its sequestered nest in the woods.
The woods were shaggy with leaves …

That's about all that I remember.
It was a long time ago.

There is a scarecrow in a field
Ruing the way and directing my life.
Time has worn the clothes right off
And wind has spun the straw to gold.

6
When daylight comes first lavender then blue,
Stay with me, voices,
Your shelter, enter my bed clothes, my mouth,
Take my breath for the words that are quiet
Without us
And my eyes for those who cannot see their path.
Sing now, voices, when I wake.

7
On the other side of the world,
I lit a thin yellow candle
The night you drove home in the rain.

I lit a candle and waited in my cell for word to come.

We danced in the square by the fountains,
Your gold earrings catching the sun, catching
The eye of every man and woman.
Your hands cast drift nets as you sang.

You played in the wind in my hair.
You teased.
You took my hand
And the world was jealous of me for being with you—

caught in a sudden rain,
Huddled under the eaves for the rain that will never end

But rise and take us up and across in a boat,
Adrift,
    on fire,
A light
To find the path in the privacy of night, passage to a room where

Behind us, doors to the past have closed
And with no thought at all, you lift me up,
Dropping
my ragged clothes
to join—lover to lover
Changing your body for mine,
My body for yours.

The darkness is wet.
The wet roads bend in the darkness. The light
Plays tricks.

I write this from my cell
Beside a candle I have lit
When you are finding your way in the dark forever.

8
Along the avenues
The travelers are months and years.

The ones who float past on park benches
Have taken their lives for granted.

For many years
People have perished along the avenues.

They walk by
And then they turn and disappear.

Others have taken off their shoes
To share a pot of tea.

I am surprised by a cloud
So complete in its wandering.

Chapter 49

Pakistan, 2007

MOHAMMED AND NASIR TOOK turns driving up to Abbottabad from Islamabad. Each time one came, Ayesha hitched a ride. Sometimes Altaf came, too. But it was Ayesha who brought him magazines, checked his stitches, and sat in his room to talk usually longer than one of the men wanted to stay. She brought other things too: nuts, apples, dates, figs, oranges, red carrots, grapes; and she put them in his room. "Please, Ayesha, we have families to get back to," Nasir once said. Ayesha would grudgingly get up and say goodbye a half dozen times until one of her friends would threaten to leave her there.

She still couldn't read very well and not at all in English, but one day she had among her own things a copy of *Frog and Toad* in Urdu, which belonged to one of Mohammed's children.

"I know that story," Barranca said.

"Really? I can read it, too," she said with a big smile.

"Will you read it to me?"

"But you don't know Urdu."

"Actually, I do."

Ayesha looked surprised, but she opened her book and read *Frog and Toad are Friends*. When she got to the end, she exclaimed: "I just love this book!"

"It's all about respect, isn't it?" Francisco smiled.

"Yes!"

She adjusted her chair. "What do you plan to teach me today?"

"Chess. It's not a game I like very much, but there is a chessboard here."

"Why don't you like it?" Ayesha asked.

"It's all about moving in straight lines … Horizonal and diagonal lines. There's nothing wrong with that. It's pure Euclidean geometry. It's just that …"

"What's that? What is 'Euclidean'?"

"Euclides was a Greek mathematician who contributed to the invention of geometry. It's just that it doesn't reflect nature very well, or people. We are more like swirls and jags and eddies than rectangles or squares. And the very notion of a perfect circle is … well … 'perfect,' and perfection doesn't exist. The world isn't as ordered as Euclides thought."

Ayesha thought about this.

"You mean, someone like me would not fit into his world very well. I'm not a black piece or a white piece, not a man or a woman."

"Something like that."

"But I fit in your world, right?" she asked with a little trepidation in her voice.

"Of course, yes. You experienced a terrible tragedy when you were young, but you've gone on to be a fine person. That makes you unique, not the tragedy."

Ayesha liked this assessment. Excitedly, she remembered to tell him: "You know, Mohammed and his friends have been working on something and we think they may have found someone who can help you."

"Oh … that's very good of them, but you'll understand if I don't want to raise my hopes."

"It's the United Nations. That's important, isn't it?" she asked, innocently.

"Very important, but how can they help?"

"Well, not all of the United Nations—just one man who works for them. Mohammed found him in Islamabad and spoke to him in hypotheticals, you know, to size him up. Well, the guy is leaving Pakistan soon, but tomorrow he is coming to see you."

Barranca listened to this news matter-of-factly, but without any enthusiasm. Since seeing Tomás in Mumbai and having to say goodbye to him there, he'd resigned himself. He would die in Pakistan. He would no longer be able to sit in this room. It was April and soon he will have been missing for five years. Not even Ayesha or Mohammed could budge the heavy stone inside him. He had given Mohammed the email account number to send and receive messages to and from Nicaragua. Tomás was working on something; he hadn't forgotten. But hope had long since dwindled away.

He gave his last little letter poems to Ayesha, and the address in Cuba, and made her promise to send them to his wife (via Nicaragua) when it was time, meaning when he was dead, whenever that day might come. He never told Ayesha his real name or about Cuba. She didn't know what Cuba was, anyway, or Nicaragua or Mexico. Ayesha protested his pessimism but eventually promised just to avoid further discussion about it.

Ayesha and Barranca had become very close friends despite Barranca's habit of keeping secrets. She, on the other hand, was often shockingly open.

"Do you want to see it?" she asked once, pointing between her legs.

"What?" Barranca swallowed. "Is that something you need to show me?"

"Not particularly. Just thought you would be curious—that's all."

"No. I'm not," Barranca had replied.

And on another occasion, Ayesha wanted to know "what it is like for a man to be with a woman." Barranca found this surprisingly difficult to explain. He started with a surface description, explaining in purely anatomical language.

"No!" Ayesha said, "I already know all that. I want to know what it feels like—you know—in your heart."

For Ayesha, the penis was a phantom limb, an elusive ghost that still haunted her. So Barranca tried again to explain.

"It feels wonderful to feel yourself inside a woman."

"Explain 'wonderful'."

Barranca looked for a metaphor.

"Think of waves and imagine that the waves are made of love and they're touching you lightly. They move in and wash up the shore and recede and so on. Now imagine the waves begin to swell and burst open and in your mind you can't tell if you are male or female, or if you are the water or the shore. It's like being outside time for a while. A really big wave is moving slowly, and with an incredible force outward on the shore, but rather than feel painful, it's ecstatic."

Ayesha was satisfied with this description. She nodded, but she also thought about the men who paid her. They didn't love her. She couldn't understand how it could be enjoyable. They ejaculated in her rectum. That's what Barranca meant by the really big wave crashing.

"So when the man ejaculates, does he feel love?"

"Not necessarily. That depends. If the man loves the woman, then yes, he will feel these feelings more intensely. His feelings will mingle and join with what he feels physically."

"So why does he bother if he doesn't love her?"

"Ayesha, the men who have sex with you feel only physical pleasure that lasts a minute. Then they feel nothing."

"So, not like you and your wife."

"Right, not like that."

Ayesha secretly believed that Barranca was never going to go home; he would die in Pakistan, if not from a bomb or a bullet, then from a broken heart. Part of her wanted to comfort him, like a wife or maybe a mother. And, in truth, part of her also wanted to test him, but she didn't. She just sat down on the edge of his bed.

"You know what I really want, Barranca?"

"No, what, Ayesha?"

"A woman."

"It's okay to want that."

"They changed me into what I am. I can only barely remember it now, but even so, they didn't get all of the boy out of me. Not the one who lives in my mind. Do you get it?"

"Yes, Ayesha."

"It's a woman I want to be with."

"And you have never been with a woman?"

Ayesha shook her head *no.*

"No, but I hear it isn't so unusual in western countries."

"Ayesha, it isn't unusual here either; it's just that we don't hear about it."

"But do you think a woman would want me? Because I don't have a . . . a . . . ."

"A vagina? Ayesha, if I were a woman, I would want you. And people don't care about things like that when they love someone. What people want is to be loved and held. Everyone wants exactly what you give so much of to me—attention. If it weren't for you, my life would be unbearable."

"Really?"

"Really, you make me laugh. You astonish me by how fast you have learned to read. You can beat me at chess."

"That's because you let me win!"

"I don't. Although there is one thing … Next visit, could you bring me some news magazines instead of these fashion magazines?"

Ayesha laughed. "I will ask for news magazines. The man in the bookstore will know which ones."

Chapter 50

Pakistan, 2007

In April 2007, Mohammed and Ayesha brought two people to meet Barranca. The five of them met in Barranca's room. The two were in some way affiliated with the United Nations.

"Shall we all sit down and have a talk?" Mohammed said.

Uncle Jinnah told his first wife to bring tea out for the visitors and then he returned to what he was doing. One of the strangers was the man whom Ayesha had mentioned, but the other was a woman. Michael Kilduff was Irish, in his fifties, and had unruly, wild blond hair and blue eyes. He leaned forward with a very serious look. The woman was closer to forty, Russian, and her name was Tatiana Puchnecheva. Her hair had turned grey early, but she was striking. She too had blue eyes, and Ayesha couldn't take her eyes off her. She was "exotic," she later told Barranca.

The Irish man had most of the details that Mohammed had and maybe had surmised a few of his own, but he wanted to hear the whole thing from Barranca from the beginning. If he were to help, he needed to know exactly what he was getting himself into—the whole truth. Barranca confessed then and there that even his friends had been protected from all of the details for fear of their safety.

"Look, Yank," the Irishman said, "I get why it's difficult to talk. The day I got here the Pakis crawled right up my arse. Uh, present company excluded."

"Pakis crawl up my arse too," Ayesha said.

She always brought levity to a situation. Even when she was serious and even though the sort of humor that emerged was black irony. So Barranca began. He started by telling everyone his real name. The Russian woman knew him by his reputation.

"If you are Bolivar Collins," Tatiana said, "then the first report was true; you're alive."

"You are who?" Mohammed asked with consternation. "I read your books! I never saw a picture of you. You are Bolivar Collins?"

Mohammed couldn't repress a hint of anger in his voice. He felt he had been deceived by a close friend, which he had.

"Prince Charles did recognize you, didn't he?" Puchnecheva said. "But he denied it in the papers."

"That's right," Collins said.

"There's a problem, Collins," the Irishman said. "There aren't very many places you can go. Or, that is, there aren't many places I'd be able to fly to."

That's when Barranca had to reveal his destination.

"I have political exile waiting for me in Cuba. I can get there from one of two places: Venezuela or Nicaragua," Barranca said.

Ayesha had never heard of any of these places. She did not even know about the Spanish language. But once she heard something, she never forgot it. She hoped that by the time she was in her forties, like the lovely Russian woman, she would know as much as other people with education. Puchnecheva was still putting pieces together.

"So the Nicaraguan death certificate was faked."

"Yes, I've very good friends there, but Nicaragua is the diversion. That's where the cartel is looking for me."

Ayesha couldn't stop herself from interrupting.

"What's a cartel?"

"A cartel, sweetie, is a group of organized criminals," Tatiana Puchnecheva said.

"Oh."

Ayesha was thinking ... *She called me sweetie.*

Finally the Irishman was satisfied.

"We can get you to Ireland. From there I'll have to see."

"We?" Collins asked.

"Tatiana and I. I'm just a pilot—Air Cargo for the UN. Tatiana is the one with some pull; she's with the UN's Human Rights Watch. I didn't bring her along to meet you. I brought her to meet this young woman," he said, motioning to Ayesha.

"Me?" Ayesha exclaimed.

"Sweetie ..." the Russian woman said, looking directly at Ayesha.

There it was again! Sweetie! Ayesha thought.

"… What was done to you. It's one of the things I'm trying to stop. You, and others like you, are why I am in Pakistan. If you agree to come with me, you will be asked to tell your story. Do you think you can do that?"

"You mean … not live Pakistan anymore?" Ayesha asked, growing both afraid and excited.

"Probably forever. You need to think this over," Tatiana Puchnecheva said.

Collins laughed. It was a laugh of relief or joy for Ayesha.

"Can I hitch a ride?" he asked.

"That's the general idea, mate," Kilduff said.

"Wait. The Pakistanis will never let us leave," Collins said.

"That's why we won't be telling them," Kilduff said.

"You mean, we just fly out."

"That's right, mate. Air Cargo," he said, pointing to himself with his thumb.

The words *Air Cargo* had a souring effect on Ayesha. She had a vague memory of the words associated with her owner, Mustaf Asad. But she tried not to let her discomfort show.

"And the United Nations would know about this?"

"No, not exactly," Tatiana said. "At least not right away. I can get Ayesha the papers she needs through a contact I have in Moscow. You won't be able to get transit papers in Dublin, so you'll have to live on Kilduff's airplane until he can pull some strings to fly to Nicaragua. It isn't part of his normal route, but it can be done. We checked. We do fly there with aid packages."

"I won't blow smoke up your arse, Collins. It's a risk. Ireland might send you right back here if they catch you. As for me? I don't care anymore. After this, I'm retiring and never leaving Ireland again."

At the end of their talk the Irishman wanted an answer.

"There's one day to decide, so what's it gonna be?"

"Yes," Collins said. "Ayesha?"

"I'm a little afraid," Ayesha said, "but I like her." She pointed to Tatiana.

"You hear that?" Collins asked. "She likes you."

Tatiana smiled.

After that, everything happened quickly. A little after 1 a.m., Mohammed picked up Ayesha and her suitcase. She had a stuffed panda bear in her arms. Then he drove to the United Nations' apartments where both Tatiana Puchnecheva and Michael Kilduff were staying. From there they went to get Collins, who had been pacing the room, hobbling back and forth for over an hour. By the time all five of them were in the car, it was nearing three-thirty in the morning.

"The next part is going to be a bit dicey," Kilduff said. "The airfield is guarded, but I did some 'bird watching' from the hills up there. They always leave a gap."

Mohammed turned off his car lights and slowed down until finally he brought the car to a stop.

"All of you, be careful. There are cobras in the grass around here. Ayesha," he said, "if your stuff is too heavy, you need to leave it. You may have to run."

Tatiana patted her on the shoulder. Her suitcase was too heavy for Kilduff to lift and run with. Kilduff let her fish around in the dark to find her jewelry—her fortune—to transfer to her purse.

"They're just things, Ayesha. We'll get new things, okay?" Tatiana said.

"I have to go now before someone sees the car," Mohammed said.

There didn't seem to be enough time to say goodbye. They might never see him again.

"I hope that you and your wife and kids can return to the University of Delaware," Collins told him.

Then Mohammed drove back the way he came with the car lights off. The fence was fifty yards or more behind a coppice. Kilduff couldn't see the guards. They could all see his airplane parked near the end of the tarmac because a few of the airfield's nightlights were on. The blacked out new moon was in their favor.

"Wait here, I'm going to cut the fence."

Kilduff slowly approached the fence but he never took his eyes off the possible locations of the guards. He used bolt cutters to cut a four-foot slit in the fence and threw the bolt cutters down. Still no guards. He motioned for them to come. Ayesha, Tatiana, and Bolivar could see Kilduff in silhouette outlined by the airfield lights in front of him.

After that it was a blind dash, but Collins was slow because of his leg. He had a hold of Tatiana's hand. Then they were on board and Kilduff started up the engines. When he did, the noise alerted two men who had been lounging about at a table in one of the hangars. They came out to see the lights on the plane go on. "No flights at this time! Come on!" The guards jumped into a jeep and headed toward the plane, but Kilduff was already gaining speed.

"I've landed and taken off in some pretty dicey airfields, but this one is a piece of Mother's mince pie, so relax," he yelled back to his passengers.

By the time Pakistan could scramble their jets, Kilduff was over the Tora Bora mountains and using the mountains on the Afghanistan border to shield him from Pakistan's aircraft. An American military control tower near Kabul picked them up on radar, but Kilduff simply identified his aircraft and its number.

"Proceed," the American said.

In a little bit …

"We're over the Arabian Sea now," Kilduff said.

Ayesha, Tatiana, and Collins began to feel relieved, though for both Collins and Ayesha, it was relief and exhilaration mixed with terror. Ayesha had never flown in an airplane and she wouldn't let go of Tatiana's hand. Collins knew that they were in more danger than Kilduff was telling them. The escape wasn't real to Collins yet, and to Ayesha it all seemed unreal. Kilduff kept announcing the time, but they were flying east, counter to the earth's rotation, so 6:15 a.m. became 6:10 a.m. and so on.

Twelve hours later, they were in Ireland. Ayesha hugged Collins hard … She wanted to tell him so many things, but all she could think of was: "Goodbye, Toad."

"Goodbye, Frog," Bolivar replied.

Like that, Ayesha and Tatiana were gone. From Ireland the two women went to Russia. A couple of days later, Collins was still aboard the cargo plane that was parked inside a hanger in Dublin. He was reading *The Catcher in the Rye*, one of the books the Irishman had brought to keep him occupied, when Kilduff poked his head in the airplane door. "Ready to go? Get in the crate here just until we're fully loaded." It will take about half an hour. Collins got inside a wooden box and Kilduff nailed it shut. He could hear the rear of the plane open and other crates loaded. He didn't need to be quiet for all the noise, but he was quiet anyway. Then he heard the doors close.

In the silence, Kilduff pried the nails out of the box lid and told Bolivar: "Let's go, mate. After takeoff, you can sit in the cockpit with me. I'm flying solo. I convinced the other pilot to call in sick. Now I'll owe that horsey's arse a favor. Who cares? Eh, mate? Let's see … Where did you say that place is—what's its name—Venezuela? Relax, mate. I'm jerking you."

Michael Kilduff's plane took Bolivar Collins to Venezuela. In Venezuela, he boarded a passenger plane to Cuba.

Airplanes were taking off and landing all over the world, like birds taking flight and returning in the spring. Mohammed sent a message to Professor Martinez Saracho. Professor Martinez Saracho (or Tomás, rather) called Teodesia. Teodesia and Karli went out to look at the waves. Karli showed Athena her leash and Athena turned three very happy circles as she whipped her tail back and forth. They walked down *Avenida del Puerto* by the seawall and watched as the dark blue waves turned white with trillions of small bubbles of air. Teodesia looked at Karli.

"Today it is really happening."

Birds of all sizes flew from tree to tree. Some flew as high as they could and swooped down again to the earth. White egrets gathered in some still waters near the port. Collins looked down through the clouds at the blue water. His plane would be landing soon. At the same time, another plane was taking off in Washington D.C. and heading to Pakistan. On board was a man born with the name "Barranca" who years earlier had decided to live a fictional life. Now he was on his way to try to kill Benazir Bhutto. Also at this moment, Special Agent Robin Ward made a telephone call to Aguilar. Aguilar gave his man in Nicaragua the kill order.

A family who lived in a house on a tall hill in San Marcos were on their terrace having their morning breakfast. The man, from Australia, worked as a teacher at Ave Maria University, but this was Sunday morning, and he wasn't in school. He and his wife and daughter were having coffee and oranges in sunny yellow chairs. A green cockatoo was squawking in a tree nearby. Aguilar's sniper considered for a moment that he might not be the right man, but a mission accomplished would let him leave Nicaragua and go back to Mexico. Shooting them would be enough to satisfy Aguilar.

Months earlier, Anoosh and his wife were making love in their upstairs room when the last words he heard his wife say were … "Did you hear something?" He replied: "It was probably a bird crashing into the window. I'll put some stickers on the glass tomorrow."

Years before that, Carmelita seduced one of the guards on the promise that he would let her outside the gate. After she had sex with him, he let her go. She had already walked seven miles down the road to Culiacán on the night of a very bright and blue full moon, all the while with a melody in her head, something she heard Bolivar playing on the record player—Gershwin. A rhapsody. The Culiacán police found her body three miles outside town after a farmer spotted her and called them. "Vultures are picking at her. You need to come." The farmer stood over her body to frighten away the birds.

Ayesha and Tatiana were still holding hands—Tatiana had taken her to Red Square. Ayesha had never seen a place so big. "Tatiana, promise me you'll never leave me." It was then that Tatiana told her young friend that she had similar feelings about her, too, and nothing could come between them. Pigeons flapped and ascended in front of them.

Paco quit his job with his father's publisher, Ms. Regier, and flew back to Mexico to live in Mexico City. He was sorry and wanted to come home to see his mother and little sister, but the house in Jlalpan was vacant. Father Sebastián told Paco what he thought was true—they had gone to live in Nicaragua and his father died in a car accident, which Paco had already been told. He gave him a telephone number for Professor Martinez Saracho. "I've really been a fool," he said to Father Sebastián. "Yes, my boy, you have, but so have I. I never should have become a priest. I don't know what possessed me. Anyway, I'm going to Mexico City to teach. I might even get married."

Some of the women at the women's university skirted the authority of Nadia and the VC and petitioned the Commission and presented evidence to support the claim that Q had no business being entrusted with the next generation of Pakistan. Dr. Farooq, of the Higher Education Commission, had her removed. Mahmood sold fewer rugs that year, but business picked up again. Fatima stayed with the ISI. When vacation time came, she visited America. She wanted to see St. Louis, so she did, and she ate dinner at Talayna's restaurant. In Abbottabad, Osama bin Laden rested in his bed, suffering from typhoid right next door to Uncle Jinnah and his daughters.

Colonel Tomás appealed to President Ortega to let him quit and work in the private sector, but Ortega said, "No, you're too valuable to us." Sen. Clinton from New York was running neck and neck in the Democratic presidential primaries with Sen. Obama from Illinois. Mohammed received a letter on the day of the morning that Kilduff's airplane took off. His visa was granted, and he and his wife and children returned to Delaware. Everywhere some birds were flying; some sat in the trees and squawked; some larger birds attacked smaller birds. Ahmed took off his falcon's little leather helmet and it flew off, never to return. Other birds continued to glide and hover, rising above the noise of cities and the cruelties of mankind.

Bolivar Collins practiced saying his new name … "Robert Segovia." A passenger on the flight from Venezuela asked him, "Qué?" "My name is Robert Segovia," he said. "It's very nice to meet you." So, the man sitting beside him told him all about his business taking car parts to Cuba. After a while, Collins had fallen asleep, but woke up with a startle. He did not want any of this to be a dream. Not now. But the Captain saluted him, and was still saluting him, still smiling from his grave, and he spoke to Collins from death and the other side of the world, in Urdu of course: "You yourself were always questioning the reality of beliefs." Collins answered him in Spanish, a little defiantly, but with sincerity and respect: "Captain, I gave up philosophy a long time ago. All that matters to me now is that my wife is real and tonight the love we make will be real, and my daughter will play 'Rhapsody in Blue,' and that will be real, too." Then, like an ordinary bird, his airplane landed.

A Photographic Epilogue
(photograph of the author greeting Prince Charles upon his arrival at a women's college in Rawalpindi, Pakistan)

Acknowledgements

I wish to thank a very special professor and friend, Chris, for his help with all things naval and all things Nicaraguan. Thank you to Paquita for chasing down a thousand details. A special thanks to Marsha Dodson, Edward Corkill, Isaac Calles, Quinn Thompson, Anabel Sanchez, Sophia Andres, and Krysta Mayfield, who helped refine the seventh draft.

About the Author

Marlon L. Fick is the author of several books and the founder of the rock group, Animula. He received a grant from the National Endowment for the Arts for his poetry, in addition to the Ramon Llull prize from Spain for translation. In addition to poetry, fiction and songwriting, he teaches at The University of Texas Permian Basin, where he lives with his wife, Paquita Esteve, and their six cats and three dogs. They have a second home in Mexico City.

Other Works by the Author

Poetry and Fiction

El niño de Safo (Fuentes Mortera, 2000)
Selected Poems (Fuentes Mortera, 2001)
Histerias Mínimas (Fuentes Mortera, 2001)
The Nowhere Man (Jaded Ibis, 2015)
The Tenderness and the Wood (Guernica Editions, 2020)

Editions, Translations

The River Is Wide: 20 Mexican Poets (University of New Mexico Press, 2005)
XEIXA: 14 Catalan Poets (Tupelo Press, 2018)
The Poetry of Oujang Jianghe (Agradecidas Señas, 2021)

Music Albums

Golden Days, Animula, Navarro Productions, 2013
On the Way, Animula, Navarrro Productions, 2014
The Trails, Animula, Navarro Productions, 2022
Goodnight Sparrows, Animula, Navarro Productions 2024

Printed by Imprimerie Gauvin
Gatineau, Québec